FLIGHT PLAN

FLIGHT PLAN

ERIC WALTERS

ORCA BOOK PUBLISHERS

Published in Canada and the United States in 2023 by Orca Book Publishers.
orcabook.com

Library and Archives Canada Cataloguing in Publication
Title: Flight plan / Eric Walters.
Names: Walters, Eric, 1957- author.
Identifiers: Canadiana (print) 20220453489 | Canadiana (ebook) 20220453497 |
ISBN 9781459835115 (softcover) |
ISBN 9781459835122 (PDF) | ISBN 9781459835139 (EPUB)
Subjects: LCGFT: Novels. | LCGFT: Thrillers (Fiction)
Classification: LCC PS8595.A598 F55 2023 | DDC jC813/.54—dc23

Library of Congress Control Number: 2022948583

Summary: In this YA thriller, thirteen-year-old Jamie's flight is just taking off
when all technology fails, plunging the world into chaos. After the pilot manages
to land the plane safely, Jamie sets out on the perilous 1,200-mile journey
home with the flight crew and a small group of determined passengers.

Orca Book Publishers is committed to reducing the consumption of
nonrenewable resources in the production of our books. We make
every effort to use materials that support a sustainable future.

Orca Book Publishers gratefully acknowledges the support for its publishing
programs provided by the following agencies: the Government of Canada,
the Canada Council for the Arts and the Province of British Columbia
through the BC Arts Council and the Book Publishing Tax Credit.

Cover image by Bulgac/Getty Images
Design by Troy Cunningham
Edited by Sarah Howden

Printed and bound in Canada.

26   25   24   23   •   1   2   3   4

For those readers who asked
so passionately for me to
continue writing this world.

CHAPTER ONE

"**I WISH I COULD PUT** you right on the plane, Jamie," my grandmother said as we shuffled through the security check-in.

"I think I can make it from here, and it's not like I'm alone."

My escort, Trina, gave a little smile. Her job was to walk me—an "unaccompanied minor"—through security and then be with me until she turned me over to a flight attendant on the plane.

"He'll be supervised the entire way," Trina said.

"I'm thirteen years old, and I don't need to be supervised at all," I huffed.

"Better safe than sorry," my grandmother said. "I want to make sure you get back with your parents safe and sound."

Trina smiled. "He'll get special treatment because he's a very special little member of our family."

"Little?" I protested.

"Not little, but certainly a VIP." Trina didn't find my joke funny.

"This looks like the end of the line." She handed my boarding pass to the TSA agent.

"I'm going to miss you so much!" my grandmother said as she threw her arms around me.

"I'll miss you too." I hugged her back.

"Now, promise me you'll fly safely."

"I don't think they're actually going to let me fly the plane. How about if you *drive* safely?"

"I'm a *very* safe driver," she replied.

"It is a long trip," I said. "Just think—you'll be in your car almost as long as I'll be in the air."

She squeezed my shoulder. "Call me as soon as you land."

The TSA agent handed my pass back to Trina. My granny gave me one more quick hug and released me as I was brought to the security check.

I put down my bag on the conveyor belt and took out my iPad. I put it in a white basket and then added my phone, wallet and shoes. I walked through the metal detector, and my bag reappeared. I shoved my wallet and phone back into my pockets and put my shoes back on.

"Slip this on," Trina said. She handed me a lanyard with a big ID tag that included my information and a picture of me.

Great. "Thanks." This was embarrassing.

I slipped it over my head and then turned the ID backward so nobody could see what it was.

"It's pretty busy in here today," she said as we walked.

"Well, O'Hare is the third-busiest airport in North America."

"Have you flown through here before?"

I shrugged. "Twenty or thirty times. Chicago is a hub."

"You're obviously quite the flier!"

I was going to tell her that both of my parents were Delta pilots, but it always sounded like bragging. In a way it was. Being a pilot was a pretty impressive job. Not that I was planning on being one. I loved animals and was going to be a veterinarian.

"Why don't you take a seat and I'll check you in with the gate agent," she said.

The waiting area was empty because it was still over ninety minutes before departure. My escort and the gate agent talked and laughed and then she came back and took a seat beside me.

"You're all checked in." She paused. "I *can* sit with you until you get on the plane."

Obviously, she didn't want to wait around. "I'll be all right."

"Are you sure?"

"I think I can manage the last forty feet on my own," I said sarcastically.

We said our goodbyes, and she was on her way. I pulled off the lanyard. I wasn't some lost kid on the side of a milk carton. I unzipped my bag and placed the lanyard inside, then went to pull out my phone before changing my mind. I grabbed my book instead. I was getting close to the end, and I wanted to read what was going to happen next.

I looked up from my book. This part of the lounge was getting noisier and busier, with more than half the seats occupied. It was still well over an hour until takeoff. A man and a woman in pilot uniforms, carrying flight bags, walked past me. He had four stripes on his sleeve and she had three, which meant he was the pilot and she was the first officer. He had that sort of "pilot look"—tall, mustachioed and all confident, like he should be in a TV commercial—and she was on the young side, small and with long dark hair. If it weren't for her uniform, I never would have thought she was a pilot. She hardly looked old enough to be a flight attendant.

They stopped and chatted with the gate agents. He handed the female pilot his flight bag, and she went through the gate and headed down the bridge toward the plane. The gate agent pointed at me, and the pilot nodded and then came in my direction.

"Hello, Jamie." He smiled and offered his hand, and we shook. "I'm Stuart Daley. I'm a friend of your father's. He called to let me know you'd be on my flight today."

I guessed it wasn't just my grandmother who wanted to have me checked on.

"I'm going to start my preflight checks. Do you want to come along with me?"

"That would be great!"

I got to my feet and packed up my carry-on bag. I followed him through the gate and down the bridge to the plane, then through the door that led down a set of metal steps to the pavement below.

"You ever done an external check before?" he asked.

"On smaller planes, but never on a jet."

"That's right. Your father has his own plane. A Cessna, right?"

"Yeah."

"Do you go up with him sometimes?"

"All the time."

He grinned. "That's real flying. My son, Adam, is taking flight lessons in a Cessna. He's only a few lessons away from his solo. Now, stay close to me as we do the check. It would be a lot of paperwork if you got hit by a belt loader."

We started circling the plane. It was a fairly new two-engine Boeing. I like Boeing planes. My parents have told me they have great safety records. Captain Daley was checking the wheels, examining the rudders and wings and looking for any visible damage. Walking under the plane, we came up to the baggage handlers putting the luggage on board. He waved, and they waved back as we continued the inspection.

"Adam and I are also building an ultralight together. A little father-and-son activity."

"Wow. That's amazing!" Ultralights are small one- or two-seat planes.

"It's basically finished except for attaching the wings. If all goes well, we're going to take it up sometime this month."

"That's a lot different than flying one of these," I said, gazing up at the jet.

"Big difference. That's being as free as a bird. This plane is so automated it sometimes feels like I'm a computer programmer instead of a pilot."

We headed back up to the stairs leading to the bridge.

"Does your son want to be a pilot?" I asked.

"That's the plan. University and then flight school. That's where I met your father."

We were greeted at the hatch by a flight attendant.

"Hey, Julia, good to know you're running the show today," he said.

"New crew member?" she asked, gesturing to me.

Captain Daley laughed. "Some of our new pilots don't seem much older than him."

"Are you talking specifically about me?" a female voice asked.

Just inside the plane sat the woman I'd seen with Captain Daley earlier. Up close she looked even younger.

"Not you specifically, but really, didn't you get asked for ID when you ordered a beer the other night?" Captain Daley joked.

"Probably something that hasn't happened to you for a *long, long* time," she said, laughing.

"No argument there. It's been a while. Jamie, this is Captain Kim."

She came over, and as we shook hands, I realized she wasn't much taller than me.

"I'm pleased to meet you, Captain Kim," I said.

"I'd much rather you just call me by my first name...Doeun."

I always addressed pilots more formally, but she'd asked, so I guessed I could do that. Besides, she didn't look that much older than me.

I nodded. "Doeun. What language is that? And does it have any particular meaning?"

"It's Korean," she said. "The first syllable—*Do*—means 'principle and reason' and the second syllable—*Eun*—translates to 'silver,'" she explained.

"Personally, I think she's worth her weight in gold as a pilot," Captain Daley said with a chuckle.

"I'm glad you think so," Doeun replied, grinning. Then her smiled faded. "It does get tiresome explaining to airport security that I actually am a pilot."

I gave her a questioning look.

"This morning they wanted to double-check my ID because they didn't believe me. Captain Daley had to offer them reassurance."

"You shouldn't take it so personally," Captain Daley replied with a shrug. "This is one of the first times you've flown out of here, and they're just being careful for security reasons."

"But it *is* personal." She turned directly to me. "Your father is a pilot. What does he look like?"

I hesitated for a second. "Well, he and Captain Daley could be brothers. My mother is a pilot too."

"But does she look like me?" Doeun asked, raising her eyebrows.

"She's older and taller and—"

"And not Asian?" Doeun asked.

I nodded.

"When you first saw me, did you think I was a pilot?" she asked.

"Yeah, of course."

"You did?" She sounded surprised.

"You're wearing the uniform. It's not like they give them away."
I paused, then added, "My mother told me that to be a female pilot,
you have to be better than the males."

She laughed. "You and I are going to get along just fine. Glad
you're able to join us for our flight today."

"Me too," Captain Daley said warmly. "Now, I suppose we
should be getting back to the flight. I was hoping Jamie could join
us on the flight deck for pre-check."

I raised my eyebrows. I'd figured I was just going to my seat
before the other passengers boarded.

"No problem with me," she answered.

"I thought it would be nice for you to have somebody closer to
your age in the cockpit." Captain Daley gave me a wink.

Doeun turned to me. "Does your father make the same sort of
lame dad jokes?"

"All the time. I thought it was a pilot thing," I answered.

"Not me. I'm a pilot, but I'm *seriously* cool."

"And I'm not?" Captain Daley asked.

"Sure you are. Most *definitely*. The *king* of cool," she replied
sarcastically.

"Hey, a little respect for your elders...although I admit you're
pretty cool. Jamie, Doeun is a certified scuba instructor, does some
serious free climbing and plays bass in a rock band."

"And I probably am closer to Jamie's age than I am to yours."
She turned to me. "I'm twenty-eight, and you're, what, fifteen?"

"Thirteen." I often had people thinking I was older because I
was tall for my age. I didn't mind it, since it meant people took me
a bit more seriously.

"And Stuart, what are you, fifty-seven, sixty-five...?"

He started laughing. "Forty-five on my next birthday, which
means you *are* closer to his age than mine." He headed through the
cockpit door. "Shall we start the checks?"

I followed them onto the flight deck. He settled into the pilot seat on the left, and Doeun took the right-hand seat. I pushed down the jump seat behind them and sat.

"Looks like this isn't your first time on a flight deck," Doeun said.

"Two pilots as parents means I've seen a lot of these," I said, setting down my bag.

They pulled out their logbooks and started going through the before-takeoff checklist item by item. They were throwing around lots of technical terms and numbers that I didn't understand. I knew it was best never to disturb a pilot during this process.

I reached into my bag and pulled out my book again. I was coming up to a good part—the asteroid was getting ready to hit Earth and would probably kill all life on the surface. Thank goodness the main characters were part of a survival group—random people who'd come together and were relocating to caves and caverns well below ground level. They'd survive the apocalypse. At least, I hoped they would.

CHAPTER TWO

"JAMIE?"

I looked up.

"That must be a pretty good book," Doeun said.

"It is." I turned it so she could see the cover.

"*End of Days.* Sounds like dystopian, end-of-the-world stuff."

I nodded. "It's my favorite genre."

"Mine too. You must have read *The Hunger Games.*"

"Yeah, but I also like the classics, like *Brave New World* and *1984.*"

"See, I thought you two kids might have things in common," Captain Daley said.

Julia walked onto the flight deck. "Here's the flight manifest." She handed the papers to Doeun. "Baggage is stowed, and, with one exception, all the passengers are in their seats."

"Oh yeah, right." I got up.

"Actually, we were wondering if you'd be interested in staying up here for the entire flight," Captain Daley said.

"Up here, definitely!" I grinned. "If that's allowed."

"We make exceptions for certain employees and their families. Besides, I'm the captain, so unless somebody has an objection, you can stay."

"Good with me," Doeun said.

"Just one less passenger in the back. I'd be willing to send you a few more," Julia said. She retreated, closing the cockpit door. There was a loud click to signify it was now locked.

"We still have twenty-five minutes to push back if you want to read some more."

"Great. Thanks."

I was turning back to my book when a message came over the radio. "Flight 751, this is the tower. We have a departure window that's just opened if you're able to leave slightly early. Over."

"This is flight 751. How soon is that window opening and closing?" Captain Daley asked.

"Opens in five and closes in ten minutes."

"Copy. Will be able to take advantage. Slot us in."

"I'll check with the crew," Doeun said.

Before she could, a message came over the PA.

"Attention," Julia announced, "doors are armed and cross-checked."

"That's our signal," Captain Daley said. He took the PA. "Good afternoon, passengers, this is Captain Daley, and I have some unexpected news. We are not going to be leaving at our original time. Instead we're going to be departing twenty-five minutes ahead of schedule."

A cheer came from the back of the plane.

"We have clear skies and no reports of turbulence. Our flight time will be two hours and thirty minutes, and with a tail wind and the early start, we can expect to arrive thirty-five minutes ahead of schedule. I hope you enjoy your flight."

After a few more communications with air traffic control, we were nearly set to go. Once the pilots finished their pre-taxi checklist, they engaged the controls, and the plane shuddered and then started slowly backward. I knew that these first few feet could be the most delicate. With their long wings, aircraft at terminals crowded with other planes and then on busy tarmacs filled with service vehicles and other aircraft are at risk of colliding with other vehicles. Some of the worst accidents in aviation history happened on the ground. Takeoffs and landings are the most risky parts of flight.

I looked at the panel. There were so many controls and dials and levers. Some were lit and others blinked as the pilots activated them or turned them off. I looked out the windshield as we swung out and the top of the terminal disappeared. We slowed to a stop and then started moving again, this time forward. The engines got louder as we picked up speed and bumped along. I listened to the messages flying back and forth between the two pilots, the air traffic controller and the cabin crew.

We came to a stop on the taxiway, and a big jet came racing along the runway in front of us. This was all part of the dance going on around us, with planes landing, taking off and taxiing, and the support vehicles loading or unloading baggage and fueling the planes.

We started forward again, the engines roared louder, and we sped up. We were swinging around, which meant we were coming up to our runway. We stopped, and the engine noise lessened.

"Looks like we're third in line," Doeun said. She turned slightly around. "*Walking Dead* fan?"

"Graphic novel or the TV show?" I asked.

"Both."

"Love the graphic novels and the first five or six seasons of the show."

Doeun gave a thumbs-up. "Perfect answer. We'll talk more when we're in flight."

We bumped forward again. I figured we were now second for takeoff.

"Where are your parents today?" Captain Daley asked.

"My mother just got back from a long-haul to Europe, and my father has a couple of days off."

"That's always precious time when everybody is home." It was true. I was looking forward to us all being together. It didn't happen very often.

"Flight 751, you are cleared for takeoff," the air traffic controller said.

"Roger that," Captain Daley replied. "Captain Kim, you have the controls."

She placed her hands firmly on the control column. She was the pilot flying. Captain Daley put a hand on the throttle and slowly began to push it forward, giving the plane thrust. He was monitoring the controls and could use the throttle to stop the flight in the event of an emergency. We started moving along the runway, gaining speed.

"Thirty knots...thirty-five...forty," Captain Daley called out.

He kept announcing the numbers as he pushed the throttle forward and the engines got louder, the rumbling stronger, the bumping more pronounced.

"Sixty-five...seventy..."

I could feel us lifting off, and I sat up as high as I could in my seat, trying to look through the windshield. Then there was a gigantic thump and bounce as we hit back down to the runway!

"Abort, abort, abort takeoff!" Captain Daley yelled.

CHAPTER THREE

"WE'VE LOST ALL POWER!" Doeun called out.

The lights on the panel were dark, and the light I'd been using for reading was out.

"Executing emergency braking!" Captain Daley exclaimed.

The plane was bumping along, but there was no sound from the engines. They had died along with all the lights and controls.

"I'm struggling to keep it running straight. It's pulling to the left!" Doeun said.

Her voice was calm, but I could hear the fear in her words.

"Slowing down…slowing down…no readings."

Captain Daley grabbed the PA. "Assume crash positions. Everybody assume—"

He realized the PA was as dead as everything else.

"Braking, braking, braking," he said.

"Are we going to run out of runway?" Doeun asked.

"It'll be close. Reducing speed."

There was another big bump, and only the buckle kept me from flying out of my seat. I could hear screaming coming from the cabin. There was more bumping and then we came to a stop. Silence. No engines, no radio, no conversation. A cloud of dust and dirt appeared in the front of the plane. We were tilted on an angle, pitched slightly forward.

"What happened?" I gasped.

"We lost all power," Captain Daley said. "We lost everything."

"Tower, this is flight 751...and there's no radio," Doeun said.

"Let's get everybody onto the tarmac," Captain Daley said. "Jamie, you stay close to me."

The two of them undid their buckles, and I did the same. Captain Daley opened the cockpit door to the sound of screaming and crying. The cabin was dim, but I could see that some things had fallen out of the overhead bins. Julia and the other flight attendants were giving orders for people to be calm and stay in their seats. Some people had already gotten up and were removing their luggage. The flight attendants had them sit back down.

"What happened?" Julia asked.

"Catastrophic power loss in all systems. Any injuries?" Captain Daley answered.

"I don't think anything too serious. We're deploying the emergency slides."

I could see the other two flight attendants—one male and the other female—working to remove the emergency exit doors. I was trying not to freak out. It helped that they seemed so in control. Doeun and Julia went to open the main cabin hatch. They opened the door and tossed it out and to the side. There was a sudden hiss, and I saw the slide inflate.

"You go first," Julia said to me. "Help people at the bottom."

Before I could even think to react, she moved me over to the door. I hesitated a half second and then, with a little push on the back, I hit the slide. I shot down to the bottom and quickly jumped to my feet. We weren't on the runway anymore. We were on a grassy section, and at the front was a high stone fence topped with metal and barbed wire. The nose of the plane was *over* the fence. We'd stopped within feet of crashing into it. This was unbelievable.

I startled back to reality as a woman hit the slide, screaming as she came barreling down. I reached out for her arm and grabbed her as she hit the bottom. She looked shocked and scared. I pulled her over to the side just before a man came shooting down behind her.

"Jump and slide!" Julia yelled from the top.

Another woman came down, and the man and myself braced her at the bottom. I looked past him to where two other slides were operating. More people were coming down and starting to gather on the ground. It was all happening so quickly.

Julia came down the slide next, and Captain Daley appeared at the top.

"I'm going to do a full search of the plane," he called down and then disappeared.

I caught sight of his head passing by one porthole and then a second, and after that I couldn't see him anymore. Julia and the other two flight attendants were moving passengers away from the plane. A couple needed to be helped by others, and I could see some blood oozing from a man's head. Maybe he'd been hit by falling luggage.

"We don't have answers yet," Julia yelled out in response to all the questions that were being thrown at her by a few vocal passengers.

Lots of people were sitting down on the grass. There was a man in a wheelchair, and I thought he must be injured. Then I remembered seeing him in the terminal in his chair. He and the woman standing beside him had matching track suits and medals around their necks. Some of the people were in tears, others looked shocked or scared or angry. I couldn't tell how I felt yet.

"Where are the emergency vehicles?" Doeun asked. "They should be on the way by now."

I looked toward the terminal. Nobody was coming. Nothing was moving. There were other planes stopped on the runway, frozen in place. The terminal looked dark. The lights on the tower and on the antenna and communication arrays were dark.

"What's happening?" I asked. There was a catch in my voice—I felt uneasy even asking.

"It wasn't just our plane. It's the tower, the terminal and other planes," Doeun replied.

Captain Daley came down the slide at the back of the aircraft. He must have finished the search and found the plane abandoned. He brushed past passengers and questions and came over to where Doeun and I stood.

"This is really wrong," he said. "I'm not sure what happened—or what's still happening."

I turned back toward the plane and looked beyond the fence at the road. It was lined with cars, but none of them were moving. People were out of their vehicles. Had they stopped to stare at us? Then, beyond the rows of stopped traffic and buildings, I saw a pillar of black smoke rising into the air. And a second pillar rose up, farther in the distance. Two planes had taken off just before us.

"Okay, everybody, can I have your attention!" Captain Daley yelled out, and the crowd went silent. "I know you all have lots of questions, but the important thing is that we're safe and off the plane."

"But it's more than just our plane, isn't it?" a man called out.

That was pretty obvious, but it didn't mean Captain Daley knew what was happening.

"We need to move to the terminal. Let's help those who are injured, get medical aid and answers. We're all okay," he answered.

We started moving. The flight attendants were keeping us in a group, like sheepdogs guarding a flock of sheep. One man was leaning heavily against another, hopping on one leg, and two men were carrying a woman between them.

People were pulling out their cell phones. That was a great idea—I could call my granny and let her know I was fine. I had to talk to her before this hit the news, and then I'd ask her to call my parents. I pulled it out and turned it on. There was nothing. Not just no signal, but nothing. The phone was dark and dead. Was it out of power? Then I noticed it wasn't just my phone. Others were holding up their phones and looking at them, but nobody was actually using them. They were complaining that their phones were dead. Had the cell towers also lost all power?

Off to the side another plane had its emergency slides out, and there were more crowds on the tarmac. Then I started looking farther away. There were other planes sitting on the runways and taxiways, and none of them were moving. I could see a dozen from here. Just then, right before my eyes, the emergency chutes of another plane activated. Every plane out here was evacuating their passengers and crew.

"I don't get it," I said. "What is this? What could cause all of this?"

"I have no idea," Julia replied, looking shaken. "But it's all the planes. All at once. And there are no emergency vehicles or baggage trams or even supervisory cars or trucks moving. And no cell phones. Why would there be no cell phones or radios?"

A passenger started yelling at another flight attendant. He was demanding answers about what was going on. Another passenger joined in, and then another and another.

"You stay right with me," Julia said. "You are not to leave my side for any reason."

She walked toward the agitated passengers, but before she could get there, Captain Daley and Doeun were at the scene. I expected Captain Daley to calmly reassure them. That wasn't what happened.

"Stop it *now*!" Captain Daley yelled. "You harass my crew and I'm going to have you arrested as soon as we reach the terminal. Do you understand?"

The first man mumbled something I couldn't hear, and the second edged away, looking at his feet. The third shut up, looking like a little boy caught doing something wrong.

Captain Daley turned to face the passengers from our plane. "Let me be honest. I don't know what's happening. I'm going to get you back to the terminal, and we're going to take care of things and take care of you. Panicking or getting angry is not going to solve anything." He was trying to sound calm and reassuring, but I figured he was as scared and confused as the rest of us.

A number of passengers yelled out encouragement and agreement.

We started walking again. There were other groups off to the side and behind us. Everybody was headed to the terminal. Our group merged with another, and then some baggage handlers joined in. We started up a ramp, and some firefighters came running out of the building, carrying all their equipment. Off in the distance a plane was fully engulfed in flames. It looked as if the hull had shattered in two, like it had smashed down hard against the runway. Had this plane been landing when it lost power? Is this what would have happened to us if we'd been two minutes earlier and already in the air? I felt a chill go up my spine, and my legs suddenly felt wobbly. We'd been seconds away from crashing.

"Everybody inside," Julia yelled. "Everybody into the terminal."

CHAPTER
FOUR

JULIA CAME OVER TO WHERE I was sitting and stooped down so that we were eye to eye.

"How are you doing?"

I shook my head. "I don't know…stunned."

"We're all stunned. At least it's quiet now. I'm surprised that the backup generator hasn't come on yet," Julia said. "This is a post-disaster facility. Things like the backup generator are supposed to work no matter what has happened."

There was plenty of light streaming through the terminal windows, but the lights themselves hadn't come back on.

"Just sit tight. We're going to get more information and figure things out in the next few minutes," she said.

I politely nodded my head, although I thought there was no way they were going to figure out anything that quickly. What we knew was that whatever had happened had affected everything. Planes that were on the ground lost power and couldn't get up, and those already in the air had either glided in for a landing or crashed. We also didn't have any "ears." All radio and cell-phone communication had stopped at the exact same second. There were no computers. Out in front of the terminal, hundreds of vehicles had just stopped dead in their tracks.

I'd been told that people had been sent out of the terminal and outside the boundaries of the airport to investigate. They reported that some of the clouds of black smoke we could see were planes that had crashed. I thought again how we had been no more than a few seconds away from getting into the air. I could be dead right now. If we had already been in the air, we would have crashed. I couldn't get my head around it.

Two more of the planes that had crashed had been coming in for a landing. There was the one we'd seen in flames and shattered, and the other had managed to hit the ground on a glide pattern. Nobody had died, but there were walking wounded—sprains and cuts and bruises. Others' injuries were more serious and were being treated in the terminal infirmary. Medical staff had wanted to transfer them to the nearest hospital, but there were no ambulances running.

People who lived locally had been advised to leave the terminal and go home. Nobody seemed to need much encouragement. They all wanted out. Some people's destinations were only a few miles away, while others had a thirty- or forty-mile journey. That would have been a short car or taxi ride if there were cars or taxis still running. Instead it was going to be a long walk. How long would it take to walk that far?

Others had been given chits to stay at the hotels used by the airlines. There were a couple dozen hotels that weren't far away, and people would be able to walk there. It wasn't like anyone had much luggage. Everything except their carry-ons were locked in the cargo holds of the planes or the basement of the terminal.

I tried to figure out where my granny would be. She had dropped me off two hours before my flight, and her place was a ninety-minute drive from the airport. If she had left immediately, she would have gotten home. Then again, maybe this was something that had hit just around the airport. Maybe everything was still okay where she was. I'd thought about how long it would take to walk to my granny's house. Even if I knew the way, it was still almost a hundred miles. It might as well be on the moon.

My parents would have heard about this by now and would be worried. No, they would be *terrified*. At least they would have been reassured that I was still on the ground when it happened. Since our flight wasn't scheduled to leave so early, they'd have made that assumption. They wouldn't know that we'd been just seconds away from lifting off and crashing down.

Julia and I watched as Captain Daley and Doeun, along with the two other flight attendants—Fede and Amanda—came out from the airline's back room.

"Maybe we're going to get some more answers," Julia said, gesturing to them.

Judging by their expressions, they had either no news or bad news.

"It looks like this is widespread," Captain Daley reported. "A member of the control tower also operates a ham radio and has been in communication with some of his buddies."

I frowned. "What's a ham radio?"

"Ham radio uses specific radio frequencies for people to communicate, to talk to each other. Some people do it as a hobby."

"And those radios still work?" Julia asked.

Captain Daley nodded. "Some of them. Those that have battery-powered backup or generators. And he thinks the ones that are still working are the older models," Captain Daley said. "Those with transistors."

"As opposed to computer chips?" Fede asked.

He spoke with a Spanish accent. He had been calm and reassuring and friendly with the passengers, even when things were breaking down.

"All the things that are *not* working have computer chips," Fede added.

Captain Daley looked thoughtful. "That might be the case, but I'd say it's a little early to confirm that."

"Those ham radios don't have a very large broadcast reach, do they?" Julia asked.

"They do have limits," Doeun confirmed. "But the signals can ripple out from one operator to the next."

She turned to me and realized from my expression that I was confused.

"Let's say you yelled out hello at the top of your lungs to somebody a hundred yards that way." She pointed down the lobby of the terminal. "They could hear you and then turn and yell to somebody else a hundred yards farther along, who could turn to somebody a hundred yards down from there. Ultimately you could get a message to somebody a hundred *miles* away if there were enough people."

"Right," I said. "So this guy here on the radio has talked to others, who've talked to others, who've talked to others even farther away."

"Exactly," Captain Daley replied. "We know that this outage is in effect for at least five hundred miles in all directions."

Doeun covered her mouth in shock. "That's huge!" she exclaimed. I felt a chill go down my spine.

"That means we probably don't have anybody who can give us answers or help us out. Not now and maybe not for a while," Captain Daley said.

I could tell he was working hard to sound calm and in control. That was what pilots did. They were trained to hide their emotions. And fears.

"Which means we're on our own," Doeun added.

"It would be easier if we were," Captain Daley said. "But we have a plane out there and dozens of passengers who are our responsibility."

"And just how are we going to play out that responsibility?" Julia asked, eyebrows raised.

"By doing first things first. Amanda"—he pointed to her—"you're based here in Chicago, right?"

"Yes, I live in Naperville. It's about twenty-five miles away," Amanda said in a quiet voice.

"And that's where you live with your husband and kids."

"Yes. We have three children."

"You need to head home."

She furrowed her brow. "I don't want to desert the rest of you and the passengers."

Captain Daley spoke firmly. "You're not deserting us. You're going to be with your family. I'm just sorry I can't offer you a way to get there."

"If I start walking now," she said, "I can be there in seven hours. Thank you. Thank you so much." She paused. "I suppose I'd better get going."

She exchanged hugs with the rest of the flight crew and then hurried off. I wished I were just a few hours from home instead of twelve hundred miles. If I walked twenty-five miles a day, it would take almost fifty days to get there. But I realized, in a strange way, knowing the exact length of that journey was almost reassuring.

"What about the rest of us?" Fede asked, looking to the captain.

"Somebody needs to secure our plane by staying with it."

"I can do that," Doeun said.

"And I can help her," Fede offered.

"Excellent," Captain Daley said. "Julia, you and I, along with Jamie, are going to go back to the hotel where all our passengers were sent."

"I'm not sure what we can do for them," she said nervously.

"Neither am I. I just know that once they set foot on our plane, they became our responsibility, and we can't just abandon them."

"I guess you're right," she agreed.

"Then I suggest we get to it. Doeun, we'll be back tomorrow, probably early."

"That sounds good," Doeun said. "And who knows, maybe by tomorrow everything will be back up and working."

Captain Daley didn't answer. I wanted him to agree with her, but really, what did he know? What did anybody know?

CHAPTER
FIVE

OUTSIDE THE TERMINAL THERE WAS a traffic jam of stalled cars and trucks and taxis. There was no motion, no sound, no smell of exhaust caught under the overhang of the roof. A lot of vehicles' hoods were up, as the drivers had attempted to figure out what was wrong before they realized it wasn't just their vehicles but the world that had gone wrong. Most cars had been abandoned, but some people continued to stand by or sit in them, not knowing what else to do. The taxi drivers stood together in little clusters, talking.

"This is eerie," Julia said.

"It's like a zombie movie without the zombies," I added.

As we passed people, a few called out questions to us about what was going on. They obviously figured that because Captain Daley and Julia were in uniforms, they might have more information. A couple of police officers stood beside a motionless police car, and I had the same urge to ask them, but what was the point?

Nobody knew anything except what they could see with their own eyes. Assuming they believed what they were seeing.

"The hotel isn't far," Captain Daley said. "You can see it from here. The blue building just off to the left."

The hotel was about ten stories tall and just outside the fence. I knew from my parents that flight crews always stayed at the closest hotel possible. Each airline had a deal with specific hotels to guarantee rooms for crews.

As she scanned around, taking it all in, Julia let out a sigh. "How are they going to fix all of this?" she asked.

"There are people way smarter than us figuring it out right now," Captain Daley replied.

"I mean, how long do you think this is going to take?" I asked. "I have a soccer game tomorrow."

Captain Daley chuckled. "I think that game is probably going to be postponed. I do wish we could get word back to our families to let them know we're all right."

"My husband is always worried about me flying," Julia said. "So he'll be beside himself. At least you know your wife can take care of things."

"She's a police captain," Captain Daley explained to me. "And she's got our son, Adam. He'll help out taking care of our younger ones, the twins."

"He's the one you're building the ultralight with, right?" I asked.

"Yes. He's sixteen, but he's really mature for his age. I hope that whatever is happening here isn't happening there." His expression was grim.

"But..." I paused. "If other places were all right, wouldn't they have sent planes or rescue units to help?"

"The kid has a point," Julia agreed.

"It's only been three hours. Let's give them a chance. In the meantime, we'll take care of what we can," Captain Daley said.

We headed off the airport grounds. Somehow I thought that magically things would be better or different as we got farther out. They weren't. Just more unmoving abandoned cars and people on foot. There were lots of people on foot. Many, traveling in the same direction as us, were dragging suitcases.

"Look!" I yelled.

There was a car moving along the street—a single car among all the broken-down vehicles. It was bright red. It wasn't going very fast, as it had to weave in and around the cars and the people walking on the road. We watched as a group of men tried to wave it down and block it. But the car kept coming, horn blaring, and ran right through them as they jumped out of the way! It bumped up on the sidewalk, still honking, scattering the people who were already there, and then passed right by us.

"I thought it was all vehicles," I said.

"That's a 1972 Camaro," Captain Daley said. "Do you know what that means?"

"That you like Camaros?" Julia asked with a quiet laugh.

"That it's old. With the exception of some Volkswagen cars, which had fuel injection systems even in the sixties, most cars from the seventies don't have computers."

"You mean Fede could be right. This could be about computers," Julia said.

"Think of the things that aren't working," Captain Daley said. "Cars, airplanes, cell phones, electrical power."

"Radio communications, and even the backup power generator at the airport, would be computer-controlled," Julia added.

I wrinkled my nose, trying to think it through. "So the systems all got hacked?" I asked. "All at once?"

"This is good news—or at least I think it is," Captain Daley said. "If it's a computer problem, then they just debug, reset and reprogram all the systems."

"It could be that simple?" I asked.

"I don't know about simple, but knowing the cause is halfway to fixing the problem," Captain Daley replied.

The hotel hadn't looked far away, but it wasn't as close as it appeared. Walking there was a lot different than driving. We continued moving. Some of the people we passed looked like they thought this was some sort of strange joke, but most looked worried. There were those who seemed desperate and scared. Others were *scary*. They looked angry, talked loudly, and there was something dangerous about them even when they weren't saying anything threatening. I was glad I was with Captain Daley and Julia. I got the feeling they both knew how to take care of business. Captains and flight crews always seemed that way to me.

I heard a sound and turned around—two police officers on horses rounded the corner of a building. The animals were huge, and the officers sat tall in the saddle. One of them looked directly at us and then changed their course to head our way.

They pulled up in our path and towered over us.

"Are you a pilot?" one of the officers asked Captain Daley.

"Captain and flight-crew member."

"What's it like at the airport?" he asked.

"No power, no communications, no flights, a couple of crashes, no computers. There were some officers stationed at the doors."

"Any rioting there?" the second officer asked.

"Everything is calm—wait, has there been rioting out here?" Julia asked.

"Nothing that we couldn't take care of. Horses have a certain effect on crowds."

I looked way up at him, in his uniform, a gun strapped to his side, atop a big, big animal, and figured the effect was somewhere between respect and fear.

"It wasn't really as much rioting as looting," the other officer said. "As soon as the power went out, the security systems went down, and people started to take advantage of the situation."

"It's terrible that would happen," Julia said, her expression darkening. "Terrible."

"Do you have anything that's working?" Captain Daley asked. "Cars, communications, anything?"

"No vehicles. It's been the mounted division and the bicycle officers that have been moving from place to place. Thank goodness one part of our equipment is still functioning." He reached down and patted the gun in its holster.

"Have you had to use weapons?" Julia asked, eyeing the gun warily.

"A couple of warning shots were fired into the air to clear a mob looting downtown. That and the horses scatter a crowd pretty well. Where are you three headed to?"

"Just there to the Brunswick Hotel," Captain Daley said.

"Good. There's going to be a curfew imposed at ten this evening. Stay inside and stay safe."

They clip-clopped away toward the airport, and we continued on.

"Your parents have probably stayed at this hotel," Julia said to me. "Our airline has a separate wing, about a dozen rooms, that are always on reserve for Delta crews."

There were a few cars stalled in the circular driveway and a dozen or more people standing in front of the building. The crowd was loud, and as we got closer, I could tell they were angry. I felt uneasy.

"If you're looking for a room, they don't have any," a woman said as we walked up.

"Thanks, but I think we're all right," Captain Daley replied.

The automatic door didn't open as we approached, and we walked up to one of the other doors. Captain Daley pulled on it and it didn't open. He tried a second door, getting the same result. He peered inside, using a hand to protect his eyes from the glare, and then knocked really loudly. A man appeared at the glass. He scowled, then suddenly smiled. He pushed open the door.

"I didn't know it was you!" he said. "Come on in."

Captain Daley let Julia lead, and I followed. The man pulled the door closed behind us, and it clicked loudly as it locked again. There were no lights, and with the curtains pulled, the lobby was pretty dark. The man was introduced to me as Renaldo, and he was the hotel manager.

"We had to lock the doors," he explained. "People were demanding rooms that we just don't have. It was starting to get ugly."

"The terminal wasn't much better. Our passengers, the ones we sent over, they got rooms, right?"

"We didn't have rooms, but we didn't turn them away. We set up cots and extra beds and blankets in the banquet hall for forty-four passengers from your flight. We were able to get them all something to sleep on."

"Thanks for taking care of them," Captain Daley said as he gave Renaldo a pat on the back.

"We're all trying the best we can," Renaldo said as he walked behind the counter. "We have the usual rooms reserved for your airline's flight crews."

"Two members of our crew won't be joining us tonight. They're staying with the plane."

"Do you want three rooms or two?" the manager asked.

"One room with two double beds and a couch is all we need," Captain Daley said.

Julia gave him a questioning look. "I just want us to stay close tonight," he replied, and she nodded in agreement.

"And if it's possible, can we still get something to eat?" he asked.

"If you don't mind serving yourselves. I'm down to a skeleton staff. Some didn't show up, and others asked if they could go home to check on their families."

"If my family wasn't twelve hundred miles away, I'd be doing the same thing," Julia said.

"Do you have enough food for everybody?" Captain Daley asked.

"Just before the power stopped, there was a delivery of supplies for our complimentary breakfasts. We have more than a week's worth of cereal, bread and supplies for pancakes. Of course, with no power there's no toast or pancakes..." He trailed off."

"I was wondering how many extra crew rooms you have that are empty."

Renaldo thought for a minute, then said, "Eleven."

"Please open them up to our passengers. You have my authorization."

The manager nodded. "I'll take care of it."

We walked down the hall, which got dimmer the farther we were from the lobby windows. We could hear the banquet hall before we got there. There were loud voices and at least one baby crying.

When we opened the door to the room, the light coming in through the windows showed the chaos. Beds and cots were pushed together. People everywhere. I could see that some of them were still clinging to their cell phones, hoping they'd come back to life. Little clusters of people stood together talking, and other people were lying down.

"You two head to our room. I'm going to talk to our passengers," Captain Daley said.

"Are you sure you don't want me to come?" Julia asked.

"There's not much to say. I'm going to try to reassure them, but I don't really have many answers. I just want to tell those who have families or friends nearby that they should go there—and that I have no idea how long this is going to last."

I felt my stomach drop. "No idea?" I asked.

He shook his head. "For now we're fine. Go to your room and get some sleep."

"Come on, Jamie," Julia said. She took me by the arm and led me down the hall.

We kept walking. "You're doing well," Julia said. "All things considered."

"Do you think this could all be fixed soon?" I asked.

"That's possible," she said and shrugged.

"But what do you think?" I asked. I knew I was repeating myself. But I needed to talk about it.

"I'm sure it'll all be fine and—"

"I can handle the truth," I said, cutting her off.

She hesitated before answering. "If it isn't fixed soon, it's probably going to get worse."

"How would it get worse?"

"This is all well before your time, but something like this happened in 2003 when the whole east coast lost power."

"But they fixed it, right?"

"They had it up in twenty-four hours, but not before there was rioting, looting and arson," she answered.

"It can happen that fast?"

"After Hurricane Katrina in New Orleans, things broke down within twelve hours," Julia said. "People died. And this is different. Bigger, more far-reaching."

I paused. "We almost died today on the plane, didn't we?"

"If we'd have been in the air instead of on the runway, there would have most likely been fatalities. As far as we can tell, every single plane that was in the air crashed." She bit her lip and blinked back tears.

It was a nightmare. "How many planes could that be?"

"It depends on the size of the disruption." She cleared her throat, getting back to the facts. "What I do know is that O'Hare has twenty-five hundred takeoffs and landings per day. If a tenth of those planes were within five hundred miles and lost power, well, you do the math."

I did. That was two hundred and fifty planes. Each would have held an average of two hundred passengers. Fifty thousand passengers were in the air when this happened.

"Let's just be grateful we're here. We'll try to figure things out starting tomorrow," she said gently.

"And what are we going to do tomorrow?" I asked.

"We'll head back to the airport," she answered. "It might be the best place to get updated information."

"And after that?"

Julia shook her head. "I wish I knew. I wish I knew."

CHAPTER SIX

I SAT UP IN BED. It took a few seconds for me to remember where I was—in a room at the airport hotel, with Julia and Captain Daley. The room was dark, but there was a little light coming in through the curtains and somebody was standing at the window.

"Julia?" I called out quietly.

"She's sleeping," came the whispered reply from Captain Daley. "It's me."

I threw off the covers and went over to join him, looking through the gap in the curtains. The city was spread out in front of us. There were no streetlights or lights from cars or windows, but there was a glow in the sky in a few places.

"Is that the sun coming up?" I asked.

"Sunrise isn't for another hour. As best as I can tell, those are fires. Buildings are on fire."

"Fires?" I gasped. "Why would there be buildings on fire?"

"It seems too coincidental to be anything except arson." He paused. "We're safe. I worked out a sentry system with passengers taking turns on watch."

I didn't know if that made me feel more secure and reassured or more scared and upset.

Julia yawned and got up from her bed. She was already dressed. She came over to where we stood.

"More fires?" she asked.

"And nobody to fight them because there are no working fire trucks," Captain Daley said.

"I can understand lots of things, but arson makes no sense," she said.

"It's raw anger and outrage," Captain Daley said grimly. "We better get going as soon as possible. I'll meet you two in the breakfast area. Please bring your bags."

He picked up his flight bag and left the room.

"How did you sleep?" Julia asked as she gave me a pat on the shoulder.

"Not so good. I couldn't stop thinking," I said.

"Almost dying in a plane crash and society breaking down can do that to you." She sighed. "What was going on in your head?"

"I was thinking about home."

"We all want to be home," she replied.

"No. I was thinking about *getting* home instead of being here," I explained.

She looked at me quizzically. "Home is a long way away, and we have no way to get there."

"We could even walk if we had to."

Julia seemed dubious. "Twelve hundred miles is a long walk. It would take forever."

"Fifty days." I'd done the math over and over again.

"I think it would take a lot longer than that," Julia said.

"If we walked twenty-six miles every day, we could do it in forty-eight days," I said, turning to her.

"That's a lot of walking."

I pointed to the fitness counter on her wrist. "How far do you walk most days?"

"Between twelve and fifteen miles."

"Then twenty-six isn't that much farther, is it?"

She laughed. "Let's put that idea on the back burner for now. Okay?"

"Okay. I guess." But I couldn't let it go that easily. "Can we at least tell the captain my idea?"

"Certainly," she said kindly. "Just not right now. Hey, let's go for breakfast."

I slipped on my shoes, and we both grabbed our bags. The hall was dark except for little bits of light coming from open doors. We could hear snippets of conversation as we passed by. I wasn't sure if anybody was sleeping.

At the dining area there were already more than a dozen people eating breakfast. The manager and Captain Daley were sitting together at a table in the corner, away from the others. They saw us and waved us over.

"Looks like you two are hard at work already," Julia said.

"Already?" the manager asked. "We never stopped last night."

"Correction. *Renaldo* never stopped," Captain Daley said. "The man is a master planner and organizer."

Renaldo sighed. "I wish I could do more."

"How many people have you made arrangements for?" Captain Daley asked.

"Twenty-three of your passengers will be leaving us today to go and stay with family or friends."

"That's great progress!" Julia exclaimed.

"So that leaves twenty-one of your passengers who will continue to stay at the hotel," Renaldo said.

"And eight of them are coming with us to the airport today to help gather supplies and equipment," Captain Daley added.

"This isn't going to end soon, is it?" Renaldo asked.

Captain Daley shook his head and got to his feet. "We'd better get going."

The two men shook hands, and then, unexpectedly, Renaldo threw his arms around the captain. He gave Julia a big hug too.

"Those who are coming with me to the airport, let's assemble in the lobby," Captain Daley announced.

Others got up or started moving as we headed out to the entrance area.

"Eight people is a lot to bring with us," Julia said under her breath.

"Some insisted on coming," Captain Daley explained quietly. "Besides, there's safety in numbers."

As they started to gather in the lobby, I realized I recognized some of them. Not just from the hotel but from the plane and the waiting room in the terminal before that.

A man dressed in a sports jacket, with short hair and sunglasses, came up first.

"Good to have you along, Phil," Captain Daley said as the two men shook hands.

"No problem. I guess the job continues for both of us."

"Jamie, this is Phillip Morgan. He's an air marshal from our flight."

I knew from my parents that many flights have air marshals. They are armed security. So this meant Phillip was carrying a gun. That was reassuring.

A youngish man and a woman wearing matching track suits were next. He was in a wheelchair, and I recognized them immediately—they just weren't wearing their medals anymore.

"Julia, Phil, Jamie, meet Sara and Noah."

Everybody shook hands and offered greetings.

"They're members of our Olympic archery team," Captain Daley explained.

"I saw you both yesterday with your medals," I said.

"Not Olympic medals this time," Noah explained. "It was a regional competition."

"Although my husband did finish fifth in the Olympics two years ago," Sara added.

"The only thing worse than fifth is fourth," he joked.

"We're just glad to have you along," Captain Daley replied. "And everybody, this is Dr. Singh." She was about the age of my mother and was dressed casually but with shiny, fancy shoes.

"Please, I'm much more comfortable if everybody just calls me Jasminder."

"I think we're all grateful to have a doctor along for the ride, Jasminder," Julia said with a smile.

"Hi," said another man, striding up. "I'm Richard, and I'm a nurse and a medical-supply representative. My luggage has medical devices, specialized tools and a lot of drug samples that we could use."

"It sounds like we have ourselves a little medical team," Captain Daley said. "The gentleman in the camo and hunting hat is Tom."

He was an older man with a long white beard. He took off his hat and gave a little bow. "As you probably figured out, I'm no doctor, and I'm not even Santa Claus. I was on a hunting trip to Canada, so I have a few things in the hold of the plane that might be helpful."

"Glad to have you along," Captain Daley offered. "And the last members of our little group are Amber and her son, Nelson."

She was young—maybe in her twenties—with short dark hair, and her son looked about five.

"I'm not a nurse or a doctor or even a hunter. I just, well, I didn't want to be left here. I feel better going with the captain back to the plane."

"Excellent." Captain Daley clapped his hands together. "Renaldo packed us water and food. Time for us to get back to the airport."

CHAPTER
SEVEN

BY THE TIME WE LEFT the hotel, the sun was almost starting to rise. Captain Daley led, and Phil let everyone else go ahead of him. I figured that being an air marshal, he was used to taking a spot where he could watch everybody and everything. Now even more I liked that he was carrying a gun.

It was still pretty dark, and totally still, and we moved along in silence. The smell of smoke hung in the air—proof that there were people close and bad things happening. It felt eerie. I kept looking around for the zombies. This was like a book or a movie, not real life.

We walked along the road between the abandoned vehicles. Where had all the people gone? It was strange that none of the vehicles could run anymore.

"Careful of the glass," Captain Daley said.

Before I could ask what glass he meant, I felt and heard it crunching under my feet. I noticed that the nearest car's windows had been smashed. And the next car's, and the next, and the next.

We came up to a large bus, the type they use to shuttle passengers between hotels and the terminals. There was a stench of burned plastic and rubber. The bus had been gutted by fire.

"Wow," Tom said. "Somebody did a number on this thing."

As the sun came up over the horizon, I could see more. Some of the cars held sleeping people. A man sat up and then climbed out the door on the opposite side from where we were walking. He looked uncertain and then gave a nod of his head. A woman got out, and then a second man joined them. He was carrying a baseball bat.

"Morning," Captain Daley said. "Looks like it got a little rough out here last night."

"It wasn't good. People just came along smashing windows, setting fires," he said. "We persuaded them to leave our car alone," the man said, holding up the bat.

"It was all pretty scary," the woman said, her face pale. "We're not going to be here tonight."

"We were just about to drop off my wife for her flight when this all happened," the man explained.

"Thank goodness you hadn't left," she said.

"We're going to try to get home," the man with the bat said.

"Do you live far from here?" Phil asked.

"About a two-hour drive," the woman said.

"Or a three-day walk," the man added. "But it beats being out here in the open."

The woman squinted into the distance. "This isn't just here, is it?"

"We're not sure of the full extent, but it's far-reaching," Captain Daley answered. "Do you have any food and water?"

The man shook his head.

Captain Daley opened one of the bags Renaldo had packed for us. He took out four bottles of water and two sandwiches. "Sorry, we can't spare more."

"Thank you so much!" the woman gushed. Then she burst into tears.

The trio took the supplies, thanked us again and then started on their way, the woman dragging her suitcase behind her.

We continued up the ramp leading to the terminal. The same abandoned cars and taxis waited. There were now more people coming to life. They'd been sleeping in vehicles or against the wall of the building.

We went to go inside but had to stop. The entrance was barricaded with a strange combination of benches, scaffolding and pieces of wood.

"Stop right there!" a voice yelled out. "The terminal is limited to authorized personnel only!"

Captain Daley spoke up. "I'm a Delta captain, and I have both a member of my crew and an air marshal with me."

"And the others?"

"Passengers on my flight. We're coming to recover their baggage and check on my plane and the crew we left behind to supervise it."

"Do you mean Captain Kim and Fede?" The man's tone had changed now to one of recognition.

"Yes. Are they okay?"

"They've been helping secure the airport. Please come forward."

A section of the barricade slid to the side. Captain Daley led us through the gap. As soon as we were in, it was closed back up.

Behind the barricade were five uniformed TSA officers. They all had guns strapped to their sides.

"Thanks for allowing us in," Julia said.

"You belong here. Not like the rioters," one of the two female officers said. She had her hands on her hips.

"Rioters?" Captain Daley exclaimed.

"It was bad. It started with angry passengers, and then there were others who just came here looking for trouble. It got out of hand."

"There were police officers here when we left for the hotel," Captain Daley noted.

"They all took off when the rioting began," explained another officer. "Thank goodness this place was designed for high security. Laminated shatterproof glass, limited entrances, the high barbed-wire fences around the grounds. We're one of the most secure places in the city."

"If only we'd have taken charge sooner, there would have been less damage and looting," the first woman said.

"There was looting?"

"You'll see it as you go to your plane."

"Thank you for what you're doing," Captain Daley said.

The woman shrugged. "What choice did we have? This place is ours to defend, and we took care of each other."

"Keep doing that," Phillip said, nodding at them.

Captain Daley turned to us. "We'd better get going."

As we moved away from the entrance, it quickly became dimmer. It seemed oddly quiet and calm. Most of the chairs and benches were empty, nobody moving or rushing toward a flight, frantically towing their luggage behind them. Almost...untouched.

Then we came up to the stores. Windows had been shattered, and the floor around them was littered with merchandise. At first I thought I saw bodies, but I realized there were two mannequins lying among scattered items of clothing. Beside them was a computer store that had been cleared out. The counters where the computers and iPads would have been secured in place had been ripped out or smashed. Obviously, the glass fronts of these stores weren't made of the same laminated security glass as the terminal windows, and in the dim light shards and pellets of glass glistened on the floor, crunching under our feet.

On the benches against the wall a few people were starting to get up and move. They'd been through some bad things. Maybe some of them had been part of it.

The restaurant where my granny and I had grabbed a bite to eat came into view. Broken glass, overturned tables and chairs all on their sides. The case that had held muffins and donuts was smashed and empty.

"We did the right thing in getting our passengers out of here," Julia said solemnly.

"I thought things might go bad, but I didn't expect it to happen this quickly," Captain Daley replied.

Tom crossed his arms. "I'll feel better when I have my rifle out of the hold of the plane and in my hands."

"We'll all feel better," Amber agreed. Those were the first words she'd spoken since we left the hotel.

"It's just so hard to believe all of this could happen," Dr. Singh said, shaking her head.

"Doesn't surprise me at all," Richard countered. "It's human nature."

"You must have a pretty sad view of humans," Dr. Singh replied.

"I've spent my life in sales," Richard said matter-of-factly. "You have to read people if you want to sell them things. I'm never surprised when people choose themselves over others."

We came up to a door that would lead us down to the tarmac. Captain Daley stopped.

"Noah, I'm sorry, but there are stairs, and this is the only route I know."

"If somebody can take my chair, I can handle the stairs," Noah said. "After all, I got up these stairs when we abandoned the plane yesterday—going down is much easier."

Tom and Richard volunteered.

Led by Captain Daley, Noah made his way down, using his arms to support himself on the railing as he slid from stair to stair. He was fast, and I could see how muscled his arms were. Sara was right behind him and finally, at the end of the line, was Phillip. He glanced over his shoulder into the terminal and closed the door behind him. Noah quickly got back into his chair, and we were off.

On the tarmac the world once again seemed calm and almost peaceful. Airports are usually a humming collection of vehicles moving among the airplanes, everything with flashing lights. Now there was none of that. The planes were still there, like big, dark sleeping dinosaurs. Some were parked against the terminal and the bridges, while others sat where they'd shut down, out on the taxiways and runways. The support vehicles—fuel trucks, belt loaders and catering trucks—stood in place.

We walked in silence. I noticed that Nelson was nestled against his mother. The whole group seemed to be pressing in closer together despite there being much more space in which to spread out. We went toward our plane at the end of the runway, where the tarmac had broken down under its weight—the tarmac was actually designed that way to help planes decelerate if they went too far. Our plane was on an angle, the port side sunk deeper into the mud.

"Doeun, Fede!" Julia called out.

They both appeared at an open hatch.

"We'd been wondering if you were still sleeping in," Doeun called down to us.

"How did things go?" Captain Daley asked.

Doeun raised her eyebrows. "It got pretty hairy in the terminal and started to spill out onto the tarmac."

"It went from chaotic but calm to a riot, just like that," Fede said, snapping his fingers.

"So what's the plan?" Doeun asked.

"We're going to try to get some supplies, luggage and equipment out of the hold of the airplane and then see what we can figure out from there," Captain Daley replied.

"And I know who can help us do that," Fede said.

CHAPTER EIGHT

"JUST A LITTLE BIT CLOSER," Wayne called down from the platform of the metal staircase. We pushed it forward until it touched the plane. "Okay, that's good. Lock the wheels in place."

Working with another man, Calvin, they opened the hatch to reveal a black hole. Wayne turned on a flashlight, and I could see partway in.

"Let's do this," Wayne said.

The two of them headed into the plane. Tom and Richard climbed the stairs to the platform, and everybody else waited at the bottom. The first bag appeared beside Tom, and he and Richard rolled it down the stairs. It flopped end over end and then bounced onto the tarmac.

"I've seen luggage handled rougher than that before," Julia wise-cracked.

Sara hauled away the first bag, dragging it off to the side. Tom and Richard tossed the second and third bags down the steps. I grabbed a bag, looking up and dodging another one that was bouncing down toward me. Julia, Doeun and Fede were trying to bring order to the luggage as the bags were hauled to the side. We were looking for specific ones, and we would have to unload the entire plane to find them. Julia estimated there were going to be almost two hundred bags in total.

"Don't toss that one!" Noah yelled up.

"This one looks special," Richard replied. He was holding a hard-sided, circular black case.

"And here's its twin," Tom said. He had an identical bag.

Sara climbed the stairs and retrieved the two bags. She handed one of them to Noah. He snapped it open, revealing one side filled with arrows and the other containing the bow. He pulled it out. It was long and curved, with a series of wires and wheels and pulleys. It looked very complicated and dangerous.

Sara took the two cases over to the side, and then other bags started tumbling down the stairs. I grabbed another suitcase and moved it over to the others. This process continued, bag by bag, stopping again for Tom's rifle case and Richard's case of medical equipment and supplies.

There were a few other items that had to be carried down the steps—two baby strollers; a little girl's bike with high handlebars, a pink seat and streamers; a couple of cardboard boxes that wouldn't have survived a tumble down the steps; some trunks; and four sets of golf bags.

"I don't think anybody is going to be golfing for a while," I said to Noah as I set down the last set of clubs, and he laughed.

Wayne stepped out of the hold and onto the platform. He had a small crate in his hands.

"That's all the luggage!" he called out. "But we have a couple of other passengers."

Calvin appeared behind him. He was lugging a much bigger crate. From inside the smaller one came the sound of barking. Dogs!

Soon we heard barking from the larger crate too—that dog's bark was harsh, strained, and he sounded mean.

"Let's bring them down and have a look," Julia said.

It took both Richard and Calvin to carry the large crate down the stairs. The dog seemed to be getting more unhappy with each step. They put the crate down on the tarmac.

"I didn't know we had any pets on board," Julia said. "Poor things must be hungry and thirsty and scared."

"The big one looks scarier than he does scared," Tom noted.

Fede undid the latch of the small crate. The dog inside was small—maybe fifteen pounds—and looked like a poodle, all groomed and fancy. Fede picked it up, and it snuggled in against him.

"Here's some water," Amber said. She handed Fede one of the bottled waters.

"And this can be a bowl," Nelson said.

It was the Styrofoam shell that had held one of the sandwiches. Fede poured the water in and set down the little dog, and it instantly started lapping up the water.

"Should we let the big one out?" Richard asked.

"Not yet," Captain Daley said, eyeing it warily. "Let's give it food and water through the bars first."

"I have a bit of my sandwich left," I offered.

I rummaged around and found the container. I'd left part of the crust and a little bit of meat. I came over to the crate.

"Keep your fingers clear," Dr. Singh warned. "I don't want to be stitching you up."

I dangled the crust over the top of the crate and then slowly lowered it down through the bars. The dog greedily took it. He was obviously hungry, but there was a gentleness to the way he grabbed it with his teeth.

Julia took a slip of paper from one crate and then the other. "The little one is named Mia, and the big one is Godzilla."

"That name fits," Tom joked. "He looks like he could destroy Tokyo."

I poured some water into the clamshell from my sandwich and put it close to the crate. Godzilla's tongue—it was blue—came out between the bars, and he lapped it all up. Without thinking, I reached in and gave him a scratch behind the ears, and he pressed up against the bars for more. His tail was wagging.

Julia leaned in to see better. "He looks like he's around a hundred and twenty pounds."

"I'm pretty good with dogs," Richard said. "I'm going to open the cage door a little and see how he's—" Richard was instantly bowled over as Godzilla bounced into the door and jumped out of the crate. He rushed straight over and sat down right beside me, leaning against my leg.

"Seems like he's found somebody he likes," Tom said with a smile.

I gave him a rub behind the ears, and he pushed against me harder.

"The papers say these are both rescue dogs from an organization just outside of Chicago and were being shipped east to new owners," Julia said. "The question is, what do we do with them now?"

"Mommy, can we keep Mia?" Nelson asked. Amber looked at the captain.

Captain Daley shrugged. "It's the same for them as for the other passengers. Our responsibility is to take care of them. Besides, it's not like we can just release them."

"More mouths to feed, but that one might just earn his keep," Tom noted, pointing at Godzilla.

"He seems pretty gentle," I said, giving him a pat.

"He might be gentle as a kitten," Tom said, "but just looking at him, would you want to mess with him? A dog is one of the best security systems you can have."

Captain Daley chuckled. "Then it looks like Jamie is going to be pretty secure."

"I hadn't even thought about animals on the planes," Wayne said. "When the computers went down, we lost all the cargo manifests."

I'd learned that Wayne was in charge of all the baggage handlers.

"I think we're going to have to check out every plane on the ground," he continued, looking worried.

"Sounds like a lot of work for those of us who stayed around," Calvin said.

He told us that most of the baggage handlers had left to be with their families. I wished I could do the same. Even my granny was too far away to get to on foot.

"We can't leave dogs in the bellies of the planes to die. We'd better get to it." Wayne paused. "How bad do you think this is, Captain Daley?"

"You probably know more than I do."

"I know nothing, really," he answered. "But I was thinking. Here we are at O'Hare International Airport. One of the biggest, busiest, most important airports in the world. So if there were planes still working anywhere in the country, don't you think the military would have sent some soldiers here to safeguard this location?"

"Seems like one of the first places they'd come," Captain Daley agreed.

"But here we are. Nothing. Nobody. I think whatever caused this here caused the same thing across the country. Maybe around the world."

Captain Daley nodded in agreement. "This could be a long fix."

"Maybe." Wayne scratched his ear thoughtfully. "But hey, it went off in an instant, so maybe it will come back on the same way."

That's what we all had to hope.

"Until then we're on our own. Nobody is coming to save us. Nobody is coming to rescue us," Wayne said.

I looked over at Noah and Sara, now holding their bows, and at Tom—he was holding a shotgun, a second rifle still in the case. And of course I knew Phillip had a gun holstered under his jacket. At least we had protection.

"How many people are here at the airport?" Captain Daley asked.

"All told? There must be seven or eight hundred."

"All of whom are going to need food and water," Julia said.

Wayne let out a big sigh. "I really have to start seeing what's in those planes besides the animals."

"Can we hang on to the set of stairs for a while so we can check out the cargo on our plane?" Captain Daley asked.

I knew from my parents that inside the belly of the plane there would be bags, cartons, boxes and pallets filled with all kinds of supplies. There was no telling what the cargo held. There might be things we'd find very helpful.

"Sure. We have four or five old sets of stairs. I guess they're all going to be put to use."

Wayne shook Captain Daley's hand and then he and Calvin headed back to the terminal.

"Well, everybody, we got the bags out of the hold. Now the hard part begins. Getting them off the tarmac and into the cabin of the plane," Captain Daley said.

CHAPTER NINE

CAPTAIN DALEY WAS RIGHT. Tossing the bags down a flight of stairs was a lot easier than carrying them back up. Julia and Fede took the pieces from us at the top and then stowed them in the back of the plane. The rest of us continued carrying them up the stairs. Each trip up, I had a shadow. Godzilla hadn't left my side. Even when I offered him food and water, he wouldn't take it unless I stayed right with him. He even followed me around when I took a little spin on the bike. It was so small that I had to extend my legs sideways to ride. Even then my knees almost hit the handlebars. And while the streamers seemed a little silly, it made me feel free to be riding.

I'd gone up and down the runway, avoiding the ruts and damaged tarmac our plane had created. Beyond the ripped-up tarmac and our strangely angled plane almost over the fence, I could see pillars of smoke rising from a dozen places across the horizon. The smell of smoke was everywhere, no matter which direction I rode. Why would people set things on fire? I understood stealing food and, I guess, other things that you might need, but why would you just burn things down?

I had this strange fantasy about just continuing to ride, finding a gate and just pedaling all the way home. I was thinking, How many miles could you ride a day on a bike? It had to be at least three or four times more than you could walk. It would take me no more than sixteen days to get home. Which wasn't that long.

Of course, the people who were setting fires and threatening others were why I really couldn't do that. It was too dangerous. Then I looked down at Godzilla running beside me. If he came along, nobody would bother me. I'd bring food in a backpack for both of us, and we could drink from rivers. I could just ride out the gate, and in about two weeks we'd be home and—no. It was just stupid to think about it. I didn't know the way. I didn't have maps, and it wasn't like I could use the GPS on my phone. I wasn't going anywhere by myself.

But what if we had a dozen bikes? Captain Daley could lead us. He had to know the way. We'd have Tom and Phillip with guns. Sara and Noah would have their bows and arrows as well. Noah could probably move as fast in his wheelchair as I could on this bike. Dr. Singh would take care of medical problems, along with Richard. Amber could ride a bike with a kiddie seat, Nelson in the back carrier holding on to Mia. Couldn't that all work?

Captain Daley called out to everybody that he wanted to talk, and I rode back and came to a stop with Godzilla at my side. Mia sat in Nelson's lap. It made me happy just to watch them. With all that was going on, it was nice for Nelson to have some comfort. Then again, he was so young he didn't understand how bad things were.

People took seats on the stairs in front of Captain Daley. Doeun, Julia and Fede stood with him. Tom, holding his shotgun, and Noah in his chair, holding his bow, fanned out around him. Phillip was one step removed, always on the outside, watching over everybody.

"First off, I want to let you know what we found in the cargo section of the hold. There were pallets of office equipment, including computers."

"Not very helpful right now," Sara said wryly.

"Not particularly," he admitted. "There was also a pallet of food."

A cheer went up.

"Unfortunately, most of it was dog food and baby food," Doeun said. A nervous laugh went up from everybody. "At least the dogs will be happy," she added.

"And baby food is still food. Adults can eat it," Dr. Singh said, trying to sound cheerful.

"That's disgusting," I said, wincing. "I'm never going to be hungry enough to eat baby food." I looked at Captain Daley's expression and suddenly realized it could happen.

"At least I hope it's flavors I like," Richard added, and everybody laughed again.

"There were also three bins filled with fresh fruit, bananas and mangoes," Doeun said.

"And since the shelf life of that food is only a few days, our plan is to keep what we can eat and get the rest to the terminal to help feed the people in there," Captain Daley said.

"Is that smart?" Tom asked. "Shouldn't we keep it all, you know, just in case?"

"It's going to spoil. We're in this together. Not just us but the people at the airport. Which leads me to my next discussion point. Doeun?"

"This airport is probably the most secure place in the city," she began.

"Certainly more secure than the hotel," Phillip added.

Dr. Singh looked worried. "But surely we can't just sleep in the terminal."

"Not in the terminal but in the plane itself," Doeun answered. "Julia, do you want to go over the details?"

Julia nodded. "Fede and I have figured out how we can reconfigure the plane so that seats and cushions provide reasonably comfortable sleeping arrangements."

"We have blankets and cushions, and even the life preservers can be used for pillows," Fede added.

"We'll also go back to the hotel and ask Renaldo if we can take more blankets, maybe a few cots and any food that would have been allocated for us anyway. We can use a couple of strollers for transport," Captain Daley said.

Richard frowned. "And if we don't agree?"

"You're all free to stay at the hotel or pursue any plan you want," Captain Daley said.

"I want to stay here," Amber said immediately. "Nelson and me, and I guess Mia, are going to stay."

"All those in favor of the plan?" Doeun asked.

A few hands went up. Richard was the last one to make it unanimous.

"Thanks for your endorsement," Captain Daley said. "I'm going to go back to the hotel to talk to Renaldo and offer to bring back any of our other passengers who want to join us."

"I'll come with you," Phillip said.

"And I can help," Tom offered.

"Me too," Noah added. Fede had also raised his hand, and Captain Daley gave him a nod.

"Thank you all for your offers," Captain Daley said. "But Tom, I was hoping you could stay here to, um, watch over things."

"Sure, if that's what you want," Tom said, adjusting his hat.

"We're going to leave immediately, but we might not be back until morning," Captain Daley explained.

I didn't like that idea. So far he was the one I felt safest with. "Could I come along?" I asked.

"Thanks for the offer, but I think we need you and Godzilla here to safeguard the plane," Captain Daley replied. "We'll leave right away and be back as soon as we can."

CHAPTER
TEN

I THREW OFF THE BLANKET. With Godzilla sleeping partly beside me and partly on top of me, I had more warmth than I needed. The plane itself was pretty hot. The hatches were wide open, but it wasn't like we could open the windows to get more air. Besides that, the weather had been warmer than normal for this time of year.

I looked at my watch. It was an old battery-operated watch that had belonged to my grandfather. That was probably why it still worked. The numbers and dial glowed in the darkness, the only light in the plane. It seemed like the only light in the world. It was almost three in the morning. Obviously, Captain Daley and the others weren't coming back tonight.

I shifted around. I'd been assigned a row of three seats. They weren't quite long enough for me to stretch out and now, with Godzilla sharing, not wide enough either. We each had our own little blanket, and Fede was right: the life preservers did make good pillows.

I could hear little wisps of breathing and gentle snoring around me. I wasn't surprised that people had been able to get to sleep, because Doeun had worked us hard. I'd dropped off immediately. Going through the suitcases had been sort of fun. At least, at first. It was like opening surprise Christmas presents. Of course, like real Christmas presents, finding out you were getting clothes wasn't that thrilling. That made it even more exciting when we did find useful things.

There were assorted bottles of alcohol—which made Richard particularly happy—lots of snack food, a few knives and a handgun with a box of cartridges. Doeun, as the senior member of the flight crew present, took possession of the gun and ammunition.

The best find of all was a suitcase that contained nothing but smoked meat. It was filled with sausages. The entire thing. Fifty pounds' worth. Then we found a matching bag, and it had matching meat. Who wanted to ship a hundred pounds of meat home?

Our supper was airplane food. The plane had been loaded with lunch for all 112 passengers. The meals were precooked, and since we didn't have a way to heat them, we ate them cold. Who would have thought that cold, compressed, one-day-old mashed potatoes and mystery meat would taste so good?

I shifted around, trying to settle in despite having to pee. I needed to go, but I didn't want to go outside. I wanted to wait until morning, when it was safer, but I knew that wasn't going to work. Reluctantly I hefted Godzilla out of the way and shuffled along the seats and into the aisle. The dog was right behind me. As quietly as possible, I went up through first class. Everyone seemed to be asleep.

Godzilla let out a little whine, and I shushed him. At the front, right by the open hatch, were two toilets. We'd been told not to use them, to go into the terminal instead or just out on the grass at the end of the runway. I really didn't want to go outside, but I would have Godzilla along with me. Besides, maybe he had to go too.

I stopped at the open hatch. The air was cool and fresh. It felt good. I stepped out onto the landing, and it sagged slightly with my weight. Everywhere I could see darkness. The only light was leaking down from the stars. There were a million of them. Hard to believe there were so many stars in the skies over Chicago.

I went down the rickety metal steps. There were sixteen steps and then the tarmac. I knew that because I'd climbed up and down them so many times dragging or carrying a suitcase. Reaching the bottom, I figured I'd just go into the grass and weeds off to the side.

"Couldn't sleep?"

I jumped. Godzilla moved in between me and the voice and started to growl.

"It's me, Tom. Can you call off your dog?"

I grabbed Godzilla by the collar. If he had lunged forward, could I have held him? "It's okay, boy, it's Tom. He's a friend."

Godzilla's tail started to wag.

"I have to go to the washroom," I explained.

"Come on, I'll show you where to go. I've been using my time and the ax from the airplane to make a trench toilet."

He turned, and I followed. He led me to a shallow hole that seemed to be about five feet long.

"I'll give you a little privacy."

He turned and walked a dozen paces away while I peed. It was a relief.

"What's it been like out here?" I asked.

"Things are pretty quiet on this side of the fence. Out in the city is a different thing."

"What's happening?"

"Come on and have a look." He beckoned me over.

We circled around the plane. I could see what he was talking about. There were more fires in the distance, which had been hidden from view by the fuselage.

"I just wish we weren't so close to the fence," he said.

"I wish the fence was higher," I replied.

"At least there's lots of open ground here. If this soil can grow weeds and grass, it can grow vegetables too," he said, looking around.

"I don't understand," I said, frowning.

"If you can't get food any other way, you have to grow what you eat," he said.

"But even if you planted today, you wouldn't be able to harvest for months." I hesitated for a moment. "Wait. You don't really think we'll be here that long, do you?"

He didn't answer right away. "Do you know about preppers?"

"Peppers?"

He laughed. "*Preppers*. It's people who are *prepared*. Some people call us survivalists."

"What does that mean?"

"It means that I've prepared for something like this to happen."

"But…how could you prepare for this?" I asked, spreading my arms wide.

"My house has an underground bunker, a generator, a gigantic tank of gas, medical supplies, enough food to keep me alive for a year and the weapons to protect it all."

I raised my eyebrows. "That's, um, great, I guess."

"It would be great if it wasn't for the fact that I'm here and my house is more than a thousand miles away," Tom said bitterly. "*That* I hadn't prepared for. But, short of walking, there doesn't seem to be a way to get there."

I looked at him. "You could ride a bike there in ten or twelve days."

"It sounds like you've been thinking about this."

"I have."

"For now this is the best place for us to be," he replied. "We have a fence, some security and weapons and enough food to last for twenty or even thirty days if we go on strict rations."

"Huh," I murmured. "It sounds like you've been thinking about this."

"Not much way around it. Anyway, you should probably head back up and try to get some sleep. I don't think tomorrow is going to be any less demanding."

"Thanks for being out here and watching out for us." I gave a wave.

"We're all in this together."

I started back up the stairs and stopped. I could hear something. Voices from across the tarmac. I turned and went down to where Tom was standing.

"I heard them too," he said under his breath.

"Do you want me to get somebody?"

"Not yet. Could just be the perimeter guards." There were pairs of guards on watch, patrolling just inside the fence.

"I see something. Out there toward the terminal," I said.

It looked like a few shapes moving in the darkness. The voices were getting louder. There was no question they were getting closer.

"Three or four of them," Tom said. "I think they've come close enough."

Godzilla started to growl softly. I figured he agreed with Tom.

"Stop and identify yourself!" Tom called out. I braced myself, trying to think what I'd do if these people meant trouble.

"Tom, it's us!" I recognized the voice and instantly relaxed. It was Captain Daley.

The shapes came forward until they were visible. Phillip and Captain Daley were pushing the strollers, and Noah was in his chair. Fede walked beside them. There were only the four of them. I'd expected they were bringing back other passengers.

"I thought you'd stay at the hotel and we wouldn't see you until morning," Tom said.

"That wasn't possible," Captain Daley said. "There isn't a hotel anymore."

"What?" I asked, confused.

"What do you mean?" Tom said at the same time.

Captain Daley let out his breath in a whoosh. "It's been vandalized, and parts of it have been set on fire."

I gasped. "But...but...what about the other passengers?"

"They were gone," Noah reported, eyes downcast. "Everybody is gone—the staff, other guests, even Renaldo."

"Gone where?" I asked, trying to make sense of what they were telling us.

"We don't know. They must have fled," Captain Daley said. He turned to Fede. "Now, we'd better wake up Dr. Singh to have a look at that gash."

"It's nothing," Fede said.

That's when I noticed he had a cut along the side of his head. In the thin light I hadn't seen it.

"What happened?" Tom exclaimed.

"We were attacked," Noah said. "If it wasn't for Phil, I don't know what would have happened."

I looked at Phillip. He looked upset, angry.

"Phil, we know you had no choice," Captain Daley said. "We'll all testify to that."

"That guy pulled the trigger," Noah said. "I heard the hammer go. He tried to shoot Fede. He would have if the gun hadn't jammed."

"He was pointing it right at me," Fede confirmed. "I thought I was dead. That's when that guy with the baseball bat swung at me."

"Phil, you had to fire at him," Noah said.

Phillip had shot somebody, and people were threatening to shoot them! It seemed unreal.

"You saved my life. You saved all of us," Fede confirmed.

Phil said nothing, his jaw set.

"How many were there?" Tom asked.

"Seven or eight. He was the only one with a gun, but the others were all armed with bats and clubs. One guy had a machete," Noah answered.

"I'm feeling a bit light-headed," Fede muttered.

"Sit down," Captain Daley said as he eased Fede to a seat on the bottom step.

"I'll go get the doctor," Tom offered. He hurried up the stairs. Phillip stood off to the side. He looked shaken.

Tom returned with Dr. Singh in tow. She started asking Fede questions and used a flashlight to look at the wound. In the light it looked worse. It was a nasty gash.

Captain Daley went over to Phillip. Tom joined them, and I moved in that direction as well. I wanted to hear what they were talking about.

Finally Phillip spoke. "Seventeen years as an air marshal, and the first time I take the gun out of the holster, I kill a man." He was slouched over and spoke quietly.

"You don't know if he's dead," Captain Daley said.

"I fired point-blank, two rounds, directly into his chest. The way I was taught to. We left him lying there in the middle of the road. His friends were running so fast I don't know if they'd even bother to come back to help," Phillip countered.

"Noah said the guy's gun misfired," Tom interjected.

"Yeah, I guess. I have it right here." Noah reached into a pocket and pulled out a gun.

"Can I see it?" Tom asked, and Noah passed it over.

Tom turned on a little flashlight to check it out. It was black, stubby and looked like a toy.

"It's a Saturday night special," Tom said. "It's made with the cheapest parts you can get, poorly constructed and prone to misfires. Makes sense it would jam."

With one hand he opened it up and looked inside. "No wonder it didn't fire. I bet the gun has never been cleaned. There's rust on the firing pin."

"You mean I killed a man whose gun didn't work?" Phillip asked. He put his head in his hands.

"You shot a man who tried to kill us," Captain Daley retorted. "His friends with the bats and clubs and machete *would* have killed us. Look at Fede. That swing would have killed him if he hadn't moved. You saved our lives. Understand?"

Phillip met his eyes and nodded. "I understand. I know. It's just... I killed a man. Have either of you ever killed anybody?"

"No," Captain Daley replied softly.

"Not yet," Tom said.

We all turned to him. What a strange response, I thought.

"I haven't killed anybody because I haven't had to," he went on. "I don't want to kill anybody, but I'll do whatever I need to do to survive—to help *us* survive."

"Has it really come to that?" Phillip asked. "That people would kill us over cereal and maple syrup?"

"That's what we brought back," Captain Daley explained. "The hotel has a storage shed in the parking lot, and the looters overlooked it."

Tom turned the flashlight on the strollers. The seats and baskets underneath were filled with boxes of cereal, little plastic containers of syrup and silver packets of ketchup.

"Cereal is almost as good as it gets," Tom said. "It stores forever, doesn't need refrigeration, is compact and filling. Syrup is sugar, and sugar is energy. I don't know about ketchup, but food is food."

"Tom is a prepper," I explained.

They all turned to look at me, surprised, like they didn't know I was there. Standing silently, at the edge in the dark, I figured they had forgotten about me.

"I've studied, read about, prepared for and gone to conferences on all sorts of different disaster scenarios," Tom explained.

"Was this one of them?" Captain Daley asked. He sounded interested.

"This is total societal breakdown. The most extreme." Tom started chuckling, which struck me as strange. "Funny how everybody—people I work with, friends, even family—thinks all of us preppers are crazy. Now I'm not looking so crazy anymore."

"It sounds like we're lucky to have you with us," Captain Daley said.

Tom tipped his head to the captain. "Hopefully I can be helpful. If I can get some sandpaper or even an emery board for doing nails, I can fix this gun."

"I think we can arrange that."

"It's only got three bullets, but that's better than none. Even empty it might help to flash another weapon if we need to get out of a bad situation."

Noah looked dubious. "Isn't holding an empty weapon a way to get shot?" he asked.

"It's got three bullets. Right now, showing it might be the best way *not* to get shot. Say, I'm curious, is it worth taking another trip back out to the hotel?" Tom asked.

Captain Daley shook his head. "We got what we could. It was bad. The whole place is gutted. There were bodies. A couple of them were from our flight. I recognized a hotel staff member."

My stomach flipped. Bodies. Dead people. Could it have been us, if we'd stayed?

"Any sign of law enforcement out there?" Tom asked.

"No, none."

"Figures." Tom clucked his tongue. "Individual officers desert to protect their own families, and the system collapses."

"My wife wouldn't let that happen," Captain Daley said. "She's a police captain in our town. She'd make sure people are safe."

"In some survival scenarios, law-enforcement officers create pockets of control," Tom allowed. "Little areas where they can protect people. If you can't control the big areas, you provide safety in smaller ones. I guess that's sort of what the airport has become." He paused. "At least for now."

Those last four words were scary. We were safe here right now, but for how long?

"You said *town*," Tom said. "How big is the place you're from?"

"It's called Eden Mills. It's about fifty-five thousand people," Captain Daley replied. That was near where my family lived.

Tom nodded. "I'm from Milton, about twenty-five miles away from where you live. Being smaller is good. Big cities are going to be the worst."

"And we're here beside the third-biggest city in the country, with almost three million people," Noah commented.

"It's worse than that," Captain Daley said. "There are almost *ten* million people in the greater Chicago area, and we're smack-dab in the middle of it."

"This isn't the best place to be," Tom agreed. "Fewer the people, fewer the problems."

"I'm afraid I won't be able to arrange a flight out of here," Captain Daley replied wryly.

"Definitely not," Tom said, "but we do need a flight plan to get out of here...and save ourselves."

CHAPTER
ELEVEN

MORNING MADE EVERYTHING BETTER AND worse all at once. Having light meant we could see all around us and know that we were safe. It also meant we could see well beyond us and know how bad things were.

It had taken me a long time to get back to sleep. I'd tossed and turned for at least an hour. Maybe it would have been better if I didn't know certain things. I tried to picture the hotel. I knew what it had looked like the day before. I imagined what would have happened if we'd been staying there instead of in the plane. It made me feel sick.

"Breakfast is served!" Fede called out. "Time to get up, sleepyheads! Breakfast will be served on the tarmac, like a meal on a really, really big patio!"

I shifted Godzilla over to the side and got up.

The side of Fede's face was bandaged up. People who'd slept through the night were asking what had happened. He joked he'd "cut himself shaving" and then explained that everybody would be told everything after we ate.

I shuffled along the aisle to the hatch and the stairs. There was a luggage trolley below being used as a table. There were a dozen chairs—probably brought from the terminal—surrounding it. I went down the steps with Godzilla at my side.

"Good morning, Jamie, how are you today?" Julia asked.

"Good. All things considered."

"I guess that's the best way to say it. Have a seat and eat," Doeun said.

I was hungry. I sat and Fede put down a tray in front of me—more airplane food, along with a jar of what looked like applesauce. I realized it was baby food.

"I thought we'd be having cereal for sure."

"We're trying to go through all the food that will go bad without refrigeration," he explained.

Soon we were all sitting around the table. There was lots of eating but not much talking, except for Nelson, who seemed happy and just wanted to tell everybody about Mia, who was settled in his arms. Part of me wished I too was a little kid who didn't know what was going on and just thought this was all a game.

Captain Daley stood up. "I'd like to fill in everybody about what went on yesterday." He paused. "Jamie, could you do me a favor? Since you've already been updated, I'd like you and Nelson to take the dogs out for a walk."

Nelson looked at his mother for reassurance. She nodded her approval.

It was obvious the captain didn't want Nelson to hear what he was going to tell them. I wondered if there were also things he was trying to keep from me as well.

I shoveled in the last few morsels of food—including the baby food—from my tray and got up. Nelson came and took my hand.

The two dogs trotted beside us. Mia looked like she was interested in playing, but Godzilla didn't seem in the mood and ignored the little poodle.

We left the edge of the tarmac and went into the grass. I thought back to what Tom had talked about, turning this into crops. There was no way we were going to be here that long. I couldn't let myself think that far into the future.

"Your dog is scary," Nelson said. He looked so small, his little-kid hair ruffling in the breeze.

I smiled. "Godzilla is good scary because he can protect us."

"Protect us from what?"

"You know. Any bad guys."

Nelson frowned. "There are lots of bad guys out there, aren't there?"

"Not as many as there are good guys—good people—here. There's your mother, the captain, Julia and Fede and everybody."

Suddenly Godzilla raced away. "Godzilla!" I screamed.

He kept running through the weeds, Mia running along too, trying to keep up. I saw a rabbit in the grass, dodging and turning. It looked like he was going to catch it when the rabbit disappeared into a hole. Godzilla started digging furiously, throwing dirt back between his legs.

We ran over, and I grabbed him by the collar. He was so strong. Nelson picked up Mia, who licked his face.

"Look," Nelson said. He was pointing beyond the fence.

I hadn't realized how close we'd gotten to it. There was a family on the other side—a mother, father and two small children. The father was pulling a wagon. The older boy, who was about ten, was on a bike. It would have looked like the family was just out for a stroll if you didn't notice that that the wagon was piled high with items. They stopped walking, and the parents looked over at us.

"Hello!" the mother yelled out.

Nelson and I waved. They came closer, and I felt uneasy. I was grateful for the high chain-link fence topped by strands of barbed wire that stood between us.

"You two aren't alone, are you?" the man asked.

"No, our families are over there," I answered.

The woman peered at me. "Are you living at the airport?" she asked.

"Yeah, for now." I didn't want to say anything more.

"Is it safe?"

"Is anyplace safe right now?" I asked. I turned and spoke quietly just to Nelson. "It's safe."

"Are they letting other people in?" the man asked.

"I don't know. Where are you going?"

"My brother has a farm," he answered. "Anyhow, we better get going. It's a long way to walk."

I took Nelson by the hand. "We need to get back too." The boy on the bike stared at me a minute before they all headed off down the road.

On our way back the dogs ran ahead, and Nelson ran along with them. I was so grateful the rabbit had escaped. Nelson didn't need to see a bunny killed right before his eyes. Neither did I.

As we returned, the others were just finishing up their discussion.

"Then it's agreed," Doeun said to the gathering. "Tom and I are going to the terminal to talk to people and see if we can pick up anything that might be helpful."

"Phillip and I will be doing perimeter security at the plane and along the fence," Noah added.

"And Richard and I will be going to talk to Wayne and have a look around," Captain Daley said.

"Jamie, you and your dog should go with the captain and Richard," Tom said. "Wayne seems to have a soft spot for dogs."

"Godzilla will listen to you, right?" Captain Daley asked.

"He's good as long as he doesn't see any more rabbits."

"There are rabbits here?" Tom said, perking up.

"At least one," I replied. "He chased it into a hole."

"Later on show me that hole," he suggested.

He was a hunter, so I figured I knew why. I just hoped he'd forget about it.

A few more words were exchanged and then everybody went their separate ways. I was happy to be with the captain. The five of us walked toward the terminal.

"You should take this," Doeun said as she pulled out a pistol and offered it to Captain Daley. "We found it in the luggage."

He waved it away. "You might want to hang on to it."

"We've got a weapon," Tom said. He pulled back his jacket to reveal the Saturday night special. "It's working now. At least, I'm pretty sure it is. We can't waste a bullet on a test fire."

Captain Daley took the gun from Doeun, nodding his thanks.

"Keep it hidden," Tom suggested. "Best to have the element of surprise."

We'd made it to the terminal. Doeun turned to us. "This is where we separate," she said. "Good luck!"

"You too," Richard said as Doeun and Tom headed up the flight of stairs leading into the terminal. Captain Daley, Richard and I headed around the side, where there was a large open door big enough for a truck to drive through. I realized there was light coming from inside. How could that be possible?

We stopped outside the door. "Generator?" Captain Daley asked.

"I think so. Gas-driven. I can smell it," Richard replied.

"Keep your eyes open for anything that might be useful," Captain Daley said. He turned to me. "Richard is a bit of a handyman."

We walked inside. I looked back. Godzilla had stopped at the door, like he thought there was something dangerous inside. Maybe it was Anguirus, the monster Godzilla fought in the second movie of the series. It was a bad movie—but a great monster.

"Come on, boy," I said, patting a hand against my leg. "I'll protect you from dragons."

He ran to catch us. I felt better having him at my side.

The space inside was big and cavernous, and there were abandoned vehicles everywhere, equipment thrown around and open suitcases, clothing and random items spread out on the floor.

Soon we could hear the hum of an engine and some voices.

"Hello!" Captain Daley yelled. "Wayne, are you in here?"

"This way!"

We came into an even larger space to find a dozen men and women sitting around a table. They were eating. It looked like more airplane food. I recognized Calvin and gave him a wave.

"Captain Daley, good to see you!" Wayne said in his booming voice.

"You too. You have power?"

"Not much, but enough to have some light and cook a warm meal for everybody."

"It must be nice to have a generator."

"We have two," Wayne said. "At least, two that work."

"And some that don't?" Richard asked, raising his eyebrows.

"Five more. All of them are such old pieces of junk. I'm surprised we even got one of them running."

"My friend here has some expertise with generators," Captain Daley said, gesturing to Richard. "Do you think he could have a look at them?"

Wayne didn't answer, his mouth set in a line.

"Look, how about if we get a couple of them to work, and then we get to keep one?" Captain Daley suggested. "Wouldn't it be better to have one working than two broken?"

Wayne hesitated a moment before giving a nod. "Sounds like a good trade," he said. "Calvin, could you take them to the generators?"

Calvin got up and grabbed a trolley, and we followed after him. As we walked away and deeper into the building, it quickly got much darker. Calvin flicked on a flashlight. It felt like we were walking through the hidden tunnels underneath Hogwarts. We could have used Harry Potter, or at least his magic wand, I thought, especially if we ran into some of the dark beings he'd met in those passages. There was definitely enough space here to hold a basilisk. I hated snakes at the best of times, let alone gigantic magical ones.

"Lots of stuff back here. We're not allowed to toss anything," Calvin explained. "So this is a burial ground for old equipment."

"Mind if I come back and have a look around later on?" Richard asked. "Sometimes it pays to be a grave robber."

"Just ask for me, and I'll bring you back. It's not like I've got anyplace to go." Calvin sighed.

"You're not from around here?" Captain Daley asked.

"Only moved here six months ago. My family is from halfway across the country, a little place nobody has ever heard of called Milton."

"Milton! One of our passengers, Tom, is from there. I live in Eden Mills."

"Really? That's, like, twenty-five or so miles away! What a small world!" Calvin said.

"It *was* a small world. Now it's a world away," Captain Daley said.

"Or a really, really long walk," Calvin said, nodding.

"It would take fifty days," I added.

Calvin stopped and pointed the flashlight at us. "Sounds like you've been thinking about it. Are you all going to try to get back home?"

"We're looking at lots of options," Captain Daley replied.

"If you do go, can I come along with you?"

Captain Daley didn't answer. The silence was broken by Richard.

"Calvin, what are those?" Richard asked.

Calvin spun the light so it was aimed where Richard was pointing. The light revealed a set of stairs mounted on the back of what looked like a motorized trolley.

"It's an old stair car. Junk. Everything back here is junk. Probably hasn't worked for years, maybe decades. We have six or seven of them. Those things have to be older than me."

I already knew that was a good sign, because *old* meant that there were no computer parts.

"Anyways, here are the generators," Calvin continued.

The captain and Richard helped him heave three of the generators onto the trolley. They looked heavy and old. Could Richard fix at least a couple of them?

"Look," Calvin said, turning to us. "I really want to go with you if you decide to try to get home."

Captain Daley gave a slight nod. "Like I said, I'm not sure we're heading anywhere."

"You should be," Calvin said. "I don't think the safety of the airport is going to last long."

"Why would you think that?" Richard asked.

"It got bad last night with rioters almost pushing through the terminal doors. Look, just take me if you do go. I want to see my family, my mother." He was on the verge of tears.

"That's all any of us want," Captain Daley offered.

It was all I wanted. To be with my family. Not here, miles away, wondering if they were all right.

"I'm good with my hands. I know where there are things at the terminal that could help."

Captain Daley squared his shoulders. "Calvin, if we go, you're coming with us. You have my word," he said.

Calvin threw his arms around the captain and hugged him.

Was it possible that we were going to try to get home? Was Captain Daley really thinking about it? Just the possibility made me feel better.

CHAPTER TWELVE

PHILLIP AND I WALKED ALONG the fence. On the other side there was a steady stream of people on the move. Most were heading away from the city. Some were on bikes, but most were on foot. They pulled wagons or pushed shopping carts or strollers that were filled with possessions. Sometimes they waved or called out to us. Phillip said to pretend we didn't notice them.

I thought about what Calvin had told us. Would rioters get through the doors and into the terminal? And if they did, how long before they spilled out onto the tarmac to where we were?

"There's another truck."

"It's got to be thirty-five years old," Phillip said. "I haven't seen anything newer that's still functioning."

There were also small motorcycles—dirt bikes and minibikes—and a couple of go-karts. They were all too old or too simple to involve complicated technology or computer systems.

I turned around and made out two people moving across the tarmac toward us. I shielded my eyes from the sun with my hand and focused—it was Doeun and Tom. That was a relief. I'd been getting worried because they had been away so long. Godzilla and I ran over to greet them.

They were both carrying two big white jugs of bleach. "This stuff is better than gold," Tom said.

"I still think gold is pretty wonderful," Doeun said with a laugh.

"You can't drink gold," Tom replied.

I made a face. "And you *can* drink bleach?"

"You can drink water *because* of bleach," Tom said. "I'll explain it all. Let's gather everybody together."

I suspected that nothing they were going to say would be good news. I couldn't help wondering just how bad it was going to be.

They didn't waste any time. Doeun spoke quietly to Captain Daley, and then they got everybody together except Amber and Nelson. They were sent into the plane on an errand and a promise to Amber that they'd explain everything to her later.

"If it's all right, I'm going to stay right here where I can listen and keep working," Richard said. He had the generators in pieces, in three separate piles.

"Doeun, Tom, you have the floor," Captain Daley said.

"We spoke to a lot of people," Doeun began. "TSA agents manning the exits, people from the stores, ground crew and passengers who had no place to go except the terminal."

"It's not looking good," Tom said. "Last night the looters almost got in. They had to shoot some people at one of the doors and along the fence."

"It got ugly," Doeun added. "It didn't look like they could hold them back."

"And to make it worse, some of the TSA agents, the guys with the guns, are abandoning the terminal. They were here because it was their job, but people rarely risk their lives for their jobs," Tom explained. "Now they're leaving to be with family."

"And tell them about the bleach," Doeun said.

"Sure. Does anybody know about the rule of three?" Tom asked.

"I read a book with that name," I said. "It was about surviving when society broke down."

"Probably lots of books named that. It's an old survival saying. You can live three minutes without air, three days without water and three weeks without food. The air's all around, so we don't have to worry about that." He turned to Julia and Fede. "How much water do we have, assuming everybody here drinks fifteen ounces a day?"

"I'd have to check, but probably enough for three or four weeks," Fede replied.

"When that's gone, then water will have to come from rivers or lakes or even puddles, but that water isn't reliable. It can be dirty or have parasites and make people sick. Bleach changes that. Six to eight drops for every gallon, left to sit for thirty minutes, and the water's drinkable," Tom explained. "Four bottles of bleach are enough to produce water for all of us for a long time. I'm going to try to get even more. I'll check on all the cleaning trolleys, because nobody else has figured it out yet."

"Don't we have an obligation to tell them?" Dr. Singh asked. "I mean, to help others too?"

"We have an obligation to ourselves," Tom answered.

Dr. Singh furrowed her brow. "Captain Daley, is that what you think?" she asked.

He appeared to be taken aback by her question. Then he thought for a minute.

"We'd like to help everybody...but we can't. The obligation of myself and my crew is to our passengers. The people around this table are my obligation. I want to keep us all alive and safe."

Dr. Singh paused, contemplating what he'd said. Then she gave a small nod of understanding.

"Tom," Captain Daley went on, "what else do you think we should do to keep ourselves alive and safe?"

Tom crossed his arms. "Leave here. Get away from the city. Away from the crowds."

"I see people every day outside the fence who are trying to get away," Phillip said.

"And we should be joining them," Tom said.

Richard looked up from his work. "And you expect us to leave here and just hope for the best?"

"I'm suggesting that we leave here with a plan. We take food, water, supplies, blankets and all the weapons we have to protect ourselves."

"And we just walk out carrying all those things?" Sara asked.

"Carrying, pushing, walking and riding," Tom said.

Noah cut in. "I'd feel a lot better about leaving if I knew where I was going."

"We should go where we were flying to," I answered. "To our families."

"You want us to leave here and go over a thousand miles on foot?" Sara questioned.

"It's more like twelve to fourteen hundred miles," Tom answered. "I've been looking at maps. We won't be able to take any sort of straight route. We'll have to work around problems and avoid any big cities completely."

"That would take forever," Phillip said.

"Fifty days," Julia and I said together.

"Nelson can't walk that far," Amber said. She was standing on the stairs. She had left Nelson inside the plane. "He's only five."

"Nelson won't have to," Captain Daley said. "He'll be carried, or pushed in a stroller or on a luggage trolley, or ride on something."

"Wait, Captain," Dr. Singh interjected. "Do you agree with him? Are you really thinking we should go?"

"I'm thinking we need to talk about it. Consider it," Captain Daley replied in a measured tone. I felt a stir of excitement and hope. It might be happening. We might be headed home.

"And if I decide I don't want to go, if I want to stay here? Or head in a different direction?" she asked.

"Of course. You're all free to go anywhere you want or to stay here."

"Assuming there's a *here* to stay at," Tom said. "I figure this place is going to break down soon. Maybe a few days, a week—a month tops."

"And if he's right," Captain Daley added, "we're better to leave on our own terms, with our own plan, rather than scrambling at the last minute." A few people murmured to each other, but I couldn't hear what they were saying. "Shall we put it to a vote?"

I was itching to vote yes. I just hoped enough of the others would be in favor too.

There was an awkward silence, and then people started to mumble agreement.

"Wait!" Noah called out. "Somebody's coming."

I turned around. It was a man pulling a trolley. It looked like he was straining under the load.

"It's Calvin," Captain Daley said.

We all greeted him, and as he pulled up, I could see the trolley was loaded with two large cardboard boxes and three or four metal containers—they looked almost like gigantic car batteries.

"Good to see you," Captain Daley said.

"I brought you some extra things." He lifted up one of the boxes. On the side was a picture of a bike.

"It's new, not fully assembled, but I thought it could be useful— you know, to get around or even go on a trip." He met my eyes. I nodded slightly. We were hoping for the same thing.

"That's fantastic!" Julia exclaimed.

"I might even be able to get more than these two. I also brought you the batteries from the stair vehicle you were looking at. I learned more about them from Wayne."

"Oh? Please go on," Captain Daley said.

"There are ten of them in storage. They stopped using them almost twenty-five years ago, but when they put them into mothballs, they were still working."

"If they were working, why did they replace them?" Julia asked.

"They're open cabs, so the driver gets wet or cold or snowed on. They don't move very fast—a top speed of less than fifteen miles an hour. And because they're on battery power, they have to be charged, and that charge takes eight hours or longer."

"But they still run?" Noah asked impatiently.

"They've been sitting there for a long time, but they should," Calvin said. "Assuming there's a way to charge them."

Almost in answer there came the roar of an engine, and we all turned toward the noise. Richard was standing beside one of the generators, and it was chugging away, throwing out a thin wisp of blue smoke. The sound was overwhelmingly loud.

He flipped a switch and the generator gurgled and then died.

Richard grinned. "I think we can conclude that we have a way to charge batteries. Does this mean we have a vehicle that will run?"

"I think I can make that happen," Calvin said.

A car—even a stair car—would make a trip so much easier. This was big.

Captain Daley spoke up. "I want you all to know that Calvin wants to join our group if we decide to leave."

"Wayne doesn't know anything about it," Calvin said more quietly, "so we're going to have to sort of sneak the vehicle out. He's pretty possessive of all the equipment."

Noah chuckled. "We're going to sneak out a gigantic stair car?" he asked.

"When things all go crazy, it's going to be easy as pie. Especially since we're not going to be sticking around long enough for him to ask us to give it back," Tom said.

There was a lot of laughter—nervous laughter.

"Calvin," Captain Daley said, "we were just about to put our future to a vote, and you deserve to be part of it."

CHAPTER
THIRTEEN

"EAT UP," FEDE SAID. "We don't want to waste anything."

We were trying to use up the last of the airplane food. It was the remaining parts of the meals that hadn't gone bad but soon would. They figured it was better in our stomachs than being tossed. Tom said it was like putting as much "fuel in our tanks" as we could.

I snuck a little piece of carrot off my plate and slipped it to Godzilla. He gobbled it down. Nelson, sitting beside me, giggled slightly. He'd been doing the same thing with Mia, who was, as always, sitting on his lap.

My hand brushed against the backpack at my feet. It was reassuring that it was there, but scary that it was soon going to be used. We each had a separate backpack full of supplies. All of us, including Calvin. Each pack contained a change of clothing, an extra pair of walking shoes, a box of cereal, two bottles of water, a small plastic bottle of bleach, ten jars of baby food and a blanket. They were what Tom called go bags, so if we got separated we each had the basics. I was going to work very hard not to get separated. I'd done some trading to get my favorite flavors of the baby food— that might sound funny, but some flavors were better than others. Apple/strawberry/banana was a cut above everything else, and turkey and gravy actually reminded me of Thanksgiving.

The backpacks themselves were reused bags we'd found in overhead storage, and the clothing and shoes were taken from the luggage itself. I was starting out with my sneakers and had somebody else's shoes as my backup. Other people, including Dr. Singh and Richard, ditched their dress shoes for better walking shoes.

The rest of the food, including all the smoked meat, cereal, packaged airplane snacks, the rest of the baby food and the dog food, and the medical supplies and other pieces of equipment were on the luggage trolley. We hoped we could rig the trolley to be towed by the stair car. If not, we'd be pulling it ourselves.

One of the escape slides had been removed from the plane and then cut up to provide two pieces of nylon big enough to act as covers—basically crude tents—against any bad weather.

The generator was the bulkiest, heaviest piece of equipment. Richard had managed to get all three of them working. We were taking one of them, and the other two had already been returned to Wayne. That was the deal—although I guess the deal hadn't included stealing a stair car.

Whether to let Wayne know what we were doing had taken up a lot of discussion. Dr. Singh and Captain Daley had wanted to talk to him, let him know and negotiate for the vehicle. They wanted his permission. Tom and Calvin—mostly Calvin—had finally convinced them that negotiating could result in our losing it completely. Calvin told us that Wayne could be a pretty difficult guy, and he was getting less reasonable with each passing day. People were becoming more scared, Tom pointed out, and this made them more dangerous.

I had one more thing in my bag—something I'd written up the night before when I couldn't sleep, thinking about what we were going to do and whether we actually *could* do it. It was a list of all of us.

At the top was a heading called *Crew* and under that were the names Captain Daley, Doeun, Julia and Fede. These were the people I knew I could count on. They weren't just the crew—because my parents were pilots, these people were like extended family.

The next heading was *Medical*, and there were two names, Dr. Singh and Richard. Having both a doctor and a nurse was pretty important if anything went wrong. There were so many ways we could get hurt or injured. It happening was almost guaranteed, traveling so far on foot. Their being with us was reassuring.

The third heading was *Security*, and I'd listed Phillip, as he was an air marshal, and Tom, because he was a hunter and had guns. I'd also put down Sara and Noah. Bows and arrows were weapons, especially in their hands.

Next was the label *Others*, which was Amber, Nelson and me. We didn't fit into any of the previous categories, and I didn't know how helpful any of us could be. I wanted to be more than just luggage or, even worse, luggage that had to be fed. I vowed to myself that I'd do anything I could to pull my weight.

The last name under *Others* was Calvin. He was the outsider, the one I didn't know at all. I'd wondered if it was smart to bring him along. But I'd also thought it might be even smarter to bring him and a few others too. There were fourteen of us in total. It seemed like a lot, but really, was the group large enough? Were we enough people to get away, stay safe and get home?

I ran my finger down the names one more time.

Somehow satisfied, I folded up the list and slipped it into my pocket.

It had been two days since we'd started our secret plan to leave. I was relieved that it was finally in the works. Nobody outside our group except Calvin knew anything about it. Tom had convinced us there was nothing to gain by letting people know what we were doing. It felt like we were in the middle of a spy novel or a zombie movie. In every zombie story I'd ever read, the danger wasn't just from the zombies but from other people.

I'd been part of guard duty and couldn't help seeing the people on the other side of the fence. Some waved and called out greetings, but more and more now, they moved with heads down, grim expressions on their faces. Sometimes I thought if it was so bad outside the fence, why did we want to go there, but then I remembered everything we'd talked about. We couldn't stay here.

Soon what was out there would come spilling into here. We were trying not just to get to a better place, but to our homes. That was the ultimate goal. We'd move as a group in the direction our flight would have taken us. A couple of people would split off just before we got to where I was going because their homes were on the way. As luck would have it, it turned out that Julia and her husband lived less than a mile from where I lived. Captain Daley lived on the far side of the city, and he promised to walk me right up to my front door before he went farther.

I wanted to get home so badly. I wanted to be with my mother and father. I wanted to know that they were safe and that they'd keep me safe. Leaving this place was the first step to getting there. Step by step in the right direction was how I was trying to think about it, because it would be a long journey.

Calvin had been out to our plane a few times. He had to be careful not to be seen there too often. He had taken the newly charged batteries, reinstalled them and tested the different stair vehicles until he found the one he thought worked best. He'd also taken batteries from another one of the vehicles, which Richard charged, along with a spare tire. It wasn't like we'd be able to get those things at the local Walmart if we needed them. Actually, we probably couldn't get anything from anywhere anymore.

We knew things were getting worse because more people were leaving the terminal. Tom described how it was just too big to defend. There were too many ways in and out. Ways out worked for us. We were going to go through a gate on the far south of the grounds. Calvin had gotten us gigantic bolt cutters to cut the chains that held it closed.

The plane had been scavenged for parts. Along with the medical supplies, we'd taken the flare gun, fire axes and anything that could serve as a weapon. I had a knife that had been taken from one of the suitcases. It was way bigger than anything my parents would have let me have. I had it in its leather sheath, strapped to my left leg, hidden under my pants. Having it should have made me feel safer. It didn't. The fact that I might need a knife was just plain scary.

The other weapons had all been given out. Phillip had his pistol, and Tom would have his rifle strapped to his back. Richard would carry Tom's shotgun. Doeun had the pistol they'd found in the luggage, and Captain Daley had the Saturday night special. Both Noah and Sara had their bows. They had been doing some target practicing, and they were deadly accurate. Somehow the bows seemed even more dangerous than guns. Maybe it was because we'd seen the arrows fly and hit their target, but nobody had fired a bullet at anything. The bullets were precious. Tom had lots of rounds for his two guns. Noah and Sara had fifty-three arrows, which could be reclaimed and reused. Other than Nelson, Dr. Singh was the only one without a weapon—she had refused to carry a weapon of any kind. She said it was against her principles to harm anybody. Her being a doctor, I guessed that made sense.

Calvin had gotten us another bike to go along with the two bikes he'd already found. They were all assembled and rideable. We even had a little patch kit to fix flats. People would take turns riding and walking. The little girl's bike was too small for anybody except me or Nelson. Maybe in a pinch Doeun could ride it as well.

I needed to stretch my legs. I got up, and Godzilla instantly responded. He was right at my heels. Doeun was coming down the stairs from the plane.

"You really do have a shadow. I don't think that dog would let anything bad happen to you," she said as she gave Godzilla a rub behind his ears.

"I feel the same about him." I looked down at his big brown eyes.

"Keep in mind that we're all here to take care of you," Doeun said softly. "Captain Daley will get us to where we need to get to. There's not another pilot in our company I trust more. I bet even your parents would agree with that."

I felt my shoulders sag. "I wish they were here or, I guess, that I was there. Do you think we can make it?"

"We'll make it to someplace better than here. It might take a long time, but we're going to get home." She sounded resolute. "Hey, do you know what this reminds me of?"

I shook my head.

"*Lord of the Rings.*"

I brightened a little. "Really?"

"We're like the characters in *The Fellowship of the Ring*," she replied. "A band of brave travelers who've come together on a dangerous mission. Can't you just see it?"

I turned and looked at our little group, hard at work on their preparations.

"Captain Daley is obviously Aragorn, our fearless leader. Tom, with all his knowledge, not to mention the beard, is Gandalf."

"Sometimes he acts like a dwarf, sort of like Gimli," I said, cracking a smile.

"I can see that too," Doeun agreed. "But definitely he has knowledge that nobody else has."

"And who are you?" I asked.

"Isn't it obvious? I am Arwen, the beautiful queen of the elves. You are, of course—"

"Frodo," we both said together.

"Frodo is the heart of the fellowship," Doeun said. "His size did not dictate his importance to the mission." She smiled. "I think we can both agree that small can be powerful."

I nodded. "And that must make Godzilla Samwise, my trusted companion." I gave him a pat.

"That goes without saying. He's your shadow, a faithful friend who would protect you with his life," Doeun said.

"I guess we have to hope we don't run into Ringwraiths."

"They're out there, but just like in the story, we will defeat them," Doeun said.

I laughed. "The only thing we're short is a ring."

"Actually..." Doeun pulled a ring from her finger and handed it to me. "This belonged to my grandmother. I want you to keep it in your pocket. Keep it safe for me."

I hesitated. "But why?"

"To complete the theme. When we're finished our journey, you have to give it back to me instead of throwing it into the fires of Mount Doom."

"I will." I took it from her and put it in my pocket. It seemed precious, like the ring in the books. "I just wish it gave me invisibility."

Doeun grinned. "Invisibility would be nice."

Somehow talking about the book made me feel better. We were setting out on a journey, and we could succeed. We only had to go for a long walk, and we wouldn't be fighting Orcs, Sauron or Saruman—and, hopefully, there wasn't any Gollum out there. When the sun set, darkness would be our cover and protection. We were ready.

Tom walked over to where we were standing. "It's time," he said. "See you at the gate. You're got thirty minutes to get there."

We were divided into groups. Julia walked over to the people clustered around the trolley, and I followed. I put my pack under the edge of the tarp, which was tied down and covering the supplies.

Already gathered there were Richard, Fede, Amber and Nelson, Dr. Singh and Noah. Noah had his bow on his lap. This group would take the trolley along the far edge of the tarmac to keep away from the terminal and, hopefully, stay hidden in the darkness.

"If anybody asks you where you're going, tell them it is none of their business," Tom said. "And if they try to look under the tarp?"

"We stop them," Noah said. "Simple as that."

Sara bent down and gave Noah a hug goodbye. They exchanged a few words I couldn't hear, and then it was time to go.

Sara would stay at the plane with Phillip to guard the plane, he with his pistol and she with her bow. If our plan didn't work, for some reason, we needed a place to come back to. The two of them had bikes. They would have to get to the rest of us in a hurry.

"Okay, it's our turn," Tom said to Captain Daley. The two of them were going to the terminal tunnels to help Calvin get the stair car out.

"What happens if somebody sees you taking the stair car?" I asked.

"I'm hoping they don't notice or are so shocked that they don't have time to react," Tom said. "But if they try to stop us, we'll do what we have to do."

That thought send a shiver up my spine.

"We'll try not to hurt anybody," Captain Daley added quickly.

"That's right. We're preparing for the worst and hoping for the best," Tom added. "We'll see you two outside the terminal in twenty minutes. You better get on your way."

Doeun and I started riding as they started walking. Without radios or telephones, we were going to relay information back and forth between the trolley group and Captain Daley's group.

"Sorry you don't have a better bike," Doeun said.

I glanced down at it. "I'm actually starting to like the pink streamers."

"You know you're safe with me," Doeun said firmly, as we pedaled faster.

"I may be safer than I've ever been in my life," I said. "I'm being escorted by somebody who's carrying a gun. Running beside me is a 120-pound Akita as a guard dog, and I have a six-inch knife strapped to my leg. How much safer could I get?"

She gave me a small smile. "Sounds pretty secure to me."

The terminal was now off to our right. I tried to picture Calvin in there, maybe already sitting at the wheel of the stair car, waiting to start it up and drive out.

We passed by a couple of stranded planes. The hatches and cargo holds were open. We came up to the burnt remains of one of the crashed planes. It was a blackened skeleton with the skin peeled back. The fuselage itself was in three jagged pieces, the landing gear was shattered, and the wheels had burned and burst. What would it have been like for the crew and passengers? We'd come close to knowing ourselves.

"I heard that there were over forty-five deaths on that plane," Doeun said. "Including the pilot and the first officer. It would have been worse if the flight crew hadn't acted so quickly."

I hadn't expected her to say that. We had never talked about the casualties.

We pedaled past, and I fought the urge to look back. I couldn't let myself.

"Did you always want to be a pilot?" I asked.

"Not always, but my parents told me I should aim for the sky."

"Your parents wanted you to be a pilot?"

She laughed. "They wanted me to be a doctor. It seems like *all* Korean parents want their children to be doctors, but I found I really did want to aim for the sky. So here I am."

In the dark we caught sight of the trolley crew. They were moving slowly, and I tried to figure out if they were halfway to the gate.

"Any problems?" Doeun asked them when they reached us.

"We ran into two perimeter guards," Julia said. "We told them we were looking for a plane to stay in that was farther away from the fence."

"And they bought that?" Doeun asked.

"They asked if there'd be space for them," Julia said. "Things are getting worse in the terminal, and they aren't feeling safe."

It was time to swing back by the terminal again. We were moving fast, and I started to worry about Godzilla. His tongue was hanging out. This was a long way to run, and he had a lot farther to go before this was over. I wondered if I should have put him on a leash and had him travel with the trolley.

We were just in sight of the terminal when we saw Tom. He was frantically waving his arms above his head. We skidded to a stop beside him.

"It's happening. Now! Right away!"

"But the schedule," Doeun said.

"Wayne's in a meeting up in the terminal. They're going to be out in less than five minutes!" Tom exclaimed. "I've got to get back inside." He turned and hurried off.

"I'll go get Phillip and Sara," Doeun said. "Jamie, you have to get the trolley crew to the gate fast, and get it open right away!"

She was gone before I could even think to argue. I raced across the tarmac, trying to figure how much farther they'd traveled and where I'd have to intercept them.

Suddenly Godzilla stopped running. I skidded to a stop and called for him. He slowly trotted over to me and lay down on the pavement. I called him again, but he didn't move. His tongue was sticking out the side of his mouth, and even in the dim light I could see foamy saliva. Poor dog. But I needed to keep moving. I had to tell the trolley group to hurry. I had an idea.

"Stay!" I yelled at Godzilla. "Stay!"

I wasn't sure if he was listening to me or was simply too tired to get up, but I had to go. I started pedaling, looking back over my shoulder as I went. He wasn't moving. I watched until he faded into the darkness. I'd reach the group, tell them to open the gate and then go back to get Godzilla and meet them at the gate.

I came to the end of the tarmac. The fence was just ahead of me. I looked both ways and couldn't see the crew. I biked back a bit, thinking that I'd overestimated their speed. I hadn't gone for more than thirty seconds when I almost bumped right into the trolley.

"It's all happening sooner!" I yelled. "You have to get to the gate right away!"

"Will do!" Richard called, and everyone instantly started pulling harder and moving faster. I had to get Godzilla.

"Where are you going?" Julia yelled as I turned to go.

"I'll meet you at the gate!" I yelled back over my shoulder.

I had to find Godzilla and coax him to come with me. That was assuming I could locate him in the dark and that we could find the gate in time. If I was late, the group would wait for us. I was pretty sure of that. Unless they were being chased and had no choice but to flee.

I angled myself back along the pavement, trying to follow the invisible trail back to my dog. I stood up on the pedals, coasting, trying not to move too fast, scanning the darkness to pick out Godzilla. I couldn't see him, but it was possible he could see me— or at least hear me.

"Godzilla!" I hissed. My voice vanished into the night.

I put on the brakes and came to a stop. I listened. Nothing.

"Godzilla...come!" I yelled.

I heard something now. Footsteps, but they were coming from behind me, and as I turned a man appeared in the darkness.

I hesitated for a split second and then tried to pedal away but was knocked off the bike, smashing down and sliding across the pavement. I tried to scramble to my feet, tangled up in the bike, but a foot pressed against my back, pushing me over and onto my face. I turned around. The man towered over me, a gun in his hand, aimed right at me!

CHAPTER FOURTEEN

"WHAT ARE YOU DOING OUT HERE?" he demanded.

"I was just...just riding my bike," I said.

I was hit by a beam of light. He was holding a flashlight. I looked away and used my arm to shield my eyes. My arm was scraped and bleeding. He grabbed me and pulled me to my feet. I was now standing, but he still was holding on to me. His fingers dug in and hurt.

"Don't lie to me," he yelled. "What are you doing here?"

"I got lost. I was out riding a bit and I got farther away and couldn't get back and—"

"How many of you came over the fence?" he yelled.

"I didn't come over the fence. I live here at the airport."

"I saw you talking to others who took off to the right."

I squinted at him. "How could you see anything in the dark?"

He let the beam of light move up toward his face, and I could see he was wearing something—sort of like big, fancy metal glasses.

"Night-vision goggles," I gasped.

"Tell me what you know right now, or I'm going to shoot you," he said.

"Shoot me?" He was talking about shooting me. Killing me. I was so scared I thought I was going to throw up.

"Do you think you'd be the first intruder I've killed? Now tell me how many are with you and where they are going."

"I don't know anything," I pleaded, my voice cracking, almost in tears.

"Last chance."

He brought the gun up so that it was aimed directly at my head. I froze.

There was a flash of movement, and I staggered sideways and toppled over as he was bowled off his feet. The gun and flashlight flew out of his hands and skipped across the pavement.

It was Godzilla! In the light coming from the fallen flashlight, I saw him on top of the man, who was kicking and flailing and struggling to push the dog off him. Godzilla growled and snarled, flashing teeth in the light, and then locked his jaws around the man's throat. The man stopped moving. Was he dead?

"Get him off me," he whimpered. His voice was constricted and hoarse.

I scrambled over to where the flashlight lay on the pavement. I picked it up and located the pistol and took it too. I pointed the gun at him. My hand was shaking badly.

"Godzilla, um, sit," I commanded.

He sat but didn't release his grip on the man's throat as the man groaned loudly.

"I mean, down."

Godzilla did what he was ordered, and the man groaned again as the dog dropped to the ground without releasing his grip.

I was going to call him over but figured he'd probably just drag the guy along. *Wait.*

"Release!" I ordered.

Godzilla let go, and the man dropped to the ground, clutching his neck. Through his fingers I could see damage had been done and blood was flowing.

"You need to go," I said, "but first I want those goggles."

He hesitated. "What are you going to do if I don't give them to you? Shoot me?"

That was a good question. I couldn't shoot him. Could I?

"No, I won't shoot you," I said.

He smiled.

"I'd just sic Godzilla on you again. Do you want that?"

The smile disappeared. He pulled the goggles off his head and placed them on the ground. He got up. Blood was flowing down his neck as he pressed his hands to the wound. I backed away slightly, holding the gun between us.

"Tomorrow I'm going to be looking for you and your dog," he said.

He backed away a dozen steps and then turned and ran, quickly being swallowed by the darkness.

I scooped up the goggles and picked up my bike. The handlebars were at a strange angle. It didn't matter. I could fix them later. I slipped the goggles over my head, turned off the flashlight and put it and the gun into the little basket on the front of the bike. Then I jumped on and started pedaling. Godzilla ran beside me. He was rested now.

"Thanks, boy," I said.

As long as I rode in a straight line, I'd hit the fence. Then I'd follow it along until I reached the gate. A minute later I remembered I didn't have to fumble in the dark. I stopped and pulled down the night-vision goggles, positioning them over my eyes. The world had a greenish glow. I could now see the gate—and two people standing there. The gate wasn't usually guarded!

I allowed my eyes to continue along the fence and saw the group pulling the trolley. They weren't far from the gate, but they didn't know about the guards. I had to let them know. But even if I told them in time, what were they going to do, get into a shootout? I had one more idea.

Keeping the night goggles in place, I started pedaling as fast as I could. I was going straight for the gate. The ghostly glow of the two men became bigger and bigger as I got closer and closer. I could see they were armed. This was close enough.

"Guards, guards!" I yelled.

I saw them startle and pull guns from their holsters.

"Don't shoot, don't shoot!" I called out. "I've been sent to get you!"

I slowed down and glided toward them. They looked at me and then at Godzilla.

"That's one big dog," one of them said.

"Me and him have been sent to get you. There's a mob gathering at the north fence. They need you there. We can watch this gate."

"Who sent you?" one of them asked.

"I don't know his name." They looked skeptical. I had to come up with more.

"He's big and likes telling everybody what to do, like he's in charge," I tried. "And he has a big mouth and swears a lot."

"Gary," they both said in unison.

I nodded, relieved. "Yeah, that's right, that's his name. You have to go. Hurry!"

"This better not be a false alarm," said the one guard, "or I'm going to shoot Gary myself."

They started jogging straight across the tarmac and disappeared. Within thirty seconds the trolley arrived. They were all panting, out of breath—except Nelson, who was sitting on top, eyes wide.

I waved a hello. "There were two guards, but I sent them away."

"How did you do that?" Julia asked.

"I told them the north fence was under attack and they had to go."

"Quick thinking. Richard, get the gate open."

A flashlight came on.

"Turn it off, or they'll see the light!" I exclaimed. The light went out. "Use these instead." I handed him the night-vision goggles.

"Where did you get these?" Julia asked.

"The same place I got this." I pulled the pistol out of the basket. "I took them from a guy who attacked me."

"You're starting to scare me," Julia said, but she looked impressed.

Richard reached under the tarp and removed the bolt cutters. He put the curved blades around the stem of the lock and it snapped in two, the pieces shooting across the tarmac.

The chains were released, the gate swung open, and we pulled and pushed the trolley through. We were ready to go. All we had to do was wait for the stair car.

"Let's get the trolley farther away from the gate," Richard said. "Somebody, get me the locks."

"I've got them both right here," Amber announced, handing them to Richard.

The plan was to lock up the gate after we'd all gotten through to make sure we weren't leaving an opening for people to invade the terminal. It would also make it harder for anybody to follow right behind us as we escaped. They might not even notice that this was our escape route if we could get far enough away to be protected by darkness and distance.

"I see lights!" Nelson yelled out.

We all turned in the direction he was pointing. There were the dim yellow headlights of a vehicle coming right toward us.

"Is it them?" Amber asked.

"It's too dark to—"

"It's them," Richard said. "I can see the outline of the stair car... and a couple of bikes as well."

He was wearing the night-vision goggles and could see what the rest of us couldn't.

"Wait, did you say two bikes?" Noah asked. "There should be three. Does that mean somebody didn't make it? Is Sara there?"

"I can't tell. There could be another bike behind them—wait, I see all three now!"

Then we heard gunshots.

"Muzzle blasts!" Noah yelled.

There were blasts of light followed by the sound of the guns being fired. They seemed to be directed toward the stair car—and we were in the line of fire.

"Everybody, get farther away!" Richard yelled.

I started pedaling as fast as I could and then turned around at the sound of more gunfire. I was so happy that Godzilla was right beside me. But I saw the others struggling, slowly moving the heavy trolley forward. So I rode over, stopped and jumped off the bike. Then I tossed it on the top, put my back against the trolley and started pushing. It picked up speed.

"Keep pushing! Get it as far away from here as possible!" Richard yelled. He ran back through the gate and pulled the shotgun off his shoulder.

I kept pushing and watching. I could see the lights getting closer. In those lights the three bikes appeared in front. Probably using the vehicle as cover as more muzzle blasts lit up the night.

Behind the lights of the vehicle there were other, fainter lights that seemed to be bouncing. I realized they were flashlights being held by the people pursuing and firing at the stair car!

Sara and Doeun shot through the gate, and Phillip skidded to a stop right beside Richard. He dropped his bike, and without seeing it, I knew he'd pulled out his weapon and was crouched down, ready.

"What happened?" Julia yelled.

"They saw the vehicle come out. They started firing at the car and then at us," Doeun answered.

"Is anybody hurt, was anybody hit?" Dr. Singh questioned.

"I don't think so, but I don't know. They were mainly firing at the vehicle and not at us."

"We'll soon find out," Noah yelled. "Here they come!"

The vehicle was now so close that we could hear it making a loud humming sound, the battery-powered engine whirring. As it got even closer, I could see Calvin at the wheel of the open controls, but where were Captain Daley and Tom?

It swayed as it made a turn and then loudly bounced across the metal grate. The stair car pulled in beside us, and just before it skidded to a stop, Tom and Captain Daley jumped off.

"Is everybody here?" Captain Daley asked. "Is everybody out?"

"You were the last," Doeun said.

"Lock it up!" he yelled.

Instantly Richard and Phillip each pulled on the gate, swinging it closed. I could see they were struggling to chain and lock it.

"Calvin, swing it in front of the trolley. I'll take a seat on the stairs and grab the handle of the trolley. We have to tow it away quickly!" Captain Daley ordered.

"And turn out the vehicle's lights!" Tom yelled.

Calvin hit a button, and we were thrown back into darkness.

"Everybody else get out of the way. Get on your bikes, run alongside. Folks, we've got to move!" Tom yelled.

I pulled down my bike, jumped on and started pedaling, racing ahead of the vehicle. Godzilla was at my side. Over my shoulder I saw the stair car towing the trolley. They were barely moving but then slowly picked up speed until they had caught up to me. I sped up as well, and I realized I could move faster than them but didn't want to. Instead I slowed so I was right beside them. I didn't want to leave them behind. There were people behind us firing guns, but there were probably people in front of us who were just as dangerous.

"Richard, are they coming after us?" I yelled. He was still wearing the goggles.

"Nothing, there's nothing!" he called out. "Everybody! We're safe! We made it!"

CHAPTER
FIFTEEN

I PUSHED GODZILLA OFF ME and sat up. Between his warmth and the blanket, I was hot. The coolness of the night air felt good. The sky had been clear, and there'd been no hint of rain, so we'd slept under the stars. The darkness stopped me from seeing very far, but I could clearly make out our vehicle, the bikes on their sides and the sleeping bodies all around me. Beyond that were the darkened outlines of the trees surrounding us. We'd stopped in a small patch of forest at the side of a park with a basketball hoop, tennis court and a nice little playground area. Amber had promised Nelson he could play on it in the morning if he went to sleep.

Four of our people were on watch. Before we'd settled in to sleep, they'd arranged to have a lookout in each direction. Each of them had a weapon and a whistle. It felt good to know people were on guard.

We'd traveled for a little more than four hours before we stopped. We'd never gone very fast. I'd kept up with the stair car easily on my bike. People had taken turns riding the bikes or sitting on the stairs and riding along. I'd ridden my bike the whole way.

The vehicle had started to sound different as we drove. The high-pitched hum of the engine had gotten lower and quieter through the night. Calvin had explained that this was because the batteries were running down. We'd traded speed for distance. The faster you ran the stair car, the quicker the batteries died, but we'd had to move quickly to get away from the airport.

I didn't know how many miles we'd traveled, but I knew it was less than the fifty miles per day fixed in my head.

Nobody had followed us out of the airport. And those we'd come across as we traveled had gotten out of our way pretty quickly. We were a very strange and formidable sight. The vehicle and the trolley were the heart of things. Surrounding them were the four bikes and the wheelchair. Noah had his bow in his lap. Tom and Richard had taken turns holding the rifle and sitting at the very top of the stair car. The shotgun was in the hands of whoever was at the bottom.

Godzilla had already shown he wasn't a long-distance runner. I'd coaxed him onto the stairs, and he'd snuggled in with Nelson and Mia. They looked cute together, and it reminded me of a book my parents used to read to me when I was small. It was called *Big Dog...Little Dog* and was about two dogs named Fred and Ted who were good friends even though they were nothing alike. Definitely Mia and Godzilla. Thinking about my childhood gave me a pang of sadness, which I pushed aside.

I heard quiet voices and turned. I could just make out the forms of two people sitting at a picnic bench just off to the side. I was pretty sure it was the captain and Tom.

"Come on, boy," I said quietly as I got up. My shoes were already on.

They didn't seem to notice. Maybe that wasn't so good. Sneaking up on people with weapons in the dark wasn't the smartest thing to do. I cleared my throat, and they both looked over at me.

"Come and have a seat," Tom suggested, patting the bench beside him. I sat.

Spread out on the table was a map.

"We're just plotting our route for the next few days," Captain Daley explained.

"How far did we go last night?" I asked.

"We went slightly more than twenty-two miles. Unfortunately, the first eight of those were in the wrong direction, to get around the airport. We'll try for double that tonight," Captain Daley said.

"Nighttime is the best time to travel," Tom said. "Fewer people out means fewer potential problems."

"But those people we do meet are going to be potentially more dangerous. I'm also concerned about staying in one place during the day. That makes us a sitting duck instead of a moving target," Captain Daley answered.

Tom shrugged. "There are pluses and minuses both ways."

Captain Daley turned to me. "What do you think, Jamie? Should we be moving at night and sleeping during the day, or sleeping at night and moving during the day?"

I was startled. "Me?"

"Why not?" Tom added. "New eyes to see a problem is a good thing."

"Hmm...does it have to be one or the other?" I asked.

Captain Daley leaned forward. "Go on."

"Well, what if we moved in the early morning, even starting before the sun came up?" I suggested.

"That's not a bad time to travel," Tom agreed.

"And then during the day, when we run across a good place, we could stop and take shelter," I added.

"That would also give us a chance to replace the batteries and charge the ones we take out. We could run harder and faster by doing that," Captain Daley said.

"And that would let us get moving again by the early evening so we could go until after dark," Tom added. "Those night-vision goggles you got are really going to make a difference."

Captain Daley's expression darkened. "We really didn't have time to talk about how you got them," he said. "I'm sorry you were put in danger."

I shrugged. "Nobody could have seen it coming," I replied.

"Certainly that guy didn't see it coming!" Tom said and gave a wheezy laugh. "The kid here takes a gun and gear away from a guy aiming a weapon at him."

I chuckled. "That was more Godzilla than me," I said, turning to the big dog lying at my feet.

"And was it Godzilla who figured out how to get the two guards away from the gate?" Tom asked.

"Well, he was there. He makes me feel safer."

"He makes us all safer," Captain Daley said with a smile. "Still, I wish you hadn't been put in that position." He cleared his throat. "Now. Let's get people up and moving."

I'd been on my bike since we'd set off. They'd been running the stair car fairly fast. While the people who were resting sat on the steps, they'd also set the generator up so that it was running and charging the spare batteries. It was noisy and smelly, but it was doing what we needed it to do. I was happy to be away on the bike—although not too far away.

The first part of the trip had been the quietest, before the world started to wake up. Now many other people were out along the road, mainly small groups—what looked to be families—but also some larger collections. They were sort of like traveling caravans, people who seemed to be headed in the same direction and were sticking together.

Lots of people were out gathering and carrying water. Everybody needed water. I thought about what Tom had said about the rule of three. Finding water was almost as important as breathing air.

There weren't many cars moving, and those we did see were all older, probably from before 1970. We continued to see the same simpler vehicles—more dirt bikes, a minibike that looked even smaller because of the very large man riding it and four go-karts, which appeared and disappeared together and looked like they'd been taken from an amusement park. Anything that was mechanical and moving got a lot of attention. We got a lot of attention.

People who saw us either stopped and stared or ran away. Those who didn't run often called out questions—usually where were we going and could they come along. We'd give them a smile or a nod as an answer as we kept moving.

If they followed along, running or riding beside us, they were given longer answers, usually by the captain, and these started polite and friendly—"just up the way" or "sorry, we can't bring anybody else." If people got angry, things got less friendly at our end. Tom or Richard would point the rifle or shotgun and tell them to leave us alone. It didn't feel right, pointing guns at people, but it was better than having guns pointed at us.

All of a sudden Doeun, Richard and Julia came pedaling back toward us. They had been ahead, scouting the way. Calvin stopped the vehicle, and Noah and I stopped as well. They pulled up to the side of the stairs.

"We found a place to stop. It's a burned-out dairy factory about a mile ahead," Doeun announced.

"There's a parking lot," Richard added. "Walls on two sides, a fence on the other two, and it's in the back so the view from the street is blocked, not visible to people passing by."

"Is there anybody there?" Tom asked.

"Not that we saw, but it's not like we went into the building itself," Julia reported.

"We'll have to check that out when we get there," Tom replied. "Captain?"

"Sounds good. Let's go."

The factory was three stories tall, made of red brick that had been blackened by the smoke that had billowed out of the windows, which had all been broken. Up top was a gigantic sign—*Chambers Dairy*. It looked fairly new, white and red, with a cheery, smiling cartoon cow. It had been left untouched by the fire.

We went around the side of the building. The parking lot was filled with milk trucks and cars. They'd all been abandoned where they sat when everything went down. The big gate was wide open and hanging awkwardly on its hinges. It had been forced open at some point. Just inside the gate the stair car slowed down and came to a stop. Instantly the captain, Tom, Doeun and Richard jumped into action. Two of them spread out to look at the vehicles while Richard ran back to the gate. He pulled it closed, looped a section of chain around it and locked it up with a padlock he'd been carrying. I relaxed—and then realized I should still keep my guard up. We'd just gotten here.

I leaned my bike against one of the trucks and went to get water for the dogs. Godzilla was, as always, at my heels.

"Jamie, could you keep an eye on Nelson while I help with the meal?" Amber asked.

"Of course," I said. He was a pretty easy little kid. "Nelson, help me take care of the dogs."

I removed a saucer from my backpack and poured in the water remaining in my bottle. Both dogs, side by side, started lapping it up.

"They really like each other," Nelson said.

"They're both good dogs. How are you doing?"

He looked at me. "I'm really sad," he said.

I patted his shoulder. "Oh, hey, we're going to be all right. Everybody here will take care of you."

"I'm sad because I didn't get to play at the playground," he said.

"Oh, I'm sorry." I tried not to smile. It was a relief, in a way, that this was his biggest worry. "Do you want to goof around in one of the trucks? You know, pretend to drive?"

His face lit up. "That would be great!"

We walked over to the nearest delivery truck. There was a sliding door open on the side, so we climbed in. Nelson settled into the driver's seat and grabbed the wheel, making engine sounds. *If only this truck really worked—we could all be home by the end of tomorrow.* I sighed.

Through the windshield I could see Calvin changing the batteries on the stair car. Somebody turned the generator off, and the silence was nice. Other than the top of the stair car sticking up above the dairy trucks, we were well hidden from the outside world.

I looked past the parking lot and past the fence to our surroundings. I was sure there were other people around, but I couldn't see any of them. I couldn't decide if that was good or creepy.

A few of our group had put out some food, and with the exception of Tom, Doeun and the captain, who were on watch, everybody else was already gathered around and eating.

"We need to go and eat," I said to Nelson.

He frowned. "Can I come back here and play after?"

"Of course." I looked around. There was a wide-open space at the back of the truck. "In fact, if you like we can even ask your mother if you can sleep in here."

"Really?" He clapped his hands.

"Why not? It could be fun. Maybe I'll join you."

He laughed and made a squealing sound as he put on the brakes of the truck. Then he scrambled out the door, and I rushed after him.

I went to grab a plate but there was something I wanted to do first. I walked toward where Captain Daley was standing with Tom. They both gave me a nod and kept on talking. They were looking at a road map.

"We went almost twenty-two miles this morning," Captain Daley said.

"That's a good pace," Tom acknowledged. "If we leave here by five or five-thirty, we'll be able to do a full fifty miles today."

"Leaving then should give us more than enough time for people to eat, rest and grab a few hours of sleep." Captain Daley paused. "Of course, that includes you."

"I haven't seen you taking a break either," Tom commented. "Besides, there are a few things I'd like to do before any of us gets too comfortable. Like check inside the building and establish high ground," he said, pointing up at the broken window on the third floor.

"That makes sense," Captain Daley replied. "But take somebody with you, okay?"

"Sure. Like Noah's ark," Tom said.

"What?" I asked.

"Stay in twos," he said with a wink. "Nobody should do anything by themselves. I'll ask Doeun to join me."

"Good choice," Captain Daley said. "Thanks. And Jamie, let's grab some food."

CHAPTER
SIXTEEN

IT WAS ALMOST FIVE O'CLOCK when we rumbled out of the parking lot, and I felt good. I'd gotten some sleep. I'd crawled into the back of that truck along with Nelson and his mother, and we had made sure the doors were locked. It had felt safe with a knife strapped to my leg, Godzilla sleeping beside me and the two of them plus Mia in the little truck. It had been a lot safer there than it was out here, riding on the little bike with the pink streamers. Godzilla was on the stairs and Julia was on a bike to my right. I knew she was carrying a pistol. She was no Akita, but I was pretty sure she was more intimidating than the dog when she wanted to be.

Calvin was again at the wheel of the stair car, a map at his side. Richard and Phillip had gone ahead on bikes to scout. We were going to be moving until at least after dark and for as long as it took to find a good, safe place to stop.

Tom sat at the top of the stairs, his feet dangling over the edge, looking forward. Captain Daley and Doeun were a couple of steps down. Between them were more maps. Calvin was concerned about the route for the day, while they were plotting the entire trip. This was day two, and if everything worked the way it was supposed to, I'd be home in forty-eight days.

"Nice day for a bike ride," Julia said.

I laughed. "I hope we have a lot of nice days."

"You know you don't have to ride all the way home," she said. "You can take a break sometimes and ride on the vehicle."

"I like being on the bike. I'll stop if I feel tired. Well, really tired."

The stair car suddenly came to a halt. It was too early to pull in for the night. Up ahead I saw the reason. Richard and Phillip were racing back toward us.

"The bridge over the river is blocked!" Richard yelled out.

Captain Daley and Tom came down the stairs and circled around to them.

"Blocked how?" Tom asked.

"They have a couple of cars pushed across to barricade most of it," Richard answered.

"Is there a space big enough for us to get by?" Captain Daley asked.

"It looks like we can squeeze by," Phillip replied. "But there are men. We counted at least five, and we could see that two of them have rifles. There might be more men and weapons that we couldn't make out."

"We can probably assume they're all armed one way or another," Tom said. He turned to Calvin and Captain Daley. "Is there a way around it?"

Calvin studied the map. "There's another bridge about seven miles north of here."

"That's a long detour," Tom said.

"And there's no guarantee that bridge isn't blocked as well," Captain Daley added. "And just because it's barricaded and the men are armed doesn't mean they'd harm us."

"And it doesn't mean they won't," Tom retorted. "We need a plan if we want to cross."

"Richard, Phil, did you two see anybody try to cross the bridge?" Captain Daley asked.

Richard shook his head. "We turned around as soon as we saw them."

"Most likely they're setting it up as a toll bridge," Tom explained. "They're charging people to let them pass."

"They want money?" I asked.

"Not money. Goods."

"Then maybe we could barter our way across," Dr. Singh said. "We could give them some of our food."

"What if they take our weapons or the bikes or even the stair car?" Tom asked.

"Then we'd be defenseless and unable to go much farther," Captain Daley replied. "What are you suggesting?"

"We need to see what we're up against. We need to do a little scouting mission," Tom said.

The stair car was stashed behind the stores of a small strip mall. All the store windows had been smashed, and businesses had been looted and stripped down. Most of our group would be staying with the car while a few of us investigated the barricade.

Calvin and Doeun were armed with pistols, Richard had the shotgun, and Sara had her bow. Tom had told them to stop anybody who threatened them, the vehicle or our supplies. Six of us would do the scouting—me, Tom, Captain Daley, Julia, Noah and Phillip. Tom had his rifle, Captain Daley and Julia, the pistols, and Noah, his bow.

We also had one other member with us. I'd tried to leave Godzilla behind, but he broke free and caught up to us. Captain Daley wouldn't let me take him back by myself, so Godzilla stayed.

When we got close to the bridge, we crouched behind some hedges so that we could see it while hidden.

"Look, somebody's crossing," I said, pointing.

A family started across the bridge. It was a man and a woman with two children. They were pushing a grocery cart full of stuff. The woman and children stopped at the edge of the bridge, and the man continued to move, his hands up in the air. Just before reaching the barricade, he was met by a man pointing a pistol at him. They talked, and then the man gestured for his family. The woman struggled to push the cart, and the two children—they couldn't have been any older than Nelson—clung to her legs, making it even harder.

A second man came out from the barricade as they approached. The two men then rummaged through the shopping cart.

"They're deciding on the toll charge," Tom said. "Seeing if there's anything they want."

"Why don't they just leave that poor family alone," Noah growled. "How low can people get?"

"A lot lower than stealing a few packages of food," Tom replied. "A whole lot lower."

I shivered at that thought.

The men kept removing things from the cart. Suddenly the father stepped forward. He was pushed down and the gun aimed at him again. I gasped. Were they going to shoot him?

Slowly he got up, and then they motioned for the family to move. They pushed the shopping cart forward, disappeared from our view behind one of the vehicles and then reappeared on the other side. They left the bridge and hurried off, looking behind them as they moved.

"Not friendly," Noah said.

"So what are we going to do?" Captain Daley asked.

"I have a plan," Tom said. "Well, at least an idea about a plan."

CHAPTER
SEVENTEEN

I PUSHED NOAH IN HIS CHAIR. He had his eyes closed, slumped over, pretending to be unconscious. Tucked underneath him were two pistols. Tom was limping beside us to look vulnerable. We'd seen that the men hadn't frisked any of the people who'd crossed the bridge in the time we'd been observing. We hoped we wouldn't be the first. I had the Saturday night special with its three bullets tucked into my pants. Tom had made sure the safety was on.

We'd regrouped with everyone else and told them our plan. Now the rest of the crew was behind us, just out of sight on a side street. They were giving us a six-minute head start. Timing was everything.

When we left, Godzilla had fought to come along with me. It took both Richard and Fede to hold him back and tie his leash to the trolley. He'd struggled to get free, and I could hear him barking and howling for two blocks.

"How are you both feeling?" Tom asked.

"I'm so calm I'm almost asleep," Noah replied dryly.

"It'll all be over in less than fifteen minutes," Tom said. "Remember, just look innocent and scared."

"I think I have the scared part down for sure," I replied.

"It'll be all right." Tom gave me a wink.

There was a reason it was the three of us. A kid, an older guy with a pretend limp and a third who was unconscious in a wheelchair looked less threatening. Captain Daley and Julia had originally objected to my going, but they finally agreed, mostly because I'd convinced them I'd be fine. Right now I wished I hadn't been so convincing. Still, it was important for me to contribute and not just be a burden.

I bumped Noah over the metal strip that edged the bridge.

"Hello!" Tom yelled. "Can we come forward?"

Two of the men came out from behind the barricade, and one of them waved us forward. They were both holding guns—one a rifle and the other a handgun.

"Nice and calm," Tom said. "Just remember we're trying to be the least threatening group they're going to see all day."

We walked forward. My legs were shaking, and it felt like I wasn't just pushing the wheelchair but using it to keep standing. We stopped in front of them.

"We're just wanting to cross," Tom said pleasantly.

"What do you have to pay for your passage?" the man with the rifle asked.

"We don't have any money," Tom replied.

"Money is useless. What's in the bag, Santa Claus?" They both laughed. They were cruel laughs.

Tom had a pack slung over one shoulder.

"Santa only brings things to people who have been good little girls and boys."

The man with the rifle reached forward and ripped it off his shoulder. He undid the zipper and pulled out a blanket, dropping it to the deck, and then a box of cereal.

"This is it?" he asked.

"It's all the food we have," Tom said.

"It's all the food you *had*," the man with the handgun said. He had scraggly hair, which he pushed out of his eyes.

Tom winced at him. "But what will we eat?"

"Go on a diet," he snarled. "What's wrong with him?" he asked, pointing at Noah.

"We're not sure," Tom said. "We're afraid it might be contagious."

Both men backed away, exactly as Tom had said they would. Nobody was going to search somebody who had some mystery disease.

"We're taking him to see a nurse we know a few miles away."

"Guy already looks dead," one of the men said.

"Have a little decency. This is his son," Tom replied.

I hadn't seen that coming. I tried to add sadness to my look of fear. They both nodded in sympathy.

"If you're coming across this bridge on the way back, you better have more than a box of cereal or you're going to have to swim," the rifle man said.

So much for them showing decency.

"We'll have more," Tom said. "Can we go?"

The man with the rifle shrugged. "Go on, get out of here."

I heard barking, and I turned around. It was Godzilla. He'd broken free! He was running along the road, his leash trailing after him. He turned onto the bridge and bounded toward me.

"Shoot him!" one of the men yelled. I spun around. Both men had raised their guns and were aiming at Godzilla.

"Don't!" I yelled. "He's my dog!" I ran back, and he practically knocked me over as he bounced up onto his back legs, put his front paws on my shoulders and started licking my face.

"It's okay, boy, it's okay," I told him. I pushed him off and took hold of the rope.

"Keep him off to the side!" the scraggly-haired man yelled. They still had their guns up.

Godzilla growled at them.

"Call your dog off or we'll shoot him!" he roared.

"First off, that's not a dog," Tom said in a measured tone. "That's an *Akita*. You shoot him, and you'll only annoy him. You shoot him a second time, and you'll get him really angry. Before you get a third shot in, he's going to rip your throat out."

I shortened the leash, pulling him closer. He continued to growl and show his teeth. He looked ferocious. My heart was pounding a mile a minute.

"Please, just let us go," I pleaded. "I just want to try to help my dad before it's too late."

Their faces softened, but before either of them could answer, the stair car appeared on the road. It was running at top speed, and I could hear the humming. I had no idea it could be heard from this distance. As planned, none of the bikes were trailing along. They were just down the road, hidden from view and protected if guns started firing.

"What the hell?" the man with the rifle said.

"I've never seen anything like it," said the second man.

I blurted out, "It's from the airport."

"I don't care where it's from. We could use another vehicle that still runs."

I shot a look at Tom, but he didn't look worried.

As always, Calvin was at the wheel. I couldn't see anybody else but expected that at least Phillip and Captain Daley were hidden on the stairs behind it, weapons at hand. The car stopped at the entrance to the bridge.

"Can we go?" Tom asked.

The rifle man glowered at him. "Get out of here, now!" he barked.

Tom reached down and grabbed the backpack and the blanket. He dropped them onto Noah's lap. Noah was still faking unconsciousness. Tom started pushing, and I walked Godzilla on the leash. We moved around the barricade and the other three men who were behind it. They had their weapons out—a rifle and a couple of pistols. They were staring over the barricade, focused so intently on the stair car that they weren't even looking at us. That was what we'd hoped, what our whole plan depended on. We continued to walk a few more paces.

"The people behind the barricade have fake weapons," Tom whispered.

"What?" I asked.

"A toy pistol, a flare gun and a BB gun." He turned to Noah. "You ready?"

Noah nodded. "Ready."

"Now," Tom said.

Noah reached down, pulled out the pistols and handed one to Tom as I pulled out my gun. Noah spun his chair around.

"Gentlemen," Tom said.

They didn't respond.

"Gentlemen!" he said louder.

One of them turned. He looked shocked. Then the second and the third noticed, practically jumping into the air.

Holding the gun in one hand, pointing right at them, Tom brought a second finger up to his lips to signal silence.

"I want you to put down your toy guns right now, quietly, and sit down."

They seemed frozen.

"Not telling you again," Tom said through clenched teeth. "*These* guns are real. Now!"

First one, then the other two put down their weapons. They sat down. Beside them was a pile of goods—bottles of water, food, blankets and other things they'd taken from people. They were like that troll who lived under the bridge in "The Three Billy Goats Gruff."

"What's the name of the big guy over there with the rifle?" Tom asked.

A bald man in a camo vest said, "Roy. His name is Roy."

"Shuffle over to the side," Tom commanded, and they all slid over, still on their butts. "Noah, they're yours. Anybody even tries to escape, you shoot him, okay?"

"With pleasure," Noah answered.

I didn't think he meant it, but he sounded believable, which was all that mattered.

Noah pointed his weapon at them, and Tom moved up to the barricade. I followed behind. He carefully placed his pistol on the barricade, using it for support. I did the same.

"Roy!" Tom called out.

"Not now!" Roy answered without looking back.

"No, Roy, NOW!"

Roy turned around, and his expression changed to utter and complete shock. Tom had his pistol pointed straight at his chest. I aimed at the back of the scraggly-haired man.

"Drop your weapons right now!" Tom yelled.

The other man turned around. He looked confused, like he was trying to process what was taking place and couldn't. Then for a few seconds he looked like he was going to bring his pistol up and take a shot at us.

"I'm not asking again," Tom said. "I'll shoot you both dead."

Roy lowered his rifle and placed it on the deck of the bridge. The second guy did the same with his pistol.

"Jamie, get their guns," Tom said.

I hurried around the barricade, Godzilla at my side. Godzilla put himself between me and them, growling ominously, as I picked up the weapons. The rifle almost slipped out of my hand. I'd never held a rifle before and was surprised by how much it weighed.

It was time. The stair car started moving forward, and the four bikes appeared. Pedaling fast to catch up were Fede, Dr. Singh, Amber and, on my little bike, Nelson. Mia ran along beside him.

Tom summoned the two men back and ordered them and the other three to push aside the cars that were blocking the bridge. The men did what they were told.

The stair car came to a stop. Phillip, Captain Daley, Sara and Doeun got off, all holding their weapons. I was relieved when Captain Daley took the extra guns from me.

"Are you all right?" he asked.

I swallowed, hoping my voice would stay steady. "Good, great. It went just like it was planned."

With the route clear, Calvin drove the stair car across the bridge, and everybody followed.

"Stu, Doeun and Jamie, stay here. And you'll be keeping the bikes. Everybody else, go!" Tom yelled.

"Wait!" I called, and everybody stopped. I pointed at the pile. "We should take their stuff, right? There are things we'll need. And the BB gun as well. It still fires something."

Tom laughed and slapped me on the back. "Kid doesn't miss anything. Get those things, and let's get moving!"

We gathered the stolen things and put them onto the trolley. Richard climbed to the top of the stairs and Fede, now holding the captured rifle, sat at the bottom. The vehicle hummed loudly as it accelerated away.

"Jamie," Tom said, "throw the toy guns into the river so they can't be used as a threat again."

I tossed them over the side into the fast-moving water, and they quickly sank.

"All of you, now it's your turn. Jump," Tom said, turning to the men.

"Into the river?" the bald man asked.

"You can all swim, can't you?"

"It's ten feet to the water, and the current's strong," Roy said. "You can't be serious."

Tom narrowed his eyes. "Do it before I sic the dog on you." He turned to me. "Jamie, have Godzilla attack the big one first, okay?"

"Sure," I answered without hesitating. I turned to Godzilla. "Him," I said, pointing directly at Roy. Godzilla growled and showed more teeth, as if he understood.

The men all started removing their shoes and shirts.

"If you'd been good little boys, you wouldn't have been on Santa's naughty list," Tom said. He laughed. They didn't. Apparently their sense of humor was selective.

"You'll pay for this," Roy said, standing up. "How far do you think you'll get?"

Tom blinked. "Sounds like you're giving us a good reason to just shoot you all right here."

"Please don't!" Scraggly Hair pleaded. "We're going to do what you want."

"And you?" Tom asked Roy.

He climbed up onto the metal railing. "We'll see you later." He jumped into the river. There was a loud splash. The next three men quickly followed Roy. The last man hesitated.

"I'm sorry," he said, his eyes watery. "We were just trying to feed our families, to survive."

"I know," Captain Daley said. "But other people are too. It's not right to survive by stopping others from doing the same."

The man jumped, hitting the river with a loud splash. I hurried over to the side and saw him, and the others farther downstream, struggling in the current. As much as I disliked them, I hoped they'd be all right.

"Okay, everybody, let's get going!" Doeun yelled.

We jumped onto the bikes and started pedaling away.

Godzilla was loping along right by my side. I knew we needed to move fast, but I also knew there was a limit to how far he could run.

"Can we slow down soon?" I asked, after a few minutes. "We've escaped."

"We'll slow down if the dog needs us to," Captain Daley said. He was reading my mind.

"But we need to get distance from the bridge and catch up to our people."

I looked over my shoulder. There was nobody following us. To the side were houses and stores. We were passing other travelers struggling along. Were they part of the group from the bridge that would sound an alarm and come after us?

"Do you think they're really going to try to catch us?" Doeun asked.

"Not sure if they will but sure they have the means to do it," Tom replied.

"I don't understand," I said.

"One of them said it would be good to have *another* vehicle that runs."

Those words suddenly came back to me.

"It's guaranteed that whatever they have will move faster than our vehicle. If they do chase us, they'll catch us," Tom reasoned.

I suddenly felt the urge to pedal faster. "Come on, Godzilla, good boy," I said to the dog, encouraging him to keep moving. It was now even more important to get farther away and catch up to the rest of our group.

I looked over my shoulder again. Still nobody.

CHAPTER

EIGHTEEN

PEDALING FORWARD AND STARING BACKWARD isn't the way you're supposed to ride a bike. I was relieved when darkness finally started to cover us. Not only were there fewer people out who might pose a threat but fewer people to see us pass by. We weren't a group that would be easily overlooked or forgotten. Captain Daley had said there were at least a dozen roads or routes we could have taken, and he'd had Calvin take us off the main road.

The guns we'd taken from the men at the bridge would help protect us. The pistol had a full magazine—twelve shots—and the rifle another eight shots. Even better, the rifle was the same caliber as the one we already had, so it could use the same ammunition— ammunition that Tom had plenty of. That meant we now had two rifles, a shotgun, five pistols and two bows, plus a BB gun.

I was still carrying the Saturday night special because nobody had asked to get it back. On top of that were the knife still strapped to my leg and, of course, Godzilla. Yet all three things still didn't seem enough.

Godzilla had run hard for us to catch up to our group. Since then he'd ridden on the stairs and fallen asleep. He'd given it all he had, not slowing us down. He was a good dog. I thought about what it would be like when we got home. Taking him for walks, playing in the park, the two of us sleeping in my bed with him taking up most of it and half of the covers. Then I thought about how everything about being home was going to be different. It was hard to get my head around. I wasn't sure I even wanted to.

Just then our vehicle came to a stop and we were joined by Phil and Fede, who had been ahead of us on the bikes, scouting.

"There's an abandoned building half a mile ahead," Fede said. "Forest behind it, nothing around it."

"Tom?" Captain Daley asked.

"Probably good to rest and change batteries. Can't be much charge left, right, Calvin?"

Calvin ran a hand through his hair. "We've been running fast. Judging by the sound of the engine, we could probably go another five miles but not much more," he answered.

"Better play it safe and get off the road instead of stalling on it. Let's get there."

"Incoming!" Richard yelled. He was on the top platform of the stairs, wearing the night-vision goggles and pointing back down the road.

I turned. I didn't need the goggles to see what he was pointing at. A set of headlights was coming down the road…and it looked like it was coming fast.

"Everybody, take your places!" Tom yelled.

We had a plan, and everybody knew what had to be done. Doeun scrambled into the seat beside Calvin. Fede climbed up onto the stairs, and they started down the road. Noah grabbed the back of the trolley and was pulled along. Tom and Phillip went to one side of the road and scrambled down into the ditch.

Captain Daley and Sara went to the other and did the same, disappearing.

"This way!" Julia called out.

The rest of us followed her, either pushing a bike along or simply running. Our job was to get away, into the trees and out of sight.

"Down, boy!" I ordered, and Godzilla dropped to the ground beside me behind some shrubbery.

The vehicle was closing in quickly. It was a truck, and I could hear its engine racing. Whoever it was, they were in a hurry to get where they were going. Calvin had brought the stair car to a stop. We wanted the truck to stop behind it, blocked from going farther and trapped between gunfire on both sides. We'd have them in what Tom had called a "kill zone." He told us this meant an ambush site where the enemy was caught in fire from different directions. I knew about the term from a video game I played. Weird that it was real life now.

There were three men standing up in the truck bed, and they started to fire at our vehicle. They were closing in and still firing. It was loud and frightening. And then we started firing back! Shots rang out, loud ones, and I could see the muzzle blasts from both sides. Its windshield was shattered, but the truck kept going, racing past the ditch where our people were hiding, speeding toward the stair car.

More shots rang out as Richard, Fede and Doeun began firing at the truck. It swerved and rocked and hit the ditch, flying up into the air, flipping over, rolling a couple of times and then settling onto its roof. And then there was silence.

Tom and Phillip climbed out of the ditch they'd been in, and Captain Daley and Sara did the same. They jogged up the road. I left my hiding spot and started running to meet them. Godzilla was at my side. We all gathered at the stair car.

"Was anybody hit?" Captain Daley asked anxiously.

"We're fine," Richard said, looking around. "But I can't see how anybody could survive that crash."

They all started toward the overturned vehicle, fanning out across the width of the road. I let them get ahead and then followed.

The truck was an older model, which explained why it had been able to run. There were no engine sounds now, but the back wheels were still slowly spinning.

"Here's one over here!" Phil yelled.

I saw there was a man in the ditch. Even in the darkness I could tell that the body wasn't right. The way it was lying there, arms and legs in different directions.

"Here's his weapon!" Phil added. He was holding up a rifle.

"Here's another body," Tom called.

He turned on a flashlight and captured the body in the beam of light.

"Look who it is," Tom said as he stood over the body.

His face was covered in mud and blood, but I still recognized him—it was Roy from the bridge.

Tom placed a hand against the side of Roy's throat. "He's dead," he confirmed. "He's been separated from his weapon, so keep an eye out for it."

I crossed the ditch and started scanning the ground as I walked. At the speed the truck was traveling, the gun might have flown into the bushes. I tripped over something. I looked down—it was his rifle. The wooden stock was splintered, and the barrel was barely attached. I was planning to leave it, but I realized it might have bullets in the magazine or chamber, so I gingerly picked it up. I clambered back across the ditch and arrived at the truck in time to hear the others talking.

"One more man in the back," Phillip said. "When the truck rolled, it crushed him. He would have died instantly."

There was another man a dozen yards in front of the truck. He was covered in blood and cuts, and judging from the smashed windshield, he'd been thrown through it. A fifth man was still in the cab of the truck. His face was smashed and his neck was at an impossible angle. I felt my stomach lurch and took a deep breath to try to keep calm.

"These men are dead, but whoever was behind the wheel isn't," Tom said. "He got out through the driver's-side window." He ran his flashlight along the ground. "And he went that way, judging by the blood and beaten-down grass. I think he's crawling."

Captain Daley winced. "He's got to be pretty badly hurt."

"He couldn't have gotten far," Calvin said. "We have to go after him."

"I don't think he's going to survive his injuries for long," Captain Daley said.

"Probably not, but we still need to find him," Tom replied. "I'll follow the tracks."

"I'll go with you," Richard offered.

Tom shook his head. "Two of us just means a chance of shooting each other. I need to go alone. While I'm gone you should clear up the scene and get us ready to move as soon as possible. We still need to put some distance between us and here."

"But it's not like they can hurt us anymore," Calvin said, leaning back against the truck.

Tom turned to him. "What do you think the others are going to do when this patrol doesn't come back?"

Of course, I thought. They were going to come looking for them.

"I'll take care of things here," Captain Daley said. "You be careful out there."

"I'll try my best." Tom headed off, following the trail.

"Calvin, how long to change the batteries on the car?" Captain Daley asked.

"Twenty minutes, but shouldn't we find a place off the road?" Calvin asked.

"If they show up now, we're caught, with or without the batteries. Better just to get to it."

Calvin nodded and hurried away.

Captain Daley looked around at the rest of us. "Richard, can you and Phillip go back down the road to our original spots in the ditches? Nobody gets by, understood?"

"Completely." Phillip gave a little salute, and he and Richard jogged off. I listened until the sound of their feet against the pavement faded away.

"Doeun and Fede, this one is harder. I need those bodies moved so they're not visible from the road. Can you do that?"

Doeun put a hand on Fede's shoulder. "We can do it. We'll start with the two guys farther away."

Captain Daley turned to me. "I keep wishing you didn't have to see all of this," he said softly.

"It's okay."

"It's not. Not for you and not for anybody your age." He let out a sigh. "I can't stop wondering what my kids are going through—what have they seen?"

I bobbed my head. "I'm sure they're fine. But hey, there's only one way to find—"

A gun blast cut me off. It was hard to be certain, but it sounded like it was coming from the direction Tom had gone.

"Get low and take cover behind the truck," Captain Daley hissed.

He dropped to one knee as I moved behind the hood of the overturned truck. Peeking out, I saw a light appear, bobbing up and down and from side to side. A flashlight being carried.

"It's me!" a voice called out. It was Tom! "Don't nobody go and shoot me."

"We hear you," Captain Daley yelled in response, getting back to his feet and striding out from behind the truck. I joined him.

Tom was panting. "I found him about forty-five yards away. His back was against a tree, and he had this in his hand." He held up a pistol. "I asked him to drop it, and he either didn't or couldn't."

"Couldn't?" I asked.

Tom stared down the road. "He might have been dead already. I couldn't take the chance. I put a round into him," he said. "Straight into the forehead."

"You shot him? You just killed him?" I felt myself get numb, my ears roaring.

"Jamie, there was no choice," Tom said. "He was as good as dead anyway."

Captain Daley put a hand on my shoulder. "I'm sorry, Jamie. I wish none of this was necessary. Are you all right?"

I nodded. "I'm okay. I'm fine." I wasn't, but I knew we had to keep moving.

CHAPTER NINETEEN

IT TOOK US ALMOST AN hour to get all the bodies moved and the truck hefted back on its wheels and pushed off into the brush. We cut down bushes and branches and piled them against it to provide camouflage. Anybody moving slowly along the road in the light of day and looking hard enough probably would be able to see it, but we hoped it would be invisible at night.

Godzilla had run beside my bike for the first hour after we set off, refusing to leave me to go and rest. Finally I had no choice but to stop riding so that he'd come onto the stairs with me. He was pretty exhausted and dropped off to sleep almost immediately.

Holding on to the railing and stepping over other people who were asleep or resting, I climbed the stairs. Tom was at the top, on the platform. He was wearing the night goggles. He sat with his rifle on his lap and his feet were dangling over the edge. He nodded at me as I settled in beside him.

"You should try to get some more sleep," he said.

"I should get back on the bike and let somebody else rest for a while."

"Everybody is fine," he said. "Fear is a pretty good motivator."

"Were you afraid?" I asked.

"Only a fool wouldn't be." He paused and met my eyes. "So. Do you want to know more about the guy I shot?"

I swallowed. "No...well...yeah, I guess."

"The guy was either dead already or going to be dead soon," he said quietly. "I just didn't want him to take me with him."

"But he was unconscious." My ears felt hot. I needed to say it, though.

"Or pretending to be, the same way Noah was when we crossed the bridge."

"I hadn't thought of that," I admitted.

"They were coming to kill us," Tom said gravely.

He was right. They'd started shooting. They weren't interested in talking.

"Do you remember how in the beginning I said we were going to have to take lives or have our lives taken?"

I nodded.

"The way home is going to involve crossing more bridges and coming across more people who will try to stop us," he said. "We're not going to let them."

I knew he was making sense. This was the way it had to be. "Are we safe now?"

"We won't be safe until we get to where we're going," Tom said.

"And you think we can get there?" I asked, my voice shaking a little.

"I'd be lying if I gave you a guarantee. What I do know is that we've crossed one more bridge and gotten another fifty miles closer. Day by day and mile by mile. That's the only way we can take it." There was something matter-of-fact about Tom, about his point of view, that helped reassure me.

Up ahead I saw Richard and Julia riding toward us. Calvin brought the vehicle to a stop.

"We found a spot to pull off," Richard yelled up.

"Lead the way," Tom replied.

The wheels of the stair car were made for traveling on the flat, hard, smooth surface of the tarmac and weren't doing so well on the dirt and gravel path that led us off the road and into the trees. I saw flashes of red and yellow and orange—tents clustered together in the woods. More tents meant more people, which potentially could mean more trouble. A couple of times I saw people peering through the trees, staring at us. We must have looked dangerous to them. We were a large group with weapons they could see, and along with the bikes, we had an actual moving vehicle. A vehicle with giant stairs on the back. The strangest-looking vehicle on the road.

"This is the spot," Richard said, raising his hand to stop our caravan.

"Let's get perimeter guards out while the tent is set up and a meal prepared," Captain Daley ordered.

Richard, Phil, Sara and Doeun fanned out in four directions to take the perimeter watch. Calvin had already removed the battery cover and was getting ready to change the batteries. I walked over to offer a hand, noticing he looked a little slower than usual.

"You must be tired," I said.

"Dog-tired," he admitted. "As soon as the batteries are replaced and I can get more gasoline to power the generator, I'm going to sleep for as long as I can."

I had an idea. "I could get gas."

"Can you do that?"

"I've seen you do it enough. It doesn't look that complicated."

It involved using a rubber tube to siphon gas out of the tank of an abandoned car or truck and into a gas container. There were lots of abandoned vehicles to choose from. We'd passed hundreds overnight, but we hadn't wanted to risk stopping.

"I doubt Captain Daley will let you go back out to the road alone," Calvin replied.

"I don't go anywhere alone," I said, pointing at Godzilla standing beside me.

"I meant with another person. If you find somebody to go with you, you can get the gas."

Captain Daley and Tom were off to the side, talking. I walked over and stopped close enough that they would know I wanted something but far enough away not to interrupt. They noticed and motioned for me to come over.

"Do you want to talk to us?" Captain Daley asked.

"Yes. Calvin needs more gas for the generator, and I volunteered to go find some. We passed some cars just before we turned off the road that I could siphon from."

"Thanks for taking the initiative, but you can't go alone," Captain Daley said.

"I could go," Tom volunteered.

"You haven't slept since the night before the bridge. You go to sleep. I'll go along with Jamie," Captain Daley said. "I'll also make sure our tracks our covered."

I had an empty gas container in one hand and a pistol in the other. Captain Daley was carrying the shotgun and an axe from the airplane, and he had the second can tucked under his arm. We walked back along the dirt track we'd driven down, and I realized what he meant by covering our tracks. The stair car had left visible tire marks that showed we'd gone down the dirt road. Captain Daley hacked off a branch from a bush and used it as a broom to sweep away the tracks.

There was more activity on the road than there had been less than an hour earlier. Everybody was wary of everybody else and keeping as wide a berth as possible on the two lanes of pavement. Captain Daley made a point of greeting and smiling at people we were passing. Some responded the same way, while it just seemed to make others more scared.

We came up to the first abandoned car, a big, fancy red BMW. We often went to the luxury cars because they used high-octane gas, which was better for the generator.

Captain Daley tried to open the two doors on the driver's side, and I did the same on the other side. They were all locked.

"Turn around and shield your eyes," he said, and then he smashed the glass with the axe.

He opened the door through the broken window and leaned in to hit the tank-lock release, and the little door popped open. Captain Daley handed me the shotgun.

"Keep both eyes open in both directions," he said. "I don't want to be surprised."

He fed the tube into the tank. "Never thought I'd be breaking into cars and stealing gas."

"I never thought I'd be carrying a gun and watching for people who are trying to kill us," I muttered.

"It's safe to say that nobody ever thought any of this could happen," Captain Daley said dryly.

"Nobody except Tom and other preppers."

"It appears they were the smart ones. I don't know where we'd be without him."

"Probably still back at the airport," I replied. I wondered what it was like there now and what had happened since we left.

"I'm trying to keep us doing the right thing as we move forward," Captain Daley said.

"Sure, of course."

He turned to me. "I mean the morally right thing. Let me explain. You see the woman and her children walking along the road? I don't see any weapons. They're probably unarmed."

I thought the same thing.

"We could easily take from them the few things they have."

I frowned. "But we wouldn't do that, right?"

"Right, and as long as I'm in charge, we never will. We'll defend and protect ourselves, but nothing more than what we have to do to survive. We're not going to become those men at the bridge, preying on others."

He started sucking on one end of the tube and then coughed and spat out gas as it started to flow. He placed the tube in the empty can, and I could hear the gas hitting the bottom.

"What I'm really worried about is sliding situational ethics," Captain Daley said.

Before I could say I didn't know what that meant, he started to tell me.

"Let me explain. It's wrong to kill somebody, right?"

"Of course."

"The Bible has it as one of the Ten Commandments—'Thou shall not kill.' The Quran says, and I quote, 'Whosoever kills a person, it shall be as if he has killed all mankind.' Buddhists say, 'Avoid killing or harming any living thing.' Every religion believes life is sacred."

"Right," I said. "But aren't there times you have to do it?" I paused and added, "Times *we* might have to do it?"

He nodded. "Yes, the ethics change in certain situations. A soldier at war, a police officer protecting somebody, or an individual who has no choice. That's where we are. We had no choice because those people were going to kill us. The ethics changed because of the situation we were in."

"I guess that makes sense."

"I believe we were justified," he said. "The only question is what more will we justify as we get more desperate, as the situation gets worse."

He took the tube from one gas can, which was now full, and put it into the second.

"If we didn't have something to eat, would we be justified in taking supplies away from other people?" he asked. "From that woman and her children?"

I cringed. "No, of course not!"

"An empty stomach can change the way you think. I just hope it doesn't make us change the way we act." I hoped not too. I really did.

The second can filled up, and he pulled out the hose.

"Let's get back. I don't know about you, but I could use something to eat and drink. I really need to get the taste of gas out of my mouth."

CHAPTER
TWENTY

I COULD HEAR THE VOICES around me before I opened my eyes. They were familiar and reassuring. The sun was warm, and tucked under my blanket I felt safe. I looked at my watch and was shocked that it was after three in the afternoon. I'd slept almost seven hours! I rolled over, and as I got up, I picked up my gun. I checked the safety again—something I seemed to do repeatedly—to make sure it was on. I tucked it in my pants pocket.

There were a few other people asleep under the makeshift tent—Tom, Calvin, Phil and Captain Daley. They had all been working or on watch when I went to lie down. There would be four more people on duty right now. Then Mia gave a little yelp, and I realized someone missing—where was Godzilla? He wasn't here beside me.

I crawled out from under the tent to look all around, calling his name. He didn't appear, but the others who were up turned to look at me.

"Have you seen Godzilla?" I asked.

"I saw him not that long ago. He went in that direction," Amber said, pointing. Nelson was asleep with his head in her lap.

"Are you sure?" I asked.

"It's hard to miss something that big," she said with a chuckle. "I thought he was going out to look for a private spot and he'd be back soon, and then I forgot about him."

I bit my lip. "I have to go and find him."

"I'll go with you," Sara offered as she got to her feet. "More eyes, more chances."

Julia looked worried. "Normally I'd say to check with Captain Daley or Tom before you head out, but I'd like them to sleep as long as possible. Anyway, we're not going to be leaving for another three hours."

"If he isn't back by then, what'll happen?" I felt my shoulders tense.

"I'm sure that won't be a problem," Julia offered.

"But if he isn't?" I insisted.

"Maybe we could wait a little longer," she replied. "But that won't be my decision."

"That's even more reason I have to look," I said. "We won't go far or be gone long."

"If you're heading in that direction," Julia said, "that's where Doeun is on duty. As long as you have her permission, you can go farther."

"Thank you."

I touched a hand against the gun in my pocket. Sara picked up her bow and slipped a quiver of arrows onto her back. We started into the woods along the path that Amber had seen Godzilla travel. I called out his name as we moved. The forest got thick quickly, and it wasn't long until we'd lost sight of our crew and even the stair car.

Doeun appeared ahead of us. "I heard you calling him. Godzilla is missing?"

"We were told he went this way," I answered.

"I haven't seen him, but he could have easily slipped by me. Wait, do you see those tents in the distance?"

I looked up and through the trees.

"We established contact with them," she said. "They're friendly. There are a dozen groups camping throughout the woods, and they're all cooperating. Maybe they can help you. I'll walk over and introduce you to one of their leaders."

As we got closer, I counted the tents. Four red and three green. In the middle was a firepit with a wisp of smoke coming out. A larger tarp sat off to the side, tied between four trees, and underneath that was a picnic bench, where three people were sitting. The scene reminded me of being on a camping trip with my parents.

I felt uneasy going to talk to strangers. Between the three at the picnic bench and those standing, there were eight people— four women, two kids and two men. There could have been more people in the tents or off in the trees or out someplace trying to get food or water. What I didn't see were weapons. That didn't mean they didn't have them, just that they weren't out in the open. Which made me even more suspicious. Was somebody hiding in the bushes with a rifle aimed at us?

"Hello, Joyce, sorry to bother you," Doeun said to a woman with curly red hair. "We're searching for a dog."

"A really big, scary-looking dog?" Joyce asked.

"Yeah, that's him!" I exclaimed. "When was he here, and which way did he go?"

"About thirty minutes ago, and he went that way, toward the creek," she replied. She got up. "I'll go with you so it'll be safe for you. The people in these camps are afraid of strangers."

"Hard to blame them," I said.

"And that's why it's even nicer of you to offer," Sara replied. "I wish there was something we could do for you."

"There is," I said.

They all turned to me.

"That person over there," I said, pointing to a man on make-shift crutches. "What's wrong?"

Joyce winced. "We hope it's just a sprain, but it could be that his ankle is broken."

I turned to Sara and Doeun. "We could have Dr. Singh look at him."

"You have a doctor?" the woman asked.

"And a nurse," I added.

"It's not just Craig who's hurt," she said. "Between the different camps, we have some cuts and infections, and two pregnant women who haven't had any medical checkups."

"We'll help however we can," Doeun offered. "But we have to be on the road before dark."

"You're welcome to stay as long as you want," Joyce said, spreading her arms. "We can always use more good people to be part of our colony."

"Well, thank you for your offer, but we have to leave," Doeun said firmly.

"How far have you already traveled?"

"We came from O'Hare," I replied.

She looked surprised. "You've covered a lot of distance already. That's more than a hundred and fifty miles."

"And we have a lot farther to go," Sara explained. "Over a thousand miles to get where we're going."

Joyce nodded in understanding. "We're only out here because our homes are gone. Set on fire or looted or it just wasn't safe to be there." I could hear the sadness in her voice and see it in her eyes. What had she been through?

"The tents are good for now, but what's going to happen when winter comes?" Doeun asked.

Joyce's face fell. "Do you really think it's going to go on that long? Do you know something?"

"We don't know anything," Doeun said, trying to sound reassuring. "I don't think anybody does."

Joyce hesitated, then said, "I hope it's all going to be worth it when you get there."

"What do you mean?" I asked.

"I hope the homes you're looking for are still there...and the people in those homes are all right."

I felt a rush of panic. My parents would be there. Wouldn't they?

"Look," Sara said, interrupting my wave of anxiety. "I'll go back and get Dr. Singh and Richard, while you two look for Godzilla. Okay?" I could tell she was trying to help, trying to move back to the problem at hand.

"And I'm going to go back on guard duty," Doeun added. "Thanks for your help, Joyce."

CHAPTER

TWENTY-ONE

RELUCTANTLY I RETURNED TO OUR camp. Joyce and I had searched, but we hadn't found Godzilla. At least he'd been seen running through the forest by a bunch of people. It was good to know he was close. The people we'd talked to promised they'd keep looking and assured me they wouldn't "shoot him." He'd scared more than a few people as he raced by. I understood. He was a scary-looking dog.

At each campsite we'd visited, Joyce had mentioned that we had a doctor and nurse who might be able to help with minor problems. There was now a pretty long lineup in front of a tent Richard and Dr. Singh had hastily set up for their examinations. Just as I got back to camp, Dr. Singh and a very pregnant woman came out of the tent. Captain Daley and Sara were standing off to one side, talking, while some of the others were gathered in the background, around our campfire.

"No luck with Godzilla?" Captain Daley asked as I approached.

"He's around," I said. "I'm sure he'll be back soon."

"Don't worry about when we're leaving," Captain Daley said. "Jasminder has made it clear that she won't go until she's examined all the patients that need to be seen."

I was suddenly grateful for the length of the lineup.

"She thinks she won't be finished until well after dark," he said. "Probably wouldn't even be the worst thing if we had to wait until morning." He paused. "We're going to find Godzilla. He's part of our crew, and we don't leave anybody behind."

Relief washed over me. "Thank you so much."

"And while we're waiting, Tom has been talking to people and found out some interesting things," Captain Daley said.

"Such as?" Sara asked.

"There's a town on our planned route that we were told we should avoid. The road there has been barricaded, and the people are pretty hostile to anybody they don't know. They've given us a safer route around it that's only a few extra miles."

"That's great," Sara said. "Nice to have found some allies on the road."

"They've also sent people to get water for us, since we're running low," he continued. "There's a spring bubbling up in the woods. It was one of the reasons they chose this spot. And best of all, they told Tom about a field along our route. It looks like it was already harvested last season, but they said that if we work hard enough and dig down deep, we'll be able to get as many potatoes as we can carry. Apparently the harvesting machines miss a fair amount."

I brightened up. "That covers two of the rule of three," I said. "Water to drink and food to eat."

"Speaking of which," Captain Daley added, "you three should get something to eat. Fede set up a fire so we can warm up our meal tonight and—" He broke off and pointed behind me, smiling. I turned around to see Godzilla walking down the path toward us.

"Godzilla!" I called out.

He heard me and started running. When he stopped in front of me, I saw there was something in his mouth. It looked like a stuffed animal. He dropped it in front of me, and when I went to pick it up, I realized it was a dead rabbit. I drew back my hand, and my stomach did a little flip.

"The dog's a hunter!" said Tom, who had just gotten back. He bent down to get the rabbit, and Godzilla growled and put a paw on top of it. Tom withdrew his hand and looked at me.

"He brought it for you," Tom said. "It's a tribute to his owner."

Reluctantly I bent down and picked it up. It was soft and wet and still warm. I held it away from me.

"A little fresh meat goes a long way in a stew," Fede said as we headed over to the fire.

I gladly handed him the rabbit. Godzilla stood up and growled.

"It's okay, boy, I gave it to him."

Godzilla went silent and started wagging his tail. He stood up on his back legs, putting his front paws on my shoulders and practically knocking me over.

"I knew that dog would earn his keep," Tom said.

We were almost ready to leave. It had been dark for more than three hours, and we were much later than we had planned because of Dr. Singh seeing every last patient. Joyce had made up for it by sending out an advance group to scout our route and make sure it was safe. She'd come back and told us it was open road.

"We're sorry to see you leave," Joyce said. "Would it be all right if I address your group before you head out?"

"Please, go ahead," Captain Daley replied.

"Thank you. I've been asked by the different families and groups here to formally thank you for what you've done," Joyce said.

"You're more than welcome. And thank you for the help you've offered to us," Captain Daley replied.

"That was only fair. I want to thank you not only for having Dr. Singh treat our people, but for just being kind," she said. "Sometimes it feels like we can't trust anybody."

"You must have been concerned when we rolled in," Tom said.

"I hate to admit it, after everything you've done for us, but when you first appeared, we thought about attacking you," Joyce said, eyes downcast.

"I'm glad it didn't come to that."

"So are we." She looked at each of us. "We want you to know you're all welcome to stay as many days as you'd like. Even permanently."

"Thank you for your offer, Joyce," Captain Daley said.

"It's safer for you here than out there," she went on. "And your staying would make us all more secure."

I couldn't help but think of Robin Hood living in Sherwood Forest and being protected and hidden by the trees. I'd loved reading about Robin Hood stealing from the rich and giving to the poor. Now, out *there*, it was mostly everybody trying to take from everybody else. These people seemed decent, and they had been kind. But I knew we should get back on the road.

"We need to keep traveling," Tom said, echoing my thoughts. "It's only going to get tougher with each day we delay."

"You really don't think waiting it out is going to work, do you?" Joyce asked.

He shook his head. "The tents are fine for now, but you need to consider something more permanent. Something to get you through the winter."

Joyce slowly nodded her head. "We hope you find your way back to your families," she said. "But if a route ahead is blocked, you'll be welcomed back here with open arms."

"That means a lot to us," Captain Daley replied. "Thank you."

"But now it's time for us to try to move forward," Tom said. "Everybody, get loaded up."

Richard, Doeun and Sara got on their bikes and started off ahead of us. I didn't ask permission but just started riding with them. Godzilla was right at my side. We left the group behind in the clearing and went into a tunnel of trees. I'd been along this road three times before, but now, in the pitch blackness, it seemed different. Clouds had rolled in, and even the faint light from the moon and stars was gone.

I was happy to be moving on, but I had to admit that at least a small part of me had wanted to stay here for a few days. Staying here was safer than being out there. Nobody could know what was just down the way or twenty miles along, and nobody could predict what we were going to run into during the next thousand miles. One thing I did know. My home was down this road. My parents were down this road. We'd keep moving forward, step by step, pedal by pedal, mile by mile. By the time the sun came up, we'd be fifty miles closer to home. That was all that mattered.

CHAPTER
TWENTY-TWO

"WHAT DAY IS IT?" I asked Doeun as she pedaled beside me.

"It's a Tuesday."

"I meant how many days has it been?"

"Nineteen since everything collapsed, and fourteen since we left the airport."

Day after day we'd continued to move forward. Half the time at night, the other half in the early morning, as soon as there was daylight. We had traveled almost five hundred miles. Unfortunately, it wasn't all in the right direction. We'd had to backtrack a couple of times and go different ways than we had planned. Detours were never good, but they were necessary. Captain Daley calculated that we'd traveled slightly less than four hundred miles toward home when we hit the road that morning. By the end of the day, all things being good, we'd have put in another thirty-five.

Doeun, Julia, Fede and Captain Daley had long ago changed out of their uniforms and into civilian clothing. What had been an advantage at the airport was a disadvantage out here. People we'd passed had wanted to talk because they'd thought the uniforms might mean more information.

That wasn't the only change. All the men had beards. Nothing to match Tom's full Santa beard, but different levels of scruffiness. Hair was longer, clothing was dirtier, and nobody had the time or water to wash up. I figured we all smelled, but the odor sort of blurred together so nobody noticed.

There were still lots of people on the road, but things were different now. Most of the groups were bigger—we figured smaller groups were coming together for protection. And they needed that protection. There were armed groups preying on people who had fewer weapons. With less food and fewer resources, people were getting more desperate. So far, our group had been large enough and armed enough that nobody had tried to take us on.

"Up ahead, over to the left," Doeun said. "Do you see it?"

Instantly the hairs on the back of my neck stood up. I scanned the side of the road. It looked like there was somebody lying there, partially in the ditch. It was probably just a body. How strange that in my mind it was "just" a body.

Richard, who was slightly ahead of us, got off his bike and swung the rifle off his shoulder, dropping to one knee and bringing the weapon up to a firing position. I stopped beside him, and Phillip came up from behind us. He and Doeun moved forward slowly, gliding without moving the pedals. Each of them held a pistol in one hand and their handlebars with the other. I left my pistol in my pocket.

They closed in on the body, guns aimed, leading the way.

"We're clear," Doeun called out.

"Don't you want a closer look, to be sure?" Richard asked.

"No need," Phillip replied. "He's been here at least a few days, judging by the flies and decomposition."

"Whoever was here before us before took his shoes, so I don't think there's much point in checking his pockets for anything valuable," Doeun added. "Let's keep moving."

We'd begun to search bodies, hoping to find things that could help us. The definition of what was valuable had changed since all of this happened. It wasn't money or jewelry or a cell phone. My useless cell phone was at the bottom of my bag, more like a memento now than anything useful. Valuable was a granola bar, or a bottle of water, or a gun, or a few bullets at least. Whatever this man had once had was long gone.

"How many bodies has that been today?" I asked.

Nobody answered at first. "I don't really keep track," Doeun said.

"You're a pilot. You keep track of everything. How many?" I asked again.

She hesitated a moment. "An even dozen," she replied. "Sorry you have to see all this." As if any of it were her fault.

"Still, we're glad to have you here, Jamie," Richard said, riding up beside me. "You're a big part of things."

I often went ahead with the scouts now while Godzilla rested on the stairs. Everyone felt we seemed less threatening with me on my little bike. Pink streamers didn't scare people.

"You are a valuable part of our fellowship, young hobbit," Doeun said with a wink.

"Frodo is important," I agreed.

"More than important—the key to the entire quest." Doeun pedaled up closer, so she was right at my side. "You still have the ring someplace safe, right?" she asked quietly.

I patted my pocket, and she smiled.

"And Samwise is also very valuable," she said.

Godzilla had started hunting more and more. Whenever we stopped moving, whether it was during the day or at night, he'd head out looking for game. It was often rabbits, but he'd brought back chickens, a wild turkey and even a cat. Every time Godzilla returned with something, he'd bring it right to me, dropping it at my feet.

We'd eaten everything he'd brought back except the cat, but I was starting to think it wouldn't be long before even a cat would be added to the stew. I thought back to our time at the airport, how I'd turned up my nose at the thought of eating baby food. Two days ago we'd used the last of the jars. I missed the baby food now. Food was food, and we didn't have enough with us to get home.

Up ahead we saw a family—who obviously had seen us as well, because they scrambled off the road and headed into the field. That happened pretty often. People we approached often got right off the road and waited on the other side of the ditch or in a field for us to pass. Some had even climbed over fences to give us our space. It happened even more often when Godzilla was running along beside me. People were terrified of him.

We shifted over to the far side of the road from where they'd gone into the field. It wasn't just them being cautious of us. There was no telling what weapons they had or how dangerous they could be. As we passed by, I gave a little wave, and they waved back.

But it wasn't really small groups like this that we feared. It was the larger ones, which were more likely to be well armed with guns and other weapons. Tom called them "vultures and wolf packs." We'd seen groups like that, but so far they'd avoided us, maybe deciding there were easier targets than us.

As well as watching for danger ahead, we also scouted for opportunity. This could be a protected place to stop and rest, potential food, fresh water or sources of gas for the generator. Luckily, there was no shortage of abandoned cars with gas in their tanks.

Off to the left we spotted five separate columns of smoke rising into the air. Outdoor cooking—and fires for heat at night—were common now. People had to eat, sure. But the smoke also signaled people's location. Did they want to attract outsiders who might try and take away their food…and maybe even their lives? Tom had shown us how to make smokeless fires—one of his many survivalist skills.

We saw more people living in tents and rough outdoor shelters now. The burned-out houses and buildings we passed explained why. So many places had been set on fire. I understood taking things—even at gunpoint—to survive, but I still didn't get arson. Looting grocery stores at least made some sense.

I thought more and more about that rule-of-three thing. Three minutes without air, three days without water and three weeks without food. The air was the only thing that was guaranteed. We had to continually look for the other two. We tried to roll as fast as we could, but we often stopped to scavenge and scrounge from the fields and forests. Tom called it "found food." He knew a lot about wild food and what was edible. The biggest problem was that when you were foraging, you weren't moving forward.

Tom had explained there was another element to the rule of three. You could live up to three weeks in bad weather without proper shelter. Whenever I saw people living in tents, I thought about that. Camping out was okay now, but what about in November or December? What if this went on that long? What if we weren't home by then? No, that wasn't possible. We'd gone one-third of the way in fourteen days, so at this rate, we'd be home well before the end of June.

"Up ahead," Doeun called out.

I saw something in the middle of the road. Was it a garbage bag or an old carpet?

"I got it," Phillip said. He started moving faster, and we dropped back. Both he and Doeun pulled out their pistols as they pedaled.

He came to a stop right by the object. He motioned for us to come forward. As I got closer, I could tell it was another body. More buzzing flies. I quickly looked away. He'd been dead for a while. We kept moving.

"Another one bites the dust," Richard said.

"I was thinking about all the bodies we find," Phillip said. "It makes you wonder how many we're missing at night, the ones at the side of the road or in the trees and fields."

"It isn't the dead bodies I'm worried about," Richard said. "I wonder how many people with weapons are in the trees or bushes beside the road, and we just can't see them."

"I've thought about that too. A lot," Doeun replied darkly. "We're doing the best we can, but what are we missing?"

"Probably a lot," I said. That idea gave me the creeps.

"We could be passing by people or things that are a danger to us, maybe even fatal, and we wouldn't know until they shot us," Doeun added.

"It's like swimming in the ocean oblivious to the fact that there's a great white shark a few feet away," Phillip said with a shudder.

"I've seen pictures like that, taken with drones," Doeun said. "People on paddle or surf boards, and there's a gigantic shark right beside them and they don't know it!"

"If it were me, I think I'd rather not know," Richard said, wrinkling his nose.

"The pilot in me wants to know everything," Doeun said, shrugging. She paused. "What I *really* wish for is a plane. Some old model, no computer chips. I'm sure I could fly it. Or, if not me, Captain Daley."

"Captain Daley said he was building an ultralight with his son," I added.

"An ultralight would probably still work," Doeun said. "It's basically a flying go-kart. No computers involved, no technology whatsoever." She sighed wistfully.

We'd often seen old cars and trucks, minibikes and go-karts on the road. We were seeing more and more of them now. Tom said he figured people were digging them out of basements, backyards, garages or junkyards now that they realized they could be made to work. A plane seemed too much to ask for—I just wished we had a truck instead of our crazy stair car. If we could travel fifty or sixty miles an hour instead of five or six miles every hour, we could be home within two days.

I looked ahead at the trees crowding the road on both sides. I thought about what Richard and Doeun had said, that we couldn't really see what was in there until it was too late to do anything about it. We were just riding along on the road, sitting ducks if somebody wanted to take a shot at us.

"Up ahead!" I yelled, and we all skidded to a stop.

"What do you see?" Doeun asked.

"The road is barricaded."

"I can see it," Richard said. "Perfect place to block off a road when there are trees to use as cover. Let's get a closer look—but not too close. Doeun, watch the left side of the road, and Phillip, watch the right. Jamie, I want you to hold back and stay well behind us."

I wasn't going to argue with staying farther away from danger.

As the three of us closed in, we could see that tires and felled trees had been piled up on both sides of the road, leaving only a small opening in the middle. Was it wide enough to let the stair car through? Behind the barricade I could make out little bumps—the heads of a few people. But that didn't mean there weren't more people I couldn't see.

"I think we've seen enough to know this could be trouble," Richard said.

"Let's report back and figure out what comes next," Doeun said.

CHAPTER
TWENTY-THREE

THE SAFEST THING WAS TO avoid the barricade entirely, but the maps showed that the closest alternate route would mean heading back almost fifteen miles. Even then, the other route passed close to a town, and there were no guarantees the road there wouldn't be blocked as well. The only choice was to move forward and deal with the people at the barricade. Probably all they wanted was a "toll" to pass through. Probably. We hoped.

"Okay, is everybody clear on their role?" Captain Daley asked.

There were a lot of nods and words of agreement.

"Let's go," Richard said.

Phillip, Richard and Sara needed to leave first, because they had the farthest to go. They were going to take a wide walk through the fields and around the forest, coming at the barricade either from the trees or from the other direction. Phillip and Richard were armed with a rifle and a pistol, and Sara with her bow and arrows.

We hoped things would go well in negotiating with the people at the barricade. If they didn't, those three were our plan B.

"All finished," Calvin said. "New batteries in place."

"She's sounding a little off today," Captain Daley said.

We'd all noticed there was a change in the "whining" of the stair car.

"This thing wasn't meant to run for this long and travel on such rough roads," Calvin said. "When we have a safe place to stop next, Richard and I'll have a look at it."

They had made some changes to the vehicle a week earlier. They'd used some pieces of metal we'd found along the road to build a little "fort" around the driver's compartment. If somebody was going to try to stop the stair car, the easiest way was to shoot the driver. Now, hidden behind the metal, the driver had the safest spot.

The supplies on the trolley had been rearranged too. Things we might want to trade for our passage had been brought closer to the edge while more important things had been buried or hidden inside backpacks. Plus, our bikes had all been tied down on top.

"It's time," Captain Daley said.

Everybody climbed onto the stairs except Tom, Noah and me. Godzilla was on a leash tied to the bottom of the stairs. He wasn't coming with me, and this was probably the only way to stop him from trying to—assuming he didn't drag the whole vehicle along with him.

"Jamie, you know you can stay with us," Captain Daley said. "It would probably make Godzilla happy."

"I'm okay."

"You're better than okay," Captain Daley said. He took one last look around at us, then clapped his hands together decisively. "Well, I think it's time, folks."

He climbed up the stairs to the platform on top. He had the shotgun.

Tom, Noah and I started moving. Godzilla started whining and barking.

"It's okay, boy, I'll be back," I yelled over my shoulder.

Noah had his bow and arrows on his lap and a pistol hidden underneath him. Tom had said that by having that weapon in plain sight, it would distract the people from looking too hard for another one. He explained that it was like a magician waving his right hand in the air when you should really be looking at what was happening with his left.

I had my pistol hidden away in a cloth holster that Sara had made for me out of an old sock. It was tucked into the small of my back and tied on. Strangely, Tom, the one who knew most about guns and how to handle them, didn't have one. He said he was there to talk, and the gun would only get in the way. If something happened, my job was to somehow get the gun I was carrying into his hands.

The same three of us led the way now as at the first barricade we'd dealt with. Tom was best at negotiating, and we figured Noah and I looked the least threatening. Obviously, Noah was in a wheelchair. But the guy wasn't just an Olympic archer. He was also as strong as an ox. He could take care of himself, and because people underestimated him, he was maybe more dangerous. I'd learned that he had been in a car accident that crushed his spine. Someone who's been through that much is sure to have some serious guts.

"How's the chair doing?" Tom asked as we walked.

"A little bit of a wobble with the left wheel. Like the stair car, this wheelchair wasn't meant for traveling this far."

"You could be riding on the stair car more often," Tom suggested.

"I always like to pull my own weight."

"Then have Richard take a look at it. That guy is a lot more than I thought he was," Tom said.

"What do you mean?" I asked.

"I had him pegged as some slick-talking salesman. He's got more to him," Tom said. "He's *solid*. Somebody you can count on."

I knew that was a real compliment coming from Tom. I liked to believe he thought of me the same way.

Richard, Sara and Phillip were part of our magic trick. Everybody would be looking down the road at us and wouldn't notice other members of our group coming through the woods. If nothing went wrong, those three would stay invisible, but if there were problems, they'd be there.

"I must admit, Jamie, you surprise me even more than Richard does," Tom continued. "I didn't think I'd be trusting a thirteen-year-old with my life."

I felt a rush of pride mixing with my anxiety. "I guess we're all trusting each other," I said.

The barricade was just in front of us. The stair car had come to a stop behind us, close enough for the crew to see us wave them forward but far enough away to stay safe.

We continued to move slowly, all together. We could see the heads of at least half a dozen people behind the barrier and at least three rifles resting on top of it, aimed at us.

"No sudden moves," Tom said. "We don't want to scare them."

"I don't think scaring *them* is going to be the problem," I muttered.

We were walking toward people we knew had guns. They were behind the barrier, and we were out in the open. They could clearly see us and the weapons we had or didn't have. We had no idea how many of them were there, and I had to assume that whatever other weapons they had were also aimed directly at us. I could feel my heart racing.

"Remember, this is just a business transaction."

"I used to do a lot of business, and it never involved weapons," Noah said.

"New rules. But this is the same as the other times, at its core. Just let me do all the talking."

"That's guaranteed," Noah said with a grim smile.

That was always the pattern. Tom talked and we listened. He was pretty convincing when he tried to talk his way through a problem or a barricade. We came to a stop.

"Hello!" Tom yelled out.

There was no response for a few seconds, and then one man, followed by a second, stepped out from behind the barricade. They were both carrying rifles.

"Can we come closer?" Tom called out.

The man in a baseball cap gestured for us to come forward.

"Here we go," Tom said under his breath.

As we walked toward them, they retreated behind the barricade. That made me feel even more uneasy. They were luring us back there with them. Then whatever was going to happen would be out of the sight of the rest of our people. As we got to the barricade, I could see that their weapons were trained on us.

Tom moved slightly in front, Noah rolling behind him, and I took up the rear. Tom stepped through the gap.

"Good afternoon, every—"

Someone knocked Tom over, and guns were aimed at Noah, and I was grabbed and pulled forward by powerful arms and thrown to the ground, landing beside Tom. Standing over us were four people—three men and a woman—with their guns aimed right at us. Two of them had rifles, and two held pistols. I looked at the guns, hoping they were toys. One was a BB gun, but the other three were deadly. I'd learned to tell what was real. That was part of the lessons Tom had been giving me.

"Search them!" the woman yelled. She was obviously in charge.

They'd already taken the bow and arrows away from Noah. One guy patted him down while another searched Tom. I raised my hands above my head and a third patted down my shirt. I was relieved when he stopped before finding the gun. The weapon underneath Noah was missed as well.

Along with the four people holding weapons and the three who had searched us, there were five who had stayed behind the barricade. Two of them were women about my mother's age. That made an even dozen. Three were watching the road in the direction we'd come, and two were watching the other way. Nobody was looking at either side of the woods.

"All three of you, get up!" one of the men yelled. He was the biggest of the bunch.

"Is this the only weapon you have?" the woman asked. She was holding the bow.

"It's the only one the three of us have," Tom said.

"Not much of a weapon." She tossed it to the ground.

"Hey, be careful with that!" Noah exclaimed.

"Shut up!" a man yelled. He aimed his rifle right at Noah's chest.

"We don't want any trouble," Tom said slowly.

"And how's that working out for you?" the biggest one asked, and all of them laughed.

"There's no need for any of this," Tom said. "We just wanted to come and talk and offer to trade for our passage through your barricade."

The woman narrowed her eyes at Tom. "What's that thing out there that you're driving?"

"It's an old airport stair car. The thing has been nothing but trouble."

"What airport did it come from?"

"O'Hare," Tom answered.

"That's over five hundred miles from here," one of them said. "Sounds like it hasn't caused too many troubles. We could use something like that."

Tom furrowed his brow. "That's one of the things we're not going to give up, but we have lots of other things we'd be willing to trade for passage."

"Trade?" the woman asked, and the others laughed.

"Yes. We have some food, clothing, flashlights and assorted supplies. We understand that trading is just what we all have to do. We know you're only trying to survive and—"

"I don't think it's our survival you should be worrying about," the woman said.

A chill went up my spine. It wasn't just what she said, but the way she said it. So calm, with no emotion, and her eyes looked dead. Like a shark's eyes. How desperate were these people? How dangerous?

"And why do you think we'd trade when we can just take?" another one of them asked.

"Come on. Be reasonable," Tom said.

"Reasonable? I need you to stop talking," the woman said as she shoved her rifle into Tom's face to make her point. "I don't like you and I don't trust you, so I don't want to hear anything more from you unless I ask you a direct question."

She pointed at me. "Kid, you answer all our questions now. And if I think you're lying or trying to trick me, I'm going to shoot him first, and then you second. Got it?"

I nodded.

"How many people are out there?"

"Six...no, seven...well, eight if you count Nelson...he's five years old."

"And what weapons do they have?"

"Um...knives and a gun, like, a pistol and a shotgun." My voice sounded tight, but I tried to keep it level.

"Anything more?" she demanded.

"Nothing. Maybe a club or something, but nothing more. Honestly."

She turned to the others. "Him I believe. Now listen closely, kid, because your life and the lives of these two depend on you."

I numbly nodded my head.

"You're going to go out and call for the others to come forward. You're going to convince them. If they don't come, we're going to put a bullet in the heads of all three of you."

"And if they do come?" Noah asked.

The woman didn't turn around. "I'm not talking to you, and if you say another word, I'm going to kill you right now."

She kept looking directly at me.

"Your choice is, you let us have what we want and we let you live," she said. "If you put up a fight, nobody's walking anywhere. You'll end up like the last group that tried to fight us." She pointed to the side of the road. "Like them."

I looked. There in the ditch were three bodies, lying facedown and partially hidden by the water at the bottom.

She glared at me. "They decided to put up a fight. Do you want to fight us, kid?"

I shook my head.

"You better do this right. Everybody's life depends on it."

I knew she was right about both parts. Our lives did depend on it, and I had to do it exactly the right way. Somebody was probably going to die. I had to hope it wasn't any of us.

CHAPTER

TWENTY-FOUR

"GET OUT THERE AND DO YOUR JOB," the man in the ball cap said as he walked me to the edge of the barricade.

"Yes, sir," I said.

"Manners aren't going to help you one bit. A bullet doesn't care how polite you are," he said. "Remember, we have a rifle aimed square at your back. If you run, you'll be dead before you get two steps. If you walk too far, you're dead. If they turn and drive away, you're going to be dead, along with the two you've left behind."

I looked back. Tom was still on the ground, and Noah was beside him in his chair. Noah couldn't pull out his gun because there was a guard standing over them. Even if he could, there were at least six of them with weapons. If he managed to shoot one or two of them, he wouldn't survive the other four gunning him down.

"It's up to you, kid. People can die or people can live. Now start walking."

I went onto the open ground. The stair car was visible but at a safe distance. They could get away if they wanted to escape. I couldn't. Neither could Tom and Noah. I walked slowly, imagining the sights of the guns boring a hole into my back. If I ran, I wondered, how many steps would I get before the bullet caught up to me?

I went out as far as I dared and came to a stop. "It's safe!" I yelled. "Come on!"

I had to think things through clearly. I had to follow the signals we'd worked out. If I waved to them with my left arm, it meant it was safe for them to come forward—there was no concern. If I signaled them with my right arm, it meant they should come forward but be very cautious and have weapons ready. I motioned to them with both arms. That meant our lives were in danger. *All* of our lives. That the people behind the barricade were going to try to kill us, and we would have to do the same if we wanted to survive.

As soon as they got the signal, Amber, Nelson and Dr. Singh would be slipping away, unnoticed, we hoped, by the people at the barricade. They'd go down into the ditch and the fields beyond that. There they'd be safe from whatever happened to the rest of us. They'd stay in hiding until we came to get them. If we didn't come, they were to run away. I knew they'd take Mia, and I hoped Godzilla would let them lead him away too.

I waved both arms once, then a second and third time. I yelled for them to come forward. They probably couldn't even hear me, but those men behind the barricade could, and they wouldn't know what I was really saying. Twelve times I lifted and waved my arms like I was trying to take off, and then I stopped. The people at the barricade probably thought I was waving so enthusiastically in order to encourage my group to come and because I was scared. I *was* scared. But what I'd done was more than that—I'd told Captain Daley that there were twelve of them.

"We will be coming forward now!" called out Captain Daley over a handheld megaphone. "Our weapons are down, and we're coming to negotiate!"

The voice was deliberately loud, so the people at the barricade could hear it. But he was also talking to Richard, Phillip and Sara. The plan was that he'd use the word *talk* if things were okay and *negotiate* if it was going to be a fight. That way, if they hadn't seen what was happening to us, they'd know to get into position.

The stair car started to move. Julia, Doeun and Fede would be riding along, hidden and protected by the stairs, and they'd each have one of the pistols or rifles. Captain Daley would be wielding the shotgun from the top of the stair platform, and Calvin was at the wheel of the vehicle, a rifle at his side.

It was time for me to get back behind the barricade. I wanted to be there before the stair car arrived. I needed to get close to Tom and somehow get my gun to him. I hoped Noah would be able to retrieve his weapon as well. We also had to hope that Richard, Phillip and Sara would be able to get close enough to do something. We had to even up the odds.

I slipped through the opening in the barricade and was barely behind it when someone grabbed me and pushed me toward where Tom was on the ground, Noah beside him.

"Stay down and don't move, if you want to live!" one of the men said to me.

The bandits were now almost all at the barricade. Three people were peering over the top, and most of the others had crouched down so they couldn't be seen by the approaching vehicle. The leader was giving them orders. She was still calm, in control. She was scary.

"Are you all right?" Tom asked.

I nodded. "As good as I can be."

"You two, shut up!" ordered a man to the side of us. He had a pistol in his hand and one eye on us, but he seemed more interested in what was coming down the road.

"It was me," I said. "I was just telling him I'm okay."

"You're wrong. You're nowhere near okay."

"They're coming, but they're coming slowly!" somebody yelled. "Get your weapons ready!"

Our guard turned away from us. I looked at Tom, and he gave me a subtle smile. He looked calm, almost confident, like he was the guy holding the guns and in charge.

Slowly I angled myself ever so slightly so that my body shielded a view of where my gun was held even if the guard did turn around. I started to slip my hand toward it and—

"Not yet," Tom hissed.

The man spun around. He looked angry. He drew back his leg and kicked Tom in the side. Tom groaned and rolled over. He kicked him again and again, in the side and the head and—

"Stop, please!" I yelled.

He kicked him once more and then stopped. "You want me to kick you instead?"

I shook my head. I was terrified.

"One more word and you're next."

Tom coughed and spat up some blood. "Leave him alone...he's just a kid...let him go."

"Get up!" he yelled at Tom. "Get up now!"

Tom struggled to his feet. He stumbled and almost toppled over.

"Go over there."

The man motioned with his gun to the ditch on the other side, by the dead people. He made Tom walk ahead of him.

"Now!" Noah said.

I hesitated for a split second and then reached for my hidden weapon. It was partway out when the man turned around. He looked at me, and he raised the pistol and aimed it directly at me and—his eyes widened in shock as I heard a *thunk*. The shaft of an arrow now poked out of his chest. He dropped the pistol and grabbed at the arrow, falling to his knees.

Tom stepped forward and scooped up the gun from the ground. I pulled mine free, and in an instant Noah had his pistol out and was holding it in front of him.

There was an explosion of gunfire as the people behind the barrier started to fire at the approaching stair car. Tom brought up his gun and started firing, and Noah did the same. A man at the line fell forward, then a second and a third. They'd been hit! Two of the others spun around, ready to fire, and an arrow shot into one of them, the featherlike fletching visible against his chest. The second man started firing, and I sensed the bullets zing by my ear. Suddenly another arrow whooshed by, leaving a bright red gash on the side of his head. He staggered, almost tumbled over and dropped his rifle.

Then everything happened at once. Richard, Phillip and Sara leaped over the ditch as the stair car barreled into the barricade, which tumbled over backward. A couple of the marauders were hit by the falling debris, and others dove sideways to get out of the way. There was a blast from above as Captain Daley fired his shotgun at a man who was firing up at him. The man spun around, toppling to the ground, the front of his chest open and gushing blood. The stair car kept moving through, toppling the barricade, and Doeun, Julia and Fede jumped off the vehicle and started firing their pistols. A woman fell to the ground as those three took cover behind some tires. It was mayhem!

"Hands up! Hands up!" Tom yelled. "Drop your weapons! Do it now or you die!"

The gunfire slowed to a few shots and stopped altogether. Then the leader dropped her gun to the ground and slowly raised her hands. I could see she was wounded—blood dripped down her side—but I couldn't tell how bad it was. A second and a third and then a fourth did the same. The others were lying on the ground. They couldn't surrender. They were too badly wounded. Or dead.

Richard and Tom came forward, weapons at the ready, as Captain Daley watched from above, his shotgun aimed.

But it was done. We'd survived. We'd won. It was over.

"Quick, somebody get Dr. Singh!" Noah yelled.

Phillip was lying on the ground, facedown, a hole in his back between his shoulder blades, open and bleeding.

CHAPTER

TWENTY-
FIVE

"HOW ARE YOU DOING? How are you feeling?"

I looked up to find Julia standing beside me. I shrugged. She slumped down to the ground beside me.

"How many?" I asked.

She knew what I meant—how many people were dead.

"Eight. Seven of them and Phillip."

I'd stood off to the side when Dr. Singh tried to help Phillip. She hadn't spent much time with him before she stood up and shook her head. I couldn't believe he was dead.

I hugged my arms around myself, trying to unsee what I'd seen. "Can we go? Can we leave?" I asked.

"Soon. Dr. Singh is still treating the injuries."

Fede had been wounded by a small bullet fragment that had hit the side of the stair car, bounced up and grazed the side of his head. He had a tourniquet wrapped around his head and, luckily, seemed fine.

Half an inch over, and he wouldn't have been fine. He would have been dead too.

Dr. Singh had said Tom had a broken rib from being kicked and could have a concussion too. Tom had joked that he "never was too smart," so the kick to his head might have "knocked some sense" into him. Dr. Singh had insisted that he spend the night sitting on the stairs. Tom and Fede were there now, talking to each other. *Wait.* If they were there, where was Dr. Singh?

"Was somebody else hurt? Who's the doctor with?" I asked.

"She's treating the people we shot," Julia answered.

I turned around to where their wounded and the prisoners were sitting. Dr. Singh was bending over one of the injured, and Richard was treating another. They were all being guarded by Doeun, who was holding the shotgun, and Sara with her deadly weapon.

There were others there now as well—five more women and almost a dozen children. They were the families of the people who had been at the barricade. They'd been camping off to the left, in the woods. After overwhelming the barricade, Captain Daley, Sara and Richard had gone to take control of the campsite. They'd captured the people there without a fight and brought them back here. It had been hard to hear them sobbing when they discovered that people— husbands and fathers and a wife and mother—had been killed. We'd had no choice. It was them or us, and we hadn't started it.

"I don't know why they're even treating them," I snapped.

"They're trained to help people—that's what they do," Julia said softly.

"But they killed Phillip!" I croaked. "They almost killed Fede! They wanted to kill us all!"

As I yelled, I noticed that a few of the campers turned to look at me. I didn't care. I glared at them. They didn't deserve to be treated. They didn't deserve to live when our friend had died!

She reached out and took my hand. "Jamie, I know why you're feeling that way. I understand."

My eyes stung with tears.

"It's hard. It's horrible, with all those bullets flying," she said. "I'm still trying to figure out if any of my bullets hit somebody, killed somebody. Did you fire your weapon?"

I shook my head. When everything had gone crazy, I'd been so scared, and everything was swirling around so much, it was like I'd forgotten I even had a gun in my hand.

"I hope we never get to the point where we'd do to somebody what they tried to do to us," Julia said. "Which is why we have to help them. Right?"

I inhaled deeply and let it out, and I felt my anger subside. I could see what she meant.

Captain Daley and Richard came out of the field, jumped over the ditch and walked toward us. They'd carried Phillip's body away and returned without it. They walked over to where the prisoners and their families were being watched.

Julia got up and offered me a hand. "Come on, you're not the only one who's curious about what's going to happen."

Captain Daley was talking to one of the prisoners.

"You can be guaranteed that Dr. Singh will treat your people the way she'd treat ours," Captain Daley said.

"I should thank you, especially after what we did," a man replied quietly.

Captain Daley gave a heavy sigh. "I wish you would have just traded with us for our passage."

"I wish that too," the man said regretfully. "That's what we did in the beginning."

"What changed?" Captain Daley asked.

The man's shoulders slumped. "We got scared. We got desperate," he said. "It was bound to lead to tragedy sooner or later." He gazed at the ground before saying, "What happens now?"

"We leave you, and we go."

"Are you taking our things—our supplies, our guns?" the man asked.

"We're going to take some things but leave you with enough supplies and food to survive. But we can't leave you with any weapons, because I'm afraid you'd turn them on us."

"We wouldn't do that," the man insisted. He paused. "It's just that… without any weapons, I don't know how we'll be able to survive, to provide for our families, to defend them."

"I don't see a way around it," Captain Daley said simply.

I looked at the man, at the women, at the kids and the wounded. Their leader was dead. The man who had beat up Tom was dead. The others looked so pathetic, so small, sitting there on the ground. It was the exact spot where we'd been pushed down and threatened. I understood what they must be thinking. What they must be feeling. Suddenly I felt different about them.

"What if we left them a couple of empty guns?" I suggested.

Captain Daley looked at me, eyebrows raised. "I'm not sure empty guns would do them much good."

"We could leave some ammunition back down the road," I said. "It doesn't have to be much, and by the time they get to it, we'll be long gone."

He paused, thinking. "I didn't expect you to be worried about them," he said eventually.

I shrugged. "They have kids to take care of. It just doesn't seem right to leave them with nothing."

Julia turned to me. "Even after what they did to us?" she asked.

"Yes. Maybe even because of it. I know what it's like to be sitting there with my life on the line, thinking I'm as good as dead."

She nodded and squeezed my shoulder.

"If we do what Jamie is suggesting," Captain Daley said, "how do we know they're not going to come looking for us? Come after us to get revenge?"

"You have my word," the man answered, "for what you think it's worth. Besides, we'd be fools to do that. We're not going looking for another fight we can't win." He seemed to be telling the truth. He looked beaten.

"Well, Jamie," Captain Daley said, "what do you think we should leave them?"

I thought for a moment. "Maybe one of the rifles, a pistol and the BB gun. It can't hurt anybody, really, but it will make them look like they're better armed."

Captain Daley was nodding his head. "Those and enough ammunition to defend yourselves but not harm anybody else."

"Thank you, thank you so much!" the man said.

"Don't thank me," Captain Daley said. "Thank him." He tipped his head in my direction.

The man turned to me. "Thank you, and I'm sorry for what we did. We didn't start off like this. We were good people just trying to survive, and it got harder and harder."

"It got harder for everybody," I said.

Captain Daley clapped his hands together. "It's settled then. I'll have Fede bring the ammunition up the road and hide it, and we'll leave the guns a short distance from here, off to the side, where you can find them," Captain Daley said.

We walked away, and Captain Daley started giving orders to prepare us to leave.

"You did the right thing," Julia said to me.

I shrugged. "What else could we do?"

"We could have left them with nothing."

"No, we couldn't. You're right. We're better than that," I said.

And then I thought, At least, we're better than that right now.

I pedaled along with Julia riding beside me. In the darkness, Richard was almost invisible in front of us. We were ahead of the stair car, scouting the route. It had been quiet so far. Whatever was off the road, in the forest or fields or in the houses we passed, had stayed out of sight.

We'd been riding as hard as the stair car would go for the past two hours. We were trying to put as much space as possible between us and the campers. They'd be fools to follow and try to attack us, but we weren't going to take a chance. Desperate times make people desperate. I got the feeling there was another reason we were moving so fast. We couldn't bring Phillip back, but we could get as far away as possible from where his death had happened.

We all knew that people were dying out here. We'd seen the bodies and the burned-out buildings, and we knew there were dangerous people around. What we hadn't experienced until now was anything happening to us. But now Phillip was gone. Fede had come a fraction of an inch away from being dead, and Tom had been hurt pretty badly. I didn't know if any of us could survive without him.

There was one positive. We were now better armed than we'd ever been, with three more rifles and a pistol that we'd taken from them. Of course, more weapons didn't mean more ammunition. My not firing meant I still had my three bullets if I needed them. Not that *that* was the reason I hadn't fired. I'd just been too scared. How could I *not* be scared with all that had happened?

From the plane almost crashing and the arson and looting to the weapons and even seeing the bodies strewn on the roadside, I could pretend this was just an adventure, a game, a book I was reading. We were the Fellowship of the Ring. We were playing, all of us just characters. And now?

Phillip was dead. That was real. Fede had almost been killed. That was real. Tom had been beaten. That was real. I'd had weapons aimed at me and bullets whizzing by my head and people threatening to kill me. And, even worse, I was sure it was going to happen again and again. What we'd been through, what was behind us, was nothing compared to what was still to come, and I wondered for the first time, deep in my bones, if we were going to make it. Would I ever see my parents again?

My whole body shuddered, and I felt a wave of tiredness overwhelm me. I slowed down and then stopped pedaling completely.

Julia turned around. "Do you need to take a break?"

I almost said I was okay, but I wasn't. "I need to stop. Is that okay?"

"Of course it is. We'll wait for them to catch up."

We moved off to the side and waited, and the vehicle quickly caught up and came to a stop slightly past us. Captain Daley bounded down the stairs, rifle in hand. Godzilla was right behind him and ran forward to greet me. I couldn't help but smile as the big dog got on his back legs and licked my face.

"Jamie's going to take a turn riding on the stairs," Julia said.

"It's about time he took a break. He's been making us all look lazy," he replied.

I climbed off my bike, and he picked it up and went to put it on the trolley. It was too small for anybody else to ride except Nelson, and there was no way he was going out to scout.

"Try to get some sleep," Julia said. "I'll go up and join Richard on point."

She took off, and I climbed the stairs, Godzilla at my side. We stepped around Doeun, who was sitting watch at the bottom, holding the rifle. We settled into one of the stairs just above her. Above us were most of the others, either sleeping or trying to sleep.

I sat down, and Godzilla snuggled in so he was more on top of me than beside me. Sometimes I'd push his smelly breath and weight away from me. Not tonight. It felt good, the warmth of him against me, knowing that he was there and I wasn't alone. He'd watch over me. As soon as we started moving, I'd close my eyes and get some sleep.

Captain Daley called to Calvin to resume driving. As the vehicle started with a jolt and a humming sound, Captain Daley jumped up onto the stairs, holding on to the railing and climbing up. He stepped over where Godzilla and I had settled in. I thought he'd go all the way to the top platform, but he stopped and sat down two steps above us.

"I wanted to thank you," he said.

"For what?"

"For your suggestion. It was the moral thing to do. It didn't feel right to leave them with nothing. You gave me a way to make it work."

I nodded and gave Godzilla a scratch. "I hope they'll be all right," I said.

"Strange—they tried to kill us, and now I'm hoping they'll be okay too. I guess it's important that we keep doing the right thing even when it gets worse out here."

I thought for a moment. "It is going to get worse, right?"

He didn't respond right away. I wasn't sure if it was because he was thinking or didn't want to answer.

"I wish I could protect you from all of this," he said, a pained expression on his face. "It would be nice to give you reassuring little lies about how everything is going to be all right, but I can't. Besides, I don't think we could have gotten this far without you."

I was taken aback. "Me?"

"Starting with what you did back at the airport to get us free to begin with. Your actions on that first bridge and since then. I know I can count on you."

I hesitated. "I didn't fire my gun back at the barricade," I said. I felt like I had to tell him.

"If you needed to, you would have. There are other ways we're counting on you. And actually, right now, I'm counting on you to get some sleep while we keep motoring."

This was something I could do. My eyes were getting heavier every second. "How much longer are we going to go tonight?"

"We're going to stop when we find a good place to get off the road. It could be soon, but it could be hours and hours. There's no telling."

"I guess that's the whole thing. There never is any way of telling," I said.

Captain Daley nodded. "I'm going to go up top to the platform. You get some shut-eye."

He got up and, with a hand on the railing, climbed up the steps, carefully stepping over those already seated or sleeping.

Godzilla shifted position, putting his massive head right by my face and giving me a big lick. I reached out and wrapped my arms around his neck. With all the things I couldn't predict, I knew Godzilla was going to be here for me. And I'd be here for him.

CHAPTER

TWENTY-SIX

THE VEHICLE LURCHED, slowed down and came to a stop. I quickly got up. The humming of the electric engine had deteriorated to a higher and higher-pitched whine over the last hour. Something must be wrong. Everybody started to climb off the stairs to see what was going on. Calvin got out of the cab and was joined by Richard, Tom and Captain Daley. They looked on while Calvin opened the battery compartment.

"Do the best you can to get things moving as quickly as possible," Captain Daley said. "I don't want to be out in the open and unable to move. I don't like being a sitting duck."

I looked up and down the road. To one side was scrub brush and small trees, and to the other, thick woods. It felt strange to be out in the morning light. We couldn't see much, but other people could see us. Over the past ten days—since the deaths at the barricade—we'd taken to traveling almost exclusively at night. We should have already stopped, but we hadn't been able to find the right place. And here on the open road was definitely the wrong place.

"I hope it's nothing serious," Tom said.

"Until we know what's wrong, we can't give you an answer," Calvin replied. "I'm actually surprised it's lasted as long as it has. Nine hundred miles is a long way."

How much longer could this vehicle last, and what would happen when it couldn't go any farther?

Calvin opened the engine compartment, and Richard leaned his rifle against the vehicle as they peered under the hood.

"I know you'll do your best and your fastest," Captain Daley said as he gave Calvin a pat on the back.

Captain Daley turned to the group. All of us were now awake, aware and anxiously looking around. Without another word needing to be said, everybody got into action. Tom, rifle on his shoulder, walked back along the road in the direction we'd come. It had taken a few days after the beating for him to get back to being himself, but he felt much better now. There was nobody better to guard the road.

Sara, holding her bow, with a quiver of arrows on one shoulder and a rifle on the other, moved forward to take a position ahead of us. She had been more responsible than anybody for our getting through that barricade. I probably wouldn't be alive without her. She had killed three people that day. Noah had worried how it would affect her, but she said it was just like target practice— nothing more, nothing less. I was sure that was just something she'd said to not be a bother. I knew she hadn't been as talkative as she was before, and sometimes I noticed a sadness in her eyes. Those people were more than targets.

Both Tom and Sara took up defensive positions at the side of the road, where they could see anybody coming but couldn't be seen themselves.

Doeun, with a pistol, and Fede, carrying a rifle, went into the woods on one side of the road. Captain Daley, with another rifle, went to the other side. We now had a sentry on every side. At least we wouldn't be surprised, although we could be overwhelmed.

"Come and get it!" Julia called out.

She and Amber were standing by the wagon. The tarp had been peeled back, and they had put out some food. We'd long ago run out of our original supplies. Who would have thought that airplane food and baby food would be so missed? Now even the extra food we'd claimed at the barricade was starting to run out. Maybe we should have taken more. Maybe we should have taken it all. Situational ethics—that's what Captain Daley had called it. If we'd known back then how hungry we were going to be, we might have taken it all.

What we mostly had were carrots and potatoes. When we had time and a safe place, we cooked them over a fire. When we didn't, we ate them raw. Either way, they would have been better with butter and salt, but we didn't have either. We also didn't have enough potatoes for the rest of the trip. We'd continued to scavenge and search fields and woods for anything edible, but it did slow us down.

Talking about food was one of the things we did a lot. Everybody had something they really missed and really wanted. For me it was ice cream. I would have loved a big double scoop of double chocolate on a waffle cone. Honestly, I would have settled for just the waffle cone.

We'd all lost weight. Tom's spare tire was gone, and Julia had been complaining that her clothes were hanging off her. We joked that this was a really fancy diet method. And it was a diet that was going to continue longer than we'd hoped.

What had originally looked like a journey of forty or fifty days now looked more like sixty or seventy days—or longer. We were traveling a shorter distance each day now. It wasn't just that the stair car was moving slower or needed to have its batteries charged more often but what was on the road. There were more barricades, more detours we had to take, more problems to try to avoid. The previous day had been the shortest distance traveled the entire trip. We'd had to double back to avoid a town, two of the bikes had gotten flat tires, and then we'd had to pull over when we came across an old truck filled with people with guns. We'd watched them as carefully and warily as they'd watched us. Thank goodness nothing had come of it. In the end we'd traveled close to thirty miles, but only a dozen of those had been in the right direction.

I realized that Godzilla wasn't at my side. That could only mean one thing—he was out hunting. He had continued to bring back prey. Sometimes it was squirrels. He managed a pheasant once. Still, it was mostly rabbit. A little bit of rabbit meat went a long way with the potatoes and carrots. It was good that he was hunting, but bad that he was doing it now. As soon as Calvin and Richard got the vehicle going again, we'd be on the move.

"Did anybody see where Godzilla went?" I called out.

"That way," Noah said, pointing in the direction Captain Daley had gone.

I jumped over the ditch.

"Wait!" Julia called. "You can't go alone!"

"Captain Daley is out there," I replied.

"I can go with him," Dr. Singh offered.

Great. The only member of the group other than Nelson who didn't carry a weapon was going to come along. That just meant I had to protect her as well as look for my dog. Julia had made me promise not to go far. If I didn't find Godzilla close by, I would be breaking that promise. I wasn't leaving without my dog.

We started into the small trees. It wasn't long before the road—and the stair car—disappeared from view.

"It's really nice out here," Dr. Singh said, gazing at the treetops. "It makes you almost forget."

I didn't think I'd ever forget, no matter what happened or changed.

"You've been handling all of this very well," she said, meeting my eyes.

I grunted noncommittally. "Everybody has."

"It's getting harder," she said, worry creeping into her voice. "I'm not sure how long I can do this."

"What's your other option?" I asked.

She shook her head. "I don't know. I just feel like giving up." Suddenly she looked so tired. As tired as I felt.

"You can't do that," I said. "We can't. We have to get home."

Dr. Singh stopped walking. "And what if when we get there, there isn't a home anymore or people we care about?" she asked. "We've all seen the burned-out houses and the bodies and—I'm sorry. I shouldn't be talking to you about any of this."

I shrugged. "It's not like you're saying things I don't know."

Suddenly Captain Daley stepped out from behind a tree. I jumped slightly, then gave a laugh of relief.

"I'm assuming you're looking for Godzilla," he said. "He went that way, chasing something. I tried to call him, but he didn't listen."

I knew what Captain Daley was going to say next, and I knew what to answer. "I'm not going to go much farther, and Dr. Singh is going with me."

"Do you have your gun?" he asked.

I nodded.

"Not much farther. If Dr. Singh says to turn around, you turn around. Even if the vehicle is ready to go and has to leave, you and I will stay and wait for Godzilla to come back, okay?"

"Okay. And thanks." Again, that made me feel much better. I would never leave Godzilla behind.

Dr. Singh and I went in the direction the captain had seen Godzilla run. I started calling for him, yelling as loud as I could. I figured that even if I couldn't seem him, he could probably still hear me. We went down a little ravine and there was a small creek, no more than a couple of feet wide. I looked at the mud on the bank, searching for the footprints of the big dog, but couldn't see any.

"Godzilla!" I cried.

"I think we should head back," Dr. Singh said.

"Just a little bit—"

"Are you two lost?" a woman's voice asked.

I looked up. A woman with short, spiky hair was standing on the other side of the little ravine. I didn't see a weapon.

"We're looking for my dog."

"If he's a big Akita, he doubled back the way you came. He had a rabbit in his mouth!"

"That's him!" I exclaimed. He was taking it back to the road to give to me.

The woman cocked her head. "Are you with the group out on the road? With that stair thingy?"

"Yeah, that's us," I said warily. "We're going back now."

"It's not safe to be out there. Do you have many weapons?"

I was about to tell her that we were armed and could take care of ourselves when Dr. Singh spoke.

"I don't have a weapon because I don't think it's right for a doctor to carry a gun."

The woman didn't answer. Instead she turned to the side. I had the feeling she was talking to people I couldn't see. Within a few seconds they became visible. Five people—all with rifles—stepped out of the bush and into the open.

"You need to get off that road as soon as possible. It's too danger-ous out there. I'd like to talk to your leader. We need a doctor."

We pulled off the paved road and onto a gravel lane. Their ancient-looking truck had a rope tied on its rear bumper, with the other end attached to our stair car, towing it along. Despite their efforts, Calvin and Richard hadn't gotten it started. We were all walking or riding bikes beside it. With us was the woman—her name was Cora—flanked by six of her people, who had guns. Between them and us we made an impressive little army. I felt relieved to be off the road. We were safer now. Not safe, but safer.

Cora had told us the road we'd been on was regularly visited by a group of what she called marauders. They were dressed all in black, drove go-karts and were heavily armed. And there were lots of them. She said they were prepared to take from everybody and stop at nothing to get what they needed. She told us we were vastly outgunned and that they'd use their weapons without thinking.

Tom had come up to each member of our group and quietly told us to keep our weapons ready—not just because of the marauders but in case these people claiming to help us turned out not to be as friendly as they seemed.

Cora was walking beside Captain Daley, and they were talking. I wanted to know what exactly they were talking about. I wove through the little crowd until I came up close to them and then jumped off my bike to walk behind them and listen in.

"What's stopped these people, these marauders, from coming after you?" Captain Daley asked.

"We have high-enough walls and enough weapons that they leave us alone. They prefer easier targets. People out on the open road," Cora said.

"Like we would have been."

"Exactly. But I'm so glad I happened upon your group. We appreciate your doctor being able to see some of our people," she said.

"Hopefully there's nothing too serious."

"A couple of late-stage pregnancies, some infections, sprains, two pretty bad cuts and one badly infected amputation," Cora said. "He was cutting wood and took off a couple of toes."

I winced thinking about it.

"That sounds awful. We do have some antibiotics that might come in handy. I'm curious...how many are in your colony?" Captain Daley asked.

"Including children, there are close to three hundred of us."

Captain Daley whistled through his teeth. "And you're able to feed that many people?"

Cora nodded. "So far. We were lucky enough in the beginning to get some milking cows, thirty chickens and a lot of seeds and seedling plants—plus we're near plenty of fields, where we've already planted crops. We'll be able to offer you something better than what you're used to eating."

"I don't think anybody here would turn down a good meal," Captain Daley said. I could hear the smile in his voice. "Except for what Godzilla brings in, we haven't had much fresh food for a while." He turned slightly. "Right, Jamie?"

I hadn't realized it was so obvious that I was listening. I reddened slightly and answered, "Godzilla's been a pretty good hunter."

"Not to mention a pretty good watchdog."

"We have a couple of hunters ourselves," Cora said, turning to me. "They managed to bag a deer last week. We're having a big venison stew tonight." She slowed to a stop. "And here we are," she announced.

Up ahead the gravel lane and the fields on both sides were blocked off by a big wooden wall at least ten feet tall. Behind it I could see houses sticking up. Once inside we'd be safe from things on the outside. The only question I still had was whether we'd be safe from the things that were inside. Was this a trap, or was Cora as nice as she seemed? I pressed my arm against my gun for reassurance.

CHAPTER
TWENTY-
SEVEN

I SAT ON THE STEPS of the front porch of the house and watched as Nelson ran by, playing with some of the kids from the neighborhood. They were all laughing and screaming the way kids do. It all seemed so normal. In fact, if you didn't turn the other way and see the crudely built wall and the armed guards, it looked like a regular neighborhood. Except that the front lawns and flower beds you might expect to see had all been plowed and were growing vegetables.

Nelson was lucky. He was a little kid. In the three days we'd been here, he had settled in like he'd always lived here. Like he belonged. I didn't feel like I belonged—but I did feel safer. Turned out they *were* nice people. They'd shared meals with us, made us feel welcome and helped Richard and Calvin fix the stair car. It had taken time, but two mechanics lived here, and they'd been the ones who really fixed it. They'd scavenged parts and got it running again, although everybody agreed they didn't know for how much longer.

While the compound had mechanics, they didn't have a doctor or a nurse. Dr. Singh and Richard had been working pretty steadily since we'd gotten here. I figured they were likely the reason we'd been invited in.

Tom had talked to their leaders about a dozen different things that could help them. He explained where they had weaknesses in their defenses along the wall and how to make raised boxes to increase food production. He also told the mechanics how to convert lawn mowers into go-karts. There was no grass to cut anymore, but there was certainly a need to move around.

His being comfortable with them made me feel comfortable. He'd come through the gate more cautious and less convinced than the rest of us. He'd pulled me aside before we even got on the other side of the wall and told me to "keep my eyes and ears open," because he thought they'd be more likely to "let something slip" in front of me, the kid, than anybody else. Luckily, nobody had said anything I thought we needed to be worried about.

I felt safer now than I had since the beginning of all this. We were behind a wall, and in a house at night. They'd given us an unused five-bedroom, three-bathroom house to stay in. Since there was no electricity, and no pumps, the way the toilets worked was to dump in a gallon of water, and it flushed everything away. I'd been sleeping on a couch in the living room, with Godzilla on a carpet beside me. These were the most comfortable nights I'd had since leaving my granny's house.

My granny. I wondered how she was doing. My uncle didn't live very far away from her. I was sure he would have gone to get her, so she wasn't alone, but all that meant was that they were suffering together. The same with my parents. How were they doing? I wished I could know and could tell them I was all right, that I was being cared for and that I was coming home. At least, I was trying to get there.

We'd be leaving this place just after sunset. I was happy to get going again but feeling uneasy. It was so much safer here. The people here had agreed to give us some supplies to help us through the next part of the trip.

Captain Daley came out of a house, along with Tom. They were accompanied by Cora and another woman named Evelyn. The two women were the leaders of this colony. That's what they called it— a colony.

I got up, and Godzilla was instantly on his feet beside me. He hadn't been out of my sight since we'd arrived. Or really, *he* hadn't let *me* out of his sight. I wasn't sure if he thought he belonged to me or that I belonged to him. I couldn't wait for my parents to meet him—and that meant leaving. I was headed toward Captain Daley when he noticed me.

"Jamie, could you do me a favor?" he called out. "Could you get everybody who's in the house and ask them to meet us by the gate?"

"Are we leaving now?"

"That's what we want to talk about. I'll see you there in ten minutes."

We all gathered in a little semicircle. Tom and Captain Daley stood at the front with Cora. The rest of us—except for Nelson—settled into the lawn chairs they'd set out for us.

"Since we're all here, we should get started," Captain Daley said. "I want to begin by thanking our hosts for all they've offered."

People started clapping.

"No, thank *you*," Cora said. "Tom, Richard and Dr. Singh have more than made up for the few meals we've offered."

"Very gracious of you to say," Captain Daley replied. "We're gathered here to talk about a further offer you want to make. Cora, the floor is yours."

I leaned in, unsure what was going on.

Cora stepped forward. "It's been our pleasure to host you," she said with a smile. "You've made us healthier, as well as better defended and prepared for the future of our colony." She paused. "And I'd like to offer to any of you, to all of you, a chance to be part of that future."

"What do you mean exactly?" Julia asked.

"You're welcome to become full-time members of this colony."

Everybody started talking at once. I just sat there, worry creeping through me.

"Please, if everybody could just stop for a minute, Tom also has things he can add to the conversation," Captain Daley said, waving his hands for us to settle down.

People became quiet, but I could tell they were as anxious as I was. Everybody was sitting on the edge of their lawn chairs as Tom stepped forward.

"What they've done here is pretty remarkable," Tom said, hands on his hips. "If we're able to get home, we can only hope that our families have done this well. You know me, so you know that I call it like I see it, and I can say with confidence that this is a good place to be if that's what you decide."

"And if people choose to stay, then the food, guns and supplies we have will be equally divided between those who join the colony and those who leave," Captain Daley said.

I felt my shoulders tightening. All I knew was I needed to get back on the road. What if everyone else wanted to stay?

"How do you divide the stair car?" Calvin asked.

"I'm afraid that won't be divided. It will go with whoever is leaving," Captain Daley said. "I hope you're not feeling too possessive of it."

Calvin shrugged. "I'm not even sure how much longer it's going to keep running."

"That's certainly a factor. This is an individual decision. Every one of us is free to choose," Captain Daley added.

"Have you decided?" Doeun asked.

"Yeah," Richard said. "What are you and Tom going to be doing?"

"We've both decided, but we don't want our decisions to unfairly affect your choices."

"It *will* affect our choices," Julia said in a strained voice. "We need to know what you two are going to do."

He hesitated before answering. "This is a fine offer. If anybody decides they want to stay, then they have my blessing and good wishes for the future."

I couldn't help but notice that he hadn't answered Julia's question.

"And," Tom added, "if you do stay, there's no question that you're going to be safer here than you will be out there."

"Safer but not necessarily safe," Captain Daley added. "We know it's going to get worse before it gets better whether you stay here or continue on the journey. No guarantees."

"Actually, there is one," Tom said, raising his index finger. "If you stay here, you're never going to get home." I felt anxiety twist in my stomach.

"Unless we stay here only until it gets back to normal," Sara countered.

"That could be a long time," Tom said. "Maybe years. Maybe never."

Everybody started talking among themselves.

"I want to go home," I said.

Nobody paid any attention to me. I stood up and said it again. This time much louder. "I want to go home."

The others got silent and turned to look at me. "I'm going home," I said. "Even if it means it's just me and Godzilla."

"We can't let you leave by yourself!" Julia exclaimed, standing up beside me.

"He won't be by himself," Captain Daley said. He let out a big sigh. "I'm leaving too." Relief coursed through me. Captain Daley. With him along, I could still make the trip. We could do it together.

"And Tom?" Richard asked. "Are you going?"

I'm going to go where I'm needed the most," he answered. I hoped he would choose to keep moving. He knew more about this situation than the rest of us combined. Plus, he was tough as nails.

"We each have to figure out what's best for us," Captain Daley said evenly. "For those coming with me, Jamie and Godzilla, we'll be leaving in just under five hours, so you have the rest of the day to decide. I'll talk individually to anybody who wants to chat," he added. "Thank you, all. This meeting is adjourned."

I was back on the front steps of the house, staring into the distance. Thinking about what lay ahead. Amber sat down beside me. "Can we talk?"

"Of course."

She sat down on the step below me. "Nelson and I are going to stay." She shrugged. "He's happy, and it's safer. Besides, I'm not sure what'll be waiting at the other end even if we do make it."

"I understand," I said. "I'm going to miss you guys." I meant it. Nelson especially.

"That's what I wanted to talk to you about." She hesitated, then went on. "If you changed your mind and decided to stay, I'd take care of you," she said. "You'd be with us."

I stared at her for a minute. Amber was nice, and I knew she meant well, but we weren't close. "Thanks, but I need to find my parents."

"What if they found you instead?" she asked, raising her eyebrows. "Captain Daley could tell them where you are, and they could come and get you."

"Did I just hear my name being used?" Captain Daley asked as he came out the door.

"Yes, I was just suggesting to Jamie that if he stayed here, you could tell his parents he's here and they could come to him," Amber explained.

I wondered what he would say. I hoped he would take my side. "You're right," he said. "If I told them, then they'd come. And that's the problem."

"What do you mean?" Amber asked, frowning.

Captain Daley folded his arms. "Because they'd have to travel five hundred miles to get him and another five hundred miles back home. That would mean traveling twice as far and would likely be more than twice as dangerous because there would only be two of them along with Jamie and Godzilla."

"I would never want that!" I protested.

"I know," Captain Daley said gently. He turned to Amber. "I assume you're going to stay, correct?"

She nodded. "It's what's best for Nelson and me."

"I agree," he said. "But what if Nelson weren't with you and instead was at the other end of this trip? Would you be staying here?"

She recoiled. "Of course not!"

"You'd take the risk to be with your son."

"I'd risk anything for him."

"Then you understand what we're doing," he said carefully. "Jamie just wants to be with his family. I need to get home. My wife and kids are waiting there, and I can't take care of them if I'm here. Does that make sense?"

"Completely," she said. "I'm not judging you for leaving." She reached out to pat my arm.

"And I'm not judging you for staying," he said. "Actually, it's probably better for those that leave if you stay here," he added.

"I agree. It's not like we can protect anybody. Even Mia can't help." She chuckled.

"Though she'd like to," Captain Daley agreed, giving Amber a smile. "Well, I think it's time. Let's go get everybody else's decision."

CHAPTER

TWENTY-EIGHT

CORA AND EVELYN HAD LEFT us alone to have our final discussion and announce the decisions to stay or go. As I stood there I realized it could end up with only Captain Daley, me and Godzilla leaving. That wasn't enough. We wouldn't make it.

"Okay, everybody, it's time to tell us your decisions," Captain Daley said. "Amber has asked me to let everybody know that she and Nelson and, of course, Mia will be staying here."

There were words of encouragement from the others. I figured we all thought it was the right choice.

"Who'd like to speak next?" Captain Daley asked.

Dr. Singh put up her hand. "I'm staying," she said. "I think this community needs me. They're also planning on linking with other nearby communities. I can help a lot of people by staying here."

Captain Daley nodded in agreement.

"I'm staying too," Calvin said.

I was surprised by that. He'd begged us to take him from the airport so he could go home. I'd kind of thought he was in it for the long haul.

"It's going to be different without you at the wheel of the vehicle," Captain Daley said. "I'm not sure if the vehicle knows how to go without you." A few people chuckled.

"I'm coming, so hopefully it won't mind me driving," Richard said.

"Or fixing it," Calvin said. "Rich knows how to keep it moving even better than I do."

"I'll do my best."

Having Richard along was important. He was a great handyman—and the more people we had, the stronger we'd be.

"Captain Daley, I want you to know there isn't anything we wouldn't do for you," Noah began.

"That goes for both of us," Sara said, putting her hand on Noah's shoulder.

"But even if we're willing to go farther, I'm afraid my chair isn't," Noah went on. "It's not going to survive another five hundred miles, and then I'd just be dead weight."

"You'd never be that," Captain Daley said solemnly. "But I respect your decision."

"We can play a role in helping defend this community," Sara added.

"The two of you up on the wall would make for a very formidable defense," Tom said.

We'd lost Sara and Noah now too. This was getting worse by the minute—and was Tom hinting that he wasn't coming either?

"You know I'm coming, Cap," Doeun said with a smile.

"I was hoping you'd make that choice," Captain Daley said.

"Choice?" Doeun asked. "Did you expect me to climb out in the middle of a flight? Flight crews back each other up."

"And that's the same for us," Julia said. "Me and Fede."

"We started this trip together and we're going to finish it together," Fede added.

I relaxed a little. There were now six of us. Seven if you counted Godzilla.

"So I guess that only leaves one person," Captain Daley said. "Tom?"

Other than Captain Daley—maybe even more than Captain Daley—Tom was the most important person. What was he going to say?

"I'll be leaving with the group," Tom said.

"You're coming!" I exclaimed, jumping to my feet. I had such a sense of relief, I felt like I might cry. I didn't want anybody to see that, though, so I pushed the feelings in and grinned so wide my cheeks hurt.

"Of course I am," he said casually. "Did you think I was going to let you and your big slobbery dog have all the fun out there without me?"

The trolley was loaded up. We now had not just more food than we'd come with but more variety too. They'd also given us extra bikes, so we had seven in total. My little bike was staying behind for Nelson to use, and I had a full-sized bike to ride—no streamers! I was grateful for the extra bikes, but it was clear why they were offered. They didn't expect our vehicle to last much longer.

Along with the bikes and extra food, we were well equipped to defend ourselves. We had Tom's rifle and shotgun, plus three more rifles and three pistols, along with extra ammunition.

I'd been told about the group that patrolled the road we were taking. It was bigger and better armed than us—and they were ruthless. They killed people, no remorse. They patrolled during the day and at night usually holed up someplace.

I touched my hand against the holster hidden underneath my jacket. It had replaced the sock. It was strapped over my shoulder and held the pistol that now had eight bullets. On my back was a package that contained eleven more rounds. I had nineteen shots instead of three.

There were hugs all around and lots of tears. I was happy to be leaving but sad to say goodbye to these people who had become like family. We were also leaving behind safety, a soft couch and hundreds of people, plus that big high wall. For a split second I thought about climbing off the bike and telling them I'd changed my mind.

About half of the colony was here to say goodbye too. I was surprised at how many of them I knew. Did I know that many people on the street where I'd lived my entire life?

Cora and Evelyn came out of the crowd and joined us.

"You're all still welcome to stay," Cora said.

"We appreciate that," Captain Daley said.

"We're leaving you some good people," Tom said.

"And some good people are leaving," Cora replied. "You need to know that if there's no way forward for you, there's always a place for you here if you have to work your way back."

"We'll welcome you with open arms," Evelyn added.

"We appreciate that offer," Captain Daley replied, giving them both a hug goodbye. "All right. We better get going."

Cora turned to the guards on the wall. "Open the gate!" she yelled.

As they did, the setting sun was framed by the open gate. It was so big and bright and orange and beautiful. We were heading out into the sunset. We were heading home.

CHAPTER

TWENTY-NINE

IN THE THREE DAYS SINCE we'd left the colony, we'd traveled
ninety-five miles. That was a longer distance than we had covered
since almost the beginning of our trip. Each mile was one mile
closer to being home and one mile farther from thinking we could
turn and go back. We were only four hundred miles away now.
We were going to make it.

The stair car was working better than before. Or maybe it was just
that it was carrying so much less weight. There was always a driver,
plus somebody riding shotgun on the platform at the top, but other
than Godzilla, nobody else was aboard. We'd been riding the bikes
beside it. We were traveling faster because we were traveling lighter.

Captain Daley and Tom had decided there was no point in
sending out advance scouts anymore. There were just too few of
us, and there was a greater risk to the scouts than there was an
advantage to the rest of us. If there was danger, it was better for us
to be together.

As we neared the end of day three, my legs were really getting tired. I'd been pedaling through the night, and I knew we wouldn't go much farther. There was a thin band of light on the horizon. Soon the sun would be up, and we'd need to find a place to camp and get some sleep away from prying eyes.

There were even more vehicles on the roads these days, as people hauled ancient cars and trucks out of storage or junkyards. Of course, no matter how strange other vehicles looked, we were the ones who drew the longest stares. It was like we were driving a dinosaur—a brontosaurus with a big sweeping neck, and the platform was the head at the top.

Every time we came up to another group of people, a sort of delicate dance went on. They were seeing if they should be afraid of us, and we were seeing if we should be afraid of them. Being afraid only made sense. Marauders had killed those people we'd seen at the sides of the road. We weren't out to kill anybody, but we weren't going to let anybody kill us. At least, not without a fight.

There were also nice people out here. Some groups had told us where to get fresh water, warned us of dangers ahead and how to get around them, and even where we could stop and have some protection. Not everybody was out to get us. In fact, we were headed right now to a place we'd been told we could pull off the road, not much farther ahead.

Tom pedaled up beside me.

"How are you feeling, kid?" he asked. He had his beard tucked into his shirt to keep it out of the way while he rode.

"Good. Hopeful."

He laughed. "Hope is a good thing in small doses and dangerous in larger amounts."

I raised my eyebrows at him jokingly. "Are you going to explain that to me?"

He chuckled. "A little bit of hope moves you forward, but too much blinds you from reality. We're doing well, but we have to keep our eyes open all the time."

I sighed. "My eyes are going to close soon. It's been a long night."

"If what we were told is right, we have less than a mile to go," Tom said.

Increasingly Tom was spending less time on the bike and more time perched on the platform. Being up top made sense because he was the best shot. He was also the oldest of us by far, and his legs didn't want to work as long or as hard. He hadn't told anybody his age, but I figured he had to be close to seventy.

Suddenly Godzilla, who had been on the platform, ran down the stairs and bounded into the field beside the road. He was gone in a flash. He'd seen something and was off to try to get it. He did this three or four times every night. He'd spot something none of us could see and be gone, chasing after it.

"That dog is a born hunter!" Tom exclaimed.

The first few times he'd done it, I was worried that he'd run off for good and I'd lost him, but each time he'd quickly catch up. Some of those times, he'd brought back whatever he was chasing. I hoped this was going to be one of those times. Rabbit made for a great breakfast. Or lunch or dinner.

"I'm going to want to take you and that dog out hunting when this is all over," Tom said.

"Do you think this is going to be over?" I had to ask. I wasn't sure myself anymore.

"Everything ends, whether it's good or bad," Tom said. "The only constant is change. Or at least, that's what Heraclitus thinks."

I frowned. "I don't know him. Is he a friend of yours?"

Tom laughed. "I'm old, but not that old. He's an ancient Greek philosopher."

"No man can ever step in the same river twice," Captain Daley said as he biked up beside us.

"You're familiar with Heraclitus?" Tom said, a twinkle in his eyes.

"His ideas about the world constantly being in flux seem pretty accurate right now."

"I'm confused," I said. "I've stepped in the same creek by our house dozens of times."

"You've stepped in the same creek, but each time it's *different*," Tom explained. "The process of you putting your foot in it changes the water forever."

"You must think my feet are a lot bigger than they are," I said with a smirk.

Tom grinned. "And speaking of feet, those shoes of yours look like they've seen better days."

I wiggled the big toe on my right foot and glanced down at it sticking out of the top of the shoe.

"Maybe it's time to start using your extra set of shoes," he suggested.

"Hey, I think I see the side road we're looking for," Captain Daley said.

Richard must have seen it as well, because the vehicle slowed down. He stopped at the turnoff. The road was narrow and unpaved but looked packed enough to support the weight of the stair car.

"Wait here and we'll check it out," Tom said. "Fede, Doeun, you're with me."

The three of them set off, leaving four of us on the road. Julia got up on the platform, rifle in hand, and started scanning up and down the road. Both Captain Daley and Richard had their rifles out. Without even exchanging a word, one of them looked at the field to the right, and the other, to the woods on the left.

Fede reappeared on the path. He called out and waved for us to come forward. Richard jumped back into the vehicle, and Julia hung on as he bumped off the road and up the path. I hesitated and looked down the road. There was no sign of Godzilla.

"Don't worry," Captain Daley said. "He'll find us. Like Tom said, your feet are so smelly he'll pick up your scent and follow the trail."

Still I paused.

"And if he doesn't, then we'll go out looking for him," Captain Daley reassured me.

He got on his bike and we started to follow after them. Then he skidded to a stop. I was instantly alarmed and whirled around, reaching for my pistol.

"It's okay," he said, realizing he'd startled me. "I just want to make sure Godzilla is the only one who'll follow us."

He pointed down at the ground. The wheels of the stair car were visible in the dirt, as were the treads of the bicycles that had gone ahead of us.

"Let's drop off our bikes and come back to cover these up," he suggested.

Captain Daley and I walked backward toward the road. As we moved, we swept a couple of branches back and forth across the path to clear away the tracks. We finished brushing them right up to the road. There was nothing left to show we'd come this way. We'd done a good job.

"We could walk back up the road a bit and look for Godzilla," he said.

"Thanks." I was worried about him—I couldn't help it.

We started off, Captain Daley with a rifle on his shoulder and me with my pistol. Tom had been teaching me how to hold the gun and aim down the sight. He told me that when the gun fired, there would be a big kickback. Of course, we'd been doing all this without actually firing. We didn't have enough bullets to waste any on target practice.

"Hopefully, we'll all get enough sleep to recharge the batteries," Captain Daley said. "And then we'll start early and make a real push for—"

He stopped in mid-sentence. I didn't have to ask why. We could hear the high-pitched roar of an engine or engines in the distance.

"Off the road!" he yelled.

I started to scramble one way before I realized he'd gone the other way. I quickly skidded to a stop and ran back to follow him. I threw myself into the bushes, and we both ducked down so we were hidden. The noise got louder and louder. It was clear that there was more than one vehicle coming. A lot more. Then they came into sight.

A bunch of little go-karts were racing along the road. They were in rows of two and three, and the noise was ear-shattering as they closed in. The first ones zipped by, and then the next pair, and three more, and more and more. Louder and louder until the last one passed our position. I could make out weapons in some of them.

"Twenty-four in total," Captain Daley said.

"Is that them? Are those the people we're supposed to be afraid of?"

"They didn't look friendly. Thank goodness we got off the road and covered up our tracks."

The noise of the machines had faded but hadn't disappeared completely. How could that be? Unless they'd stopped.

"Stay close to me," Captain Daley said. "And don't go out onto the road or into the clear."

I followed him to the edge of the road. He dropped to the ground, and I did the same. It was obvious why he'd done that. The go-kart group was no more than a hundred yards up the road.

"They're right by the path," Captain Daley said, his voice tense. "Why would they have stopped?"

Before he could answer, the engines got louder, and the go-karts started heading away. It didn't matter why they'd stopped. The important thing was that they were going. The front few sped down the road, followed by the next pair, and the next—but then two of them turned down the path, and six more followed them!

"We have to get back. We have to help them!" Captain Daley boomed.

We both jumped to our feet.

CHAPTER
THIRTY

I WAS WORKING HARD TO slow down my breathing and catch my breath. We'd run full speed along the road and down the path as far as we dared travel. Now we were creeping through the bush and scrub trees toward where we'd left our group. We were close enough that I could see the platform of the stair car, even though I couldn't see anybody on it. Had they gotten away? Had they been captured? Or maybe those guys were friendly, and they were just talking right now.

Captain Daley walked in front of me, his rifle leading the way. I had my pistol out, the safety off, aimed at the ground to one side, the way Tom had taught me. I wished I had my pack where the spare bullets were stashed. Would eight bullets be enough?

Captain Daley dropped to the ground and I did the same, right beside him. Peering through the bushes I could see the go-karts and the people who were riding them. They were all dressed in black, and most of them were still wearing their helmets.

I couldn't see any of our people. They must have heard the go-karts coming and gotten away into the bushes.

"Do you see anybody? Did they get away?" I asked.

"To the left, on the ground," Captain Daley said.

I desperately tried to see around the bushes and spotted two figures. They were on their knees, their hands placed awkwardly on their heads.

"It's Doeun and Fede. I think. Did the others escape?" My heart was pounding in my chest. This was big trouble.

"Maybe. Or...we just can't see them."

I let out a whoosh of air. "I thought you were going to say they were dead."

He shook his head. "We would have heard gunfire. I have to get closer to see what's happening. You stay right here."

He started crawling and sliding forward. I wasn't going to be left behind. I started to move, slowly slithering forward on my belly the same way he was, so that I was as invisible as possible. Captain Daley stopped and hid behind a slight rise in the earth. He took the rifle off his shoulder and rested it on the ground, aiming. I slid in beside him.

Voices rose from the clearing. I could only make out some of the words, but the people in black were angry and asking where "the others" were.

One of the men suddenly struck Fede in the face, and he tumbled backward. I gasped but kept myself from screaming out. The man stood over him and raised his hand again.

There was a gunshot! He had shot Fede, and the gun was now being aimed at Doeun!

A loud report went off beside me, and I jumped. At that same second, the man with the gun toppled to the ground. Captain Daley had fired. He fired again, and a second man grabbed his chest, staggered and fell. In the confusion Doeun scurried away on all fours, taking shelter behind the stair car, temporarily hidden from them but visible to us.

Another one of the men in black toppled over, although Captain Daley hadn't fired another shot. And then a fourth man seemed to do a dance as he spun around. He reeled a few steps and fell facedown. The shots had to be from Tom or Richard or Julia.

Then I saw movement on the far side of the clearing. Tom stepped out of the bushes, his shotgun held in front of him, and walked forward. He fired a blast, took a few more steps and fired again. One more man crumpled to the ground, and a second bent over and then slumped down. The remaining men turned and started firing at him. Tom dropped to one knee—was he hit? No, he had opened the shotgun and was reloading.

Captain Daley fired again, and I saw the bullet hit one of the go-karts near where the man was standing. More shots rang out. Tom, still on one knee, fired again and then again. After that there was silence.

Richard and Julia appeared off to the side. Their weapons still in hand and leading the way, they came forward. Captain Daley and I got up, climbed over the dirt embankment and ran to the clearing. I stopped at the edge, too shocked to move any farther. There were bodies everywhere, blood and guts and...Fede. He'd been shot! Was he dead?

Doeun was already beside him. She'd dropped to one knee and was holding a weapon—she'd picked up a rifle. Tom was yelling out orders, and I saw Richard and Julia grabbing weapons from the fallen men. A couple of them were still moving but obviously injured. One was screaming in pain. Doeun was sobbing loudly. I went toward her.

"Doeun?" I said.

She looked up at me. Her eyes were open wide in shock, sadness, disbelief. She was holding Fede. The side of his head was gone.

I turned, bent over and vomited.

"Take a bigger sip," Captain Daley said.

I tipped back the bottle and took a drink, swilled it around in my mouth and spit out the water and the taste of the vomit. Godzilla looked at me with concern. He'd come back just after the shooting stopped. He had a dead rabbit in his mouth.

"Are you feeling any better?" Julia asked, and I nodded.

She had her arm around my shoulders and was holding me. I didn't know if it was me shivering or her or both of us.

There was a gunshot, and we both jumped. I looked over in time to see Tom pointing his gun at one of the wounded men. He was down on the ground. Then there was a second shot.

"There's no choice," Captain Daley said. "They were badly wounded and—"

"I don't care," I said. "They needed to die. They killed Fede."

Tom walked toward us. His shotgun was broken open, and he ejected the two spent cartridges and placed two more shells into it. For a split second I had the strangest thought that he was coming to shoot us. How crazy. He was the reason we were still alive to begin with.

"Stu, how many of them did you say were in their group?" he asked.

Captain Daley was staring into the distance like he hadn't heard the question.

"Twenty-four," I answered for him.

"And they sent one-third of them here. That's military organization. That means when these eight don't return, they're going to come looking for them."

"They're coming back?" I exclaimed.

"It's okay," Tom said. "They're not coming yet. We have some time to figure this out."

"What's to figure out?" Richard asked bitterly. "We have to leave. We have to get away." He paused. "I wish I'd had a chance to change the batteries," he muttered, almost to himself.

"It doesn't matter, because we're going to have to leave the stair car behind."

"What?" Richard sounded shocked. "We can't leave it behind. I just need to change the batteries—I can do it quickly."

"Even with the new batteries, it's not going to start running fast. We can't outrun them with that thing, and we can't hide from them when we have it." Captain Daley made good points. Awful but good.

"Our choices are to take the go-karts or start walking through the forest," Tom said.

"If the go-karts work, then that's what we're going to use," Captain Daley replied.

I had a terrible thought. "But what about Godzilla? He can't run beside us."

"I looked at a couple of them, and there's one that's bigger. It has enough space for him to ride sort of beside you, at your feet. Don't worry. That dog is coming."

I felt instant relief. As bad as things were, I wasn't leaving my best friend behind.

"Richard, can you check out the go-karts to see if any are damaged?"

Richard answered with a salute and turned and walked away.

Captain Daley gazed blankly down at his rifle. Tom walked over and put his hands on Captain Daley's shoulders.

"You did what you had to do," Tom said.

Captain Daley gave a heavy sigh. "I know...I know."

"If you hadn't fired, Doeun would be dead as well."

Captain Daley met his eyes. "I was thinking that if I'd shot a few seconds earlier, I could have saved Fede." His face was ashen. It was hard to see. He was usually so sure of himself.

"I was watching too and didn't see it coming," Tom said. "But we can see what's going to be happening next. And that's why we have to get our heads in the game and get out of here."

Captain Daley straightened his shoulders and nodded. "How long do you think we have?" he asked.

"I don't know, but the sooner we leave, the better. We need to gather up supplies, food and all of their weapons," Tom said.

"And everybody," Captain Daley said, raising his voice for us all to hear. "If you hear the sound of engines before we have a chance to hit the road, you have to scramble into the woods. Take whatever is in your hands or at hand and just run. There's no point in having supplies that might cost you your life. We'll run that way."

He pointed across the clearing to the thickest part of the forest. I had the urge to immediately rush over that way. But I couldn't do that yet. I had to gather my things, put my pack together and get ready to move.

CHAPTER
THIRTY-
ONE

TOM USED A HAMMER TO smash the engine of a second kart. Hopefully, it was beyond repair. He'd already done that to one machine. There were eight machines, and we only needed six. Six because Fede was dead.

Richard had disabled the stair car by removing some wiring and throwing the batteries into the forest.

Julia and Doeun had searched the bodies. There were six men and two women. We'd taken their guns and also their helmets and black shirts. Well, the shirts without obvious bullet holes and blood. We wanted to dress like the marauders. Tom called it "hiding in plain sight." He also reasoned that if people were afraid of this group, they'd give us a wide berth.

We'd talked about moving the bodies into the woods, but in the end decided it was too much work when we had better things to do with the little time we had.

Fede had been carried out of the clearing and laid down under some bushes. The Fellowship of the Ring had lost another member. It seemed as wrong to leave him behind as it had Phillip, but there was no choice. Taking time to bury him wouldn't bring him back, and it might mean the rest of us dying. These eight had shown they'd kill us in cold blood with no second thoughts. There was no reason to believe the other members of their group would be any different.

"Let's get going," Tom said. "Jamie, it's time."

I climbed into a go-kart, and Godzilla went up on his back legs to shove his face into mine. Richard and Captain Daley picked him up.

"This dog has lost some weight, but he's still heavy!" Richard exclaimed.

Between the three of us, we positioned him so that he was partly beside me, partly on top of me and partly at my feet. I made sure I could still work the gas pedal and brake. I gave him a rough rub behind the ears the way he liked, and he turned and licked my face. I slipped on a helmet.

Tom handed me my pack. "I hope you have room for this."

I took it and slid it down beside me. Inside was a change of clothing, a bit of food, two bottles of water, my airplane blanket— which was getting pretty ratty and smelly—and a simplified first-aid kit.

"Glad it fits, but I don't think there's room for a rifle," Tom said. "So I guess that means that the rest of us have two rifles."

"We have lots of guns," Richard said. "I just wish we'd gotten more ammunition from them."

While the eight marauders had each carried a rifle, they didn't have that many bullets. After the shots they'd fired at us, three rifles were completely empty, and there were only twelve bullets in total between the other five.

"Maybe we should be grateful," Tom replied. "If they'd had more ammunition, it might have been a different ending to the story."

We'd used eighteen bullets and seven shotgun cartridges. We had less ammunition now than we'd had before. My gun was the exception. Once again I hadn't fired a shot. The gun was in my hand, but all I'd done was watch. Tom had said I'd done the right thing, because there was no way I could have fired accurately from that distance with a pistol, but really, I hadn't even thought about firing. So what would be the point in me even having a second gun if I couldn't fire it? In fact, I thought, maybe somebody else should be carrying the pistol instead of having it strapped to my shoulder.

"You're sure about this plan?" Richard asked.

Tom nodded. "I know that often the best thing you can do is what's least expected by your enemy."

"If that's the case, we have a *great* plan," I said. "Nobody is going to expect this."

"We have to be bold," Tom said, hitching up his pants. "To live long you have to be prepared to die fast."

"Not reassuring," Doeun said dryly.

Captain Daley gave a soft chuckle. "Well, folks, we need to get going," he announced.

One by one people climbed into their karts, and food and supplies were packed in around them. Bags and bins poked out. We were trying to carry as much as we could.

The last one to climb into a kart was Captain Daley. He reached down to the ground and grabbed some of the remaining supplies and pulled them up to store at his feet.

We were taking with us Richard's tools, whatever food we had, the axes from the plane, all the contents of the first-aid kit, the drugs we still had from Richard's store of medication, a couple of cooking pots, six plates and utensils, bleach for water sanitizing, spare clothing and shoes and, of course, our maps. Those maps were more than our guidance—they were our hope.

An engine started. Even through my helmet it was loud. Then the noise got louder as a second and a third go-kart were started. It was time. I turned the key, and my engine roared to life. Godzilla shifted and struggled, and I had the sense he was trying to get away from the sound and fumes. I wrapped an arm around his neck to both reassure him and hold him in place. There was no choice. He had to stay here.

There was a go-kart track at the amusement park by our house, so I'd driven them dozens of times. The controls were simple. Push the gas pedal, and it went. The harder you pushed, the faster it went. The brake would bring it to a stop. I pressed down slightly on the gas pedal, and the vehicle inched forward. I pressed the brake to stop.

The first kart pulled away. Tom's beard flowed out beneath his helmet and dark visor. I thought about Santa Claus abandoning his sled and reindeer and delivering presents with his go-kart. The next kart moved in directly behind him. I was next. I pushed down on the pedal, and the kart jumped forward. Without looking back, I knew the other three would be falling in line.

I caught sight of the stair car, its strange, dinosaur-like neck rising in the air. I thought about the people who'd been with us when we'd started out. About Phillip and Fede. About Noah and Sara, Dr. Singh, Calvin, Amber and Nelson and Mia. About everybody we had started our journey with who was no longer with us.

The karts kicked up dust as we moved along the path. I closed my visor to protect my eyes and lungs. I couldn't help but wonder, What if we chose the other direction? What if when we reached the road we turned to the right and raced like crazy to get back to the colony? These karts were so much faster than the stair car. We could probably ride hard all day and be back there by nightfall.

They'd open the gates and let us in. Our friends would be waiting and be so happy to see us. I could go back to the soft sofa behind that wall, and we'd be safe, and most of us would be together again.

We reached the road. Tom turned to the left, and Doeun instantly fell in beside him. I was next in line, and Julia rode beside me. In the back were Richard and Captain Daley. I was safest in the middle, but I knew I was far from safe.

We headed in the same direction the other sixteen go-karts had gone. They'd be heading our way if they came back looking for their missing people. If we ran into them on the open road, we'd have an element of surprise because they'd see us and think we were the missing people. As they drove toward us, they wouldn't suspect anything. We'd be able to get right up to them and then stop and open fire. We could shoot at least some of them, but we wouldn't be able to get them all. The rest would be shooting at us. We'd probably still be outnumbered. Would I be able to shoot back? I hoped I wouldn't have to find out.

We were on a long straightaway, and the road was empty as far as I could see. That was reassuring. What wasn't reassuring was knowing that the second we could see them, they could see us too. We came to a curve, and the brake lights of the karts ahead of me flashed red. I rounded the corner, and as I straightened out I saw people walking on the road ahead. They scrambled out of the way, running down the ditch and into the woods as we got closer. They were obviously trying to get away from us. I couldn't blame them. I'd seen what people dressed like this and driving these go-karts were capable of doing.

We hit another straightaway, and Tom picked up speed again. I didn't know how fast we were going, but it felt as if we were moving like lightning. At this speed we could travel the last four hundred miles in a day or two at most.

Tom raised a hand to signal that we were going to stop.

We slowed down dramatically, and then he edged his go-kart onto the gravel shoulder. Julia fell in behind him, and I behind her. My go-kart rocked and rolled, and Godzilla shifted and whined, anxious to be out of the kart but too scared to try to get out. I knew how he felt.

Tom continued to ride slowly until he found a little clearing behind some bushes. He moved forward to make space for us all. One by one we turned off the engines.

"I'll go back and make sure we're not visible from the road," Richard said.

"I'll go with you," Doeun offered.

"Make sure the tracks don't show," Tom said. "And if they do, cover them up as good as you can."

"I can help with that," I offered.

I struggled to get out of the kart, and Godzilla squirmed to get free. He jumped out, and I climbed out after him.

"Godzilla should stay here," Tom said. "Don't want to risk him being seen."

I reached back into the kart and grabbed his leash. I clipped it onto his collar and tied the other end to my go-kart. He whined.

"It's going to be okay, boy," I said reassuringly.

He wagged his tail to show he believed me. I wished I believed me.

CHAPTER
THIRTY-TWO

TOM WAS ON THE GROUND, asleep, quietly snoring. His beard was longer and a bit wilder these days, and he was a lot thinner—like everybody—but he still looked like Santa Claus. I guess he *was* like Santa, because he had given us all a gift. We wouldn't have been able to get this far without him.

"The waiting is the hardest part," Julia said. "Unless you're Tom."

"He does look peaceful," Doeun said with a smile.

She and Julia were on this side of the road with me and Tom. Richard and Captain Daley were positioned on the other side. They were closer to the road than us but equally hidden, their rifles trained on whatever would come by. So far there'd been some people on foot, on a couple of bikes and in an old truck. None of them had seen us hiding.

"Tom was like an action hero back there," Julia said.

"I was pretty busy hugging the ground, so I didn't notice," Doeun said with a shiver.

"He just came walking out of the woods, shotgun in hand, blasting away, but all calm at the same time," Julia replied.

"He stopped and reloaded," I added.

"And it wasn't just that he did that, but the way he did it. It was like he was walking to the store to get a quart of milk," Julia said, shaking her head in disbelief.

"I was terrified," Doeun said.

Julia put a hand on her shoulder. "We were all terrified, and we didn't have a gun aimed at our heads."

"But you didn't act like that," I said to Doeun. "You grabbed a gun, and you took cover. You even fired at them."

Doeun cocked her head. "It was strange, but it was like I was watching the whole thing from afar, like I could see myself doing it but didn't feel like it was really me."

"Don't they have a term for that?" Julia asked.

"Trauma-related disassociation is what they call it. The mind escapes when the body can't." Doeun let out a deep sigh. I looked at her questioningly. "I've been close to death before. I've had footholds give way and fallen twenty feet with only my rope keeping me from falling the next two hundred feet."

"The thought of that terrifies me," Julia said with a shudder. "I'm afraid of heights."

"And that's why you earn a living flying," Doeun joked.

"It's different. I'm *in* the plane, not hanging off the side of it."

"That doesn't guarantee much. Anybody who has flown for a while has had at least one time they thought the plane was going down."

Julia held up three fingers. "I've said my prayers, but no crash landings so far."

"I had to make an emergency landing when the engine failed in a two-engine bush plane, and I had to put it down in a field between scattered trees," Doeun said. "I've thought it was all over at times like that...but this was different."

"I guess I understand," Julia said softly. "This wasn't an accident or something that went wrong. This was somebody just wanting to kill you." She locked eyes with Doeun. "They had our stuff. They could have just let us walk away."

"That's why we couldn't let any of them walk away," I said.

They both turned to me. Their expressions told me they'd forgotten I was there.

"I'm just saying we couldn't let them walk away," I repeated. "If we didn't kill them, then they'd have killed us. They would have killed you, Doeun." My voice shook as I said it.

She nodded. "I know that, but I still don't believe it. I don't know if I could have killed her even if I knew she was going to kill me."

"You could have," Tom said. He was still lying on the ground with his eyes closed. "That part of your brain that wants to survive would have kicked in. You'd do it for your survival, and you'd do it for all of us."

"The way you did," I said.

"Yep. And just for the record, I was terrified too," Tom said, opening an eye.

"You heard us?" Doeun asked, surprised.

"I had my eyes closed but my ears open." He laughed. "I've been called a lot of things over the years, but never an action hero."

We all laughed, and the laughter felt good.

"Although I've lost so much weight I don't even have a pot belly anymore." He patted his stomach.

"I think I must be down about fifteen pounds myself," Julia said.

"Yep, the new apocalyptic diet. Plenty of exercise, a limited supply of food and unlimited amounts of fear," Tom joked.

"Anybody else think Jamie's gotten taller and older-looking since this started?" Doeun asked.

"I was thinking that," Julia said, looking at me. "Both him and the dog."

"Speaking of Godzilla, wouldn't a rabbit stew really hit the spot right now?" Tom said.

"It would," Julia agreed. "Maybe after we get through the plan."

The plan was simple. If they passed by without seeing us, we would ride out and race away in the opposite direction. If we were seen and they stopped, we'd have the advantage of cover and the first shots. If it looked like we were going to be overwhelmed, we were to abandon our positions, leave the go-karts behind, take what we could carry and run into the forest. We would then to try to meet about two miles south of here.

Godzilla's ears perked up, which caused me to listen harder. It was faint, but it was there—the sound of an engine. Was it a random truck or car, or was it the go-karts?

"Do you hear something?" Tom asked.

I listened again. "Maybe. Wait...yes...do you hear it?"

"I do," Julia said. "It's an engine."

"My old ears don't hear as well as they used to. Thank goodness the trigger finger and eyes still work well."

It was now obvious that everybody had heard the sound. It was getting louder and louder—a high-pitched whine. It could only mean one thing.

Tom got up, and we all took our positions. We had separate spots where we would hide, steady our rifles and prepare to fire. Across the road from us, Richard and Captain Daley did the same.

I tried to look up the road but couldn't see very far without revealing myself. I could hear the go-karts, though—they were closing in. The first one flashed by, then another, and then a pair after the first two, and two more behind them. I counted sixteen in all. They had to be doubling back to find the missing karts. The engine noise faded to silence as they got farther away.

The turnoff to the path they knew the karts had taken was twenty-five minutes down the road. They had to drive down that path to discover the bodies. They'd take a bit of time to figure out what had happened. We figured they'd head out in the opposite direction of where we were, assuming that whoever had done this had fled that way. At a minimum we had almost an hour, if they headed right back here, and if they didn't, more like three or four.

Captain Daley and Richard jumped up from their positions across the road. They hesitated for a second and then ran toward us. It was agreed—we had to get in the karts and take off in the direction those karts had just come from.

Once more Tom had guessed right.

CHAPTER THIRTY-THREE

WE WERE DRIVING FAST, racing along the road. Whenever we saw people or other vehicles, they hurried off the road or pulled over to the side. Once I saw weapons being pointed at us from the back of an old truck that had pulled off, but they didn't fire, just let us pass. With each minute, we were putting more space between us and the convoy of sixteen go-karts. Even if they left a few minutes after discovering the dead bodies and came this direction, we were at least forty miles ahead of them—and forty miles closer to home.

We'd never been able to travel this fast before. If the little speedometer on my kart was registering correctly, we were traveling more than thirty miles an hour. That meant that if we continued at this speed for twelve or thirteen hours, we could be home. Home!

Of course, that didn't include things like having to make detours or going through blockaded roads or barricaded bridges, and we'd have to stop for gas—I hadn't thought about that until now. How much gas was in my tank? How much gas was in any of the tanks? If one of us ran out, we'd all have to stop.

Tom and Julia slowed down dramatically, and I pushed hard on the brake pedal to avoid crashing into them. I looked beyond them. There was a barricade up ahead. It was like a gate at a parking-garage exit, and it extended across the road. Standing beside it were two men, armed and dressed in black. Off to the side were two go-karts painted like the others in the convoy. They had to be part of the same group. We were trapped.

Tom continued to drive. The gate stayed down, but one of the men waved us forward as the second stood off to the side. Their rifles remained on their shoulders. But then, why would they act any different? We were in the same black uniforms, driving the same vehicles, as their buddies. Our identities were hidden beneath the helmets and behind the face shields. They had to think we were friends.

I pushed Godzilla's head farther down so he'd be hidden from view. Having a dog with me would be hard to explain. "It's okay, boy," I said reassuringly.

I reached over and removed my gun from the holster, holding it where it couldn't be seen above the cockpit of the kart.

Tom and Julia came to a stop right in front of the gate, and Tom gave the guy a friendly wave and then a salute. Was that enough? Would the man open the gate? No, he circled around to Tom, lifted up his visor, and the two of them started talking. The man waved for the second to come forward. His rifle was now off his shoulder—then there was the blast of a gun being fired! The man beside Tom tumbled over backward. He was clutching his hands to his chest, and blood was rushing out of a gaping hole. The second man raised his gun to fire, there was another bang, and he staggered backward, his gun sagging toward the ground. Somehow he straightened up and brought the gun back up, but another shot rang out. He fell to his knees and then toppled forward onto his face. Richard got out of his kart, holding his rifle, and walked over until he stood over him.

Captain Daley ran forward and lifted up the gate to let us pass. While he was doing that, Richard dragged one of the bodies away. The captain ran back and grabbed the second lifeless body, holding him under the arms, and lugged him away.

Tom motioned, running his hand across his neck. I didn't understand what he meant. Was he saying the men were dead or—no, he wanted us to cut our engines. We turned off the go-karts.

"Can you all hear me?" he yelled.

I pulled off my helmet. Others did the same as we nodded that he could be heard.

"Before he realized that something wasn't right, the man told me that their settlement is just ahead. They have more than two hundred and fifty people who are armed."

"What?" Captain Daley exclaimed. "That can't be right."

"Plus, he knew that they're missing eight people. I tried to bluff my way through, but he looked at the number on my kart."

"What number?" Julia asked.

"Each of the karts has a serial number. The guard realized I was driving one of the missing karts but wasn't one of the people missing. They're looking for them. They're looking for us."

My whole body shuddered, and I felt a sense of panic overwhelm me.

"We have to get rid of the go-karts," Tom said gravely.

"Right here?" Richard asked.

"No. We have something to do first. And when I tell you what, you're all going to think I'm crazy."

We slowly drove through the town. We were staying close together the way Tom had told us to, and he was right—this was crazy.

There were people out on the streets, casually strolling, and it looked like some of the stores were actually open. It was surreal. We drove on the road that circled the town square. There was a band shell and a baseball field and a playground. There were kids on the swings. It was really a beautiful little town. It all seemed so peaceful and normal. Normal except for the go-karts parked on the street and the occasional man, dressed in black, walking along with a rifle on his shoulder.

Up ahead three go-karts were coming toward us. I slouched lower in the seat and pushed Godzilla down even lower so I was positive he couldn't be seen. As we came up to them, Tom raised a hand and offered them a wave. They waved back, and all of us did the same. In a world filled with hundreds of people dressed in black, wearing helmets and driving go-karts, why would anybody think we didn't belong? We were hiding in plain sight like Tom had said—and it was working. We were counting on them not being able to read the serial numbers of our vehicles and not being able to recognize us under the helmets and behind the face shields. This was so crazy that it might work.

We continued to drive, completing the circuit of the town square and heading for the road that would lead us out the other side. We kept motoring, driving slowly. I glanced over my shoulder and behind me. Richard gave me a little thumbs-up, and I could imagine him smiling behind the visor. That guy was made of steel. I took one more glance at the receding view of the town before we turned and headed along the road that soon was surrounded by fields and grass.

Then another gate appeared. We hadn't known for sure but had expected it would be there, that they'd be guarding all the roads in and out of the town. Tom and Julia slowed down, and we tightened up together. There were two men with guns guarding the gate.

Neither of them realized that weapons were being trained on them. The guard gate opened. Why would they be worried about somebody leaving town? Tom waved as we passed. Then we accelerated until we were at full speed. Now it was nothing more than a race.

How far could we get before they discovered who we were and came after us?

CHAPTER

THIRTY-FOUR

WE'D MOVED FAST FOR ABOUT thirty minutes before pulling off the road. That was as long as we could risk, because as we raced away from the town, there was no guarantee that another group wasn't moving toward it from this direction. We couldn't afford to meet a dozen riders—at least, meet them and live.

We had driven far enough from the road that we weren't visible to anybody passing by. We kept our eyes and ears open so no vehicles could sneak up on us. Richard was hidden out by the road, guarding us.

Now, I stood out of the way as Doeun and Captain Daley pushed hard against the little go-kart. It picked up speed as they gave it a final big shove, and it went into the river. There was a big splash and it instantly sunk, bubbles rising as it went down to join the other five go-karts on the bottom.

I peered into the water. Even if you looked closely and knew exactly where to look, you could barely see them down there. If the other go-karters didn't find the machines, they'd still think we were out there driving around on them. It made sense to ditch them, even though it would slow us down to a walk.

I couldn't help thinking that if only we could have kept driving fast for another day or two, we'd almost be home. But getting closer to home and closer to death all at once wasn't worth it.

Along with the go-karts we'd also weighed down the black clothing and helmets and tossed them in as well. We were dressed in our own clothing again. We wanted no connection between us and what they were looking for.

All the rifles we'd taken from them were now hidden underneath a fallen log. We figured that if they had the go-karts' serial numbers, they might have the serial numbers of the rifles too. We could have tossed them in the river too, but Captain Daley had suggested it didn't hurt to have a backup plan if we needed to double back. Of course, we'd taken all the ammunition that went with them.

Tom sat under a tree, using a pair of scissors to trim his beard. That thick white beard was the only thing the two guards had seen at the gate as we left, and this took away the last link. Satisfied, he stood up. He now looked like a scraggly, skinny, short-bearded Santa Claus. I was glad the Santa part still came through.

"Let's get ready to go," Tom said. He called for Richard, who came running over.

We grabbed our backpacks, which contained only the most essential items—food, ammunition, some tools, medicines and first-aid kit, and clothing. We had our original rifles and shotgun on our shoulders. Richard and Captain Daley picked up the water containers. They were full and heavy. Now we'd move by foot. No stair car, no bikes and no go-karts. It would be slow.

We started off in the opposite direction of the road. Captain Daley and Doeun had looked at the maps and plotted our next steps. We were heading cross-country for about fourteen miles, aiming to connect to another country road. The marauders wouldn't be looking for us there. We weren't sure what terrain we'd have to cover, but we assumed it would be a combination of forest, fields and scrub. Tom figured we'd run into people hunkered down at farms, simply trying to survive by settling on land where they could grow crops. We'd have to be prepared and aware. Our sudden appearance might frighten people into taking action against us.

Captain Daley took the lead. He'd had survival training when he was younger and had worked as a bush pilot up in Alaska. He'd learned orienting, so he knew how to use a map and compass to keep us moving in a fairly straight line. The shorter the distance we had to travel through the countryside, the better, because moving cross-country was slower. What made it even worse? We were moving in the opposite direction of home.

I fell in right behind Captain Daley, with Godzilla right at my heels. He was probably the only one of us who was glad to be on foot. Then again, he had four of them.

Suddenly Godzilla raced away, and I yelled for him to come. He skidded to a stop but didn't come back, instead staring straight ahead at a clump of trees.

"He must have seen a rabbit," Richard said with a grin.

"No, look at the hair on his back." It was standing up on end. "And he's growling."

Tom turned. His put his finger to his lips to silence everybody. He motioned for Richard and Captain Daley to move to the right and Julia and Doeun to the left. They instantly went into motion, circling with their rifles up, aiming and leading them forward.

"You're with me. Stay low and keep your eyes open. You've got my six," Tom said.

That was military talk. It meant I was covering him from behind. What he probably was doing was putting me behind him so I'd be safer.

He started forward, and I crept in behind him. Godzilla was standing as still as a statue, still staring straight ahead.

"It's all right, boy," I said as I reached his side. He disagreed and continued to growl. It was low-pitched and frightening. There was something in those trees he didn't like.

"We know you're in there!" Tom called out. "We have you surrounded. Come out with your hands in plain sight or we're going to start shooting."

There was no response. Was he talking to trees or a raccoon? No, Godzilla wouldn't have reacted this way. There had to be something, and that something could be dangerous.

"Last chance!" Tom called out. "If they don't come out, I want everybody to fire on my signal!" he yelled even louder. He wanted the people in the trees to hear him.

There were a few more seconds of silence.

"We're coming out. Please don't shoot. Please!" It was a woman, and she sounded scared.

A woman and three small children came out of the trees. Their arms were in the air and they each held a white plastic container.

"Is there anybody else with you?" Tom asked.

"We're all alone."

The kids clung to her side. They couldn't have been much older than Nelson.

A man stepped out of the woods, and I'd started to bring my gun up when I realized it was Richard. "Nobody else here!" he called out.

The children had started to cry quietly.

"It's okay," Julia said. "We're not going to hurt you. Why were you hiding?"

"We heard you coming and we saw the go-karts and we know about them and we were so scared, but there wasn't time to run away so we hid," the woman said breathlessly.

"We're not them," Tom explained.

She sounded close to tears. "But you have—had—go-karts, and you were dressed like them."

"We took their karts and clothes when they attacked us. We had to ditch them because we know they're looking for us," Tom said calmly.

"If they find you, they'll do terrible things," she said. "They'll kill you."

"First they have to find us. That's why we dumped the karts."

The woman's children still clung to her, staring at the ground. "We've seen them along the road all the time but never by the river," she said. "That's the only reason we feel it's safe to come here for water. They won't find the karts here."

"Unless somebody tells them," Tom said.

She shook her head. "We would never do *anything* to help them. Not after what they've done to people we know. *Never.*"

"We've seen what they're capable of. We're just trying to escape and get away from them," Captain Daley said.

"If you go onto the road, they'll get you. It doesn't matter who you are, they'll stop you, take your things, hurt you, even kill you," she said. "They've killed so many people." She stared off into the distance.

"We're not going to the road. We're going to head cross-country to route fourteen."

"That's a long way over some rough country," she said. "There's a wide ravine, a couple of creeks. It's easy to get turned around and lost."

"I hear you. But it's our best option because there's no other," Tom said with a dark chuckle.

"We could help," the woman offered. "My husband was born here. He knows this territory better than anybody. I know he'd be willing to lead you to the road."

"But we don't want to put you out," Captain Daley said. "We'll be all right."

"People out here have been trying to take care of each other. You're welcome to come back to our homestead and spend the night. You can start traveling in the morning. You'd be safe."

Tom and Captain Daley looked at each other. They were trying to figure it out. I was too. She seemed trustworthy to me. I couldn't say why. She just did.

"Thank you for the offer," Captain Daley said. "Lead on."

CHAPTER
THIRTY-FIVE

"THERE IT IS," HE SAID, pointing to the horizon. "Can you all see it?"

I strained my eyes and searched for what Jeff was seeing. It was a faint brown line of what looked like a dirt road. He clearly knew the land as well as his wife had said he did.

"I can see it," Richard said.

"It's still a ninety-minute walk, but if you keep the creek on your left, you'll get there," he explained.

"That would have been hard for us to do on our own," Captain Daley said appreciatively.

"It was hard enough to do even with your help," Tom said with a laugh. "I thought I was going to have to get a saddle and ride Godzilla."

We'd spent the night at the settlement that the Johnson family shared with a dozen other families. It was an old farm well off the roadways, accessible only by foot. They had some goats and a cow and had planted crops that were starting to come up. They hunted deer and used snares and traps to catch smaller animals. They seemed to be doing pretty well.

I couldn't help but notice the differences between us and them. They were in clean clothes, they had water for washing up, and they just looked healthier. We were a pretty ratty, skinny bunch compared to them.

"Thank you," Captain Daley said as the two men shook hands.

"Thank you for the rifles," he replied.

We'd given them the rifles we'd hidden and would be abandoning.

"Just sorry we don't have more ammunition to spare," Tom said.

"Ammunition we have. More weapons to fire them is what we needed. I guess we should also thank you for having taken out some of those *people*." He made a sour face and spit on the ground.

We'd told the families at the house about our journey, including our encounter with the marauders. The families had told us what had happened to them and how they'd come together as a settlement to survive. It had given me more hope that my family and neighborhood had been able to do the same thing. They'd also given us more information about the go-kart predators that were out on the road. There was no question what they'd do to us if they ever found us.

Just as at the other colony where we'd stayed, we'd been invited to join the settlement. They knew what we'd done, the skills we had and who we were. It was nice to be wanted, and we'd thought about staying for a few days—we could have rested up and let our trail get colder to the people chasing us. But we had to move forward.

Still, it was reassuring to know there was someplace we could return to if something went wrong. Of course, getting back to their settlement assumed we *could* find our way back. It had been a pretty rough crossing, and sometimes it felt like we were going in circles.

"Will you be able to get back home before dark?" Julia asked Jeff.

"It'll be touch and go. Worse comes to worst I'll just camp out for the night. You should be able to get to the road a few hours before dark."

"If we do, we'll use that time to get some rest," Tom said. "We're going to wait until nightfall to leave."

"Our people aren't out here much, but we don't think the go-karters use this road often. Still, keep your ears open," Jeff advised solemnly. "Those machines make so much noise you can get off the road before they see you, especially at night."

"We'll keep our ears and eyes wide open," Tom assured him.

"And if they do find you," Jeff said, "keep fighting as long as you have a bullet left. They don't take prisoners."

I swallowed. I could only hope and pray we had left them behind us.

We said our goodbyes and started off down the side of the hill. Captain Daley took the lead. I stayed back. I wanted to be close to Tom. Not just because I felt safe but because I'd been worried about him. He wasn't young anymore, and he'd stumbled a couple of times on our trek. Plus, I'd noticed his breath getting noisy and rasping when we climbed hills. At least it looked like it was all downhill from here to the road.

Godzilla came bounding through the trees. He had something in his mouth, but he was too far away for me to see what it was. I was just glad to see him coming back. The sun was already starting to set, and I knew we'd be on the road within the next hour or two at most.

"That dog is really something," Tom said, watching Godzilla. "I've had lots of hunting dogs, but none that ever did the hunting themselves!"

Godzilla galloped up and dropped the animal at my feet. It was a groundhog.

"How about if I make us a little groundhog stew before we start moving?" Tom asked, lifting his eyebrows at us.

"Do we have time?" Julia asked.

"I'll cut it into thin slices so it cooks fast," he said, kneeling gingerly to pick up the groundhog. "I'll make sure the fire doesn't smoke, and we're still far enough from the road to be safe."

We were in a little depression about two hundred yards in from the road, completely hidden from view. Richard was at the top of the hill, keeping an eye out. To our left was a little creek. We'd washed up, drank as much as we wanted and even filled our two water containers. The water looked fresh, but just to be safe we'd used a little bleach. We'd started out with so much of it, but we'd used a lot and left more at Cora's colony. We were two-thirds of the way home, but would the last third take us just as long or longer? We couldn't know what it would be like in a hundred miles or another few weeks. We didn't even know what it was going to be like two miles or two hours down the road.

Tom took out his knife and started to skin the groundhog. I couldn't help but think how a few months ago I would have thought that was disgusting. Now I just looked forward to the meal. I wished we had a jar or two of apple/banana/strawberry baby food for dessert.

"I want to thank you for keeping with me during the walk across the open country," he said.

I didn't know what to say, so I just nodded.

"I hope I don't hold everybody back," Tom went on. "I wouldn't want to slow folks down and keep you from your families any longer than we have to."

"We never would have made it this far without you." I paused. "You'll be okay, right?"

He finished with the pelt—it was basically in one piece—and tossed it to the side.

"I can't guarantee much, but I can promise you I'll never lie to you. It's rough out there, so who knows. What I do know is that we're all here for you. The captain and me, heck, all the others, we're going to make sure you're taken care of."

I knew they were here for me. I knew that. But I also knew he hadn't answered my question.

"Do you know what would go nice with groundhog?" Tom asked.

"A little red wine?" Doeun asked, walking over to us.

Tom gave a big belly laugh. "Fish. A little surf and turf, and you don't get more turf than *ground*hog. Jamie, how about you take our little rod and reel and try to catch us a fish?"

"I can go with you," Doeun offered.

"Thanks." I knew her offer had more to do with her keeping an eye on me than fishing. They were here for me. I knew that was true.

CHAPTER
THIRTY-
SIX

I'D CAUGHT TWO LITTLE PERCH. They weren't much, but combined with the groundhog stew, with potatoes and some greens the others had found by the river, it was pretty amazing. It was almost as good as the meal the people had given us the night before at the settlement. Two good meals for two days in a row made me feel stronger.

Richard was washing out the pot and frying pan. Everything else had already been stowed away in our packs. Even the ashes from the firepit had been dug into the ground so nobody could tell there had recently been a fire.

Captain Daley and Tom were talking off to the side. I hadn't been able to pick up what they were saying but could tell they were having an enthusiastic debate.

"Don't know if I've seen those two disagree about anything before," Doeun said.

"I just hope they eventually come to the same conclusion, because I don't want to have to vote against either of them," Richard added.

Watching them now made me nervous. As if I didn't have enough to worry about already. What were they talking about? They stopped, turned and came toward us. We wouldn't have to wait long to find out.

"We're going to be heading out in the next twenty minutes," Captain Daley said.

"Well, at least the first group is leaving," Tom added.

"First group? What do you mean?" Doeun asked.

"We're breaking into two groups," Tom answered.

"But why?" I exclaimed. "We need to stay together."

"We *are* staying together," Captain Daley explained. "We're just doing it in two groups."

I frowned. "But you always said there was safety in numbers."

"Not when that number is six," Captain Daley said. "Tom, I think it's best that you explain."

"They're looking for six people who took six go-karts," Tom said. "It's best that we don't fit that description. It's safer if our groups are smaller."

"Safer from them, but what about other things or other people?" I pressed. We all knew about the armed groups that had formed. Three people didn't seem like enough against such a threat.

"We're trying to keep ourselves safe from the danger we know. Nobody we've encountered so far compares to these people," Tom said.

"Besides, we won't be far apart," Captain Daley said.

"How far?" I asked.

"Twenty minutes or so. About one mile apart."

I shrugged my shoulders. It made sense, I had to admit. So long as we didn't get too far apart.

"Richard, you'll be with Doeun and Julia, and you three will be first," Tom explained.

"And, of course, that means that Tom, Jamie and the big dog are my traveling companions," Captain Daley added.

If we couldn't all be together, there was nobody else I'd rather be with than the two of them. And Godzilla.

"And every two hours, the advance group is to stop, hide off the road and wait for us, so we can check in," Captain Daley said. "Any questions?"

"None," Richard said briskly. "Let's get moving."

"Good luck and be safe," Captain Daley said.

Richard, Doeun and Julia put their rifles on their shoulders, picked up their packs and started off. Richard also had a water container. Julia had the axe from the plane, and Doeun had an extra bag filled with potatoes.

They headed for the road and disappeared from view for a few seconds as they passed behind some trees, and then I saw them dip into the ditch and emerge on the road. Julia turned slightly around and waved in our direction, and then they started off. They were quickly swallowed up by the darkness. I hated letting them out of my sight. There was no telling what was just up the road or what might come along from behind.

"Can we move down closer to the road?" I asked. "If somebody came along and was heading for them, we couldn't do anything to protect them from up here."

"Good point. Let's move," Tom said.

We grabbed our packs and put them on our shoulders. Rifles followed. My gun was tucked away in its holster, and both of them also had pistols. Captain Daley picked up the second water container. I knew it was heavy. Water couldn't be compressed or dehydrated. It was heavy, only getting lighter as we drank. Then the weight would be replaced by worry until we could fill it again.

We stopped in a little stand of trees two dozen feet from the road. The light from the rising moon and stars threw down enough illumination for the road to be clearly visible. My eyes and ears were open.

We'd actually had eyes on the road continually since we'd arrived. There hadn't been any go-karts, but there had been activity. We'd seen people on foot, on bikes, in a couple of horse-drawn carts and in a very noisy, old pickup truck. The sound of the engine had startled us, and we'd been relieved when the truck had come into view. There had been half a dozen people in the back, some with weapons. They'd set up guards, gathered water and loaded twenty-five or thirty big water jugs into the back, as if they had a lot of people or crops that needed water.

"We should get back out there," Tom said. "I'm not sure we can move as fast as the other group."

"Godzilla and I can keep up," I assured him.

"It's not you I'm worried about. These legs aren't getting any younger."

I wanted to say something to him, but he was right. He was older, and I knew he'd been struggling.

We went down the ditch and up onto the road. I stopped, looked and listened. We were alone. We could relax for a moment.

"How old are you, Tom?" Captain Daley asked as we walked along.

"Some days I'm thinking about three hundred." He chortled.

"Let me rephrase that. What does your birth certificate say?" Captain Daley asked.

"It just says *old* in big letters." Tom grinned. Captain Daley gave him an exasperated look. "Okay, okay. I just turned seventy-one two weeks ago."

I stopped, staring at him. "You had a birthday and you didn't tell us?" I asked.

He shrugged. "Didn't want you to throw me a surprise party or nothing. Do you have any idea how hard it would have been to pick up a cake and ice cream?" he joked.

"Not to mention presents, balloons and party hats," Captain Daley added.

We both laughed. Godzilla's ears perked up.

"But for now, how about if we move without talking," Tom said, lowering his voice. "I'd rather hear than be heard. You know how far voices can travel at night. And Jamie, you keep an eye on the dog. He'll let us know of trouble long before we know about it."

I reached down and gave Godzilla a rub behind the ears, and he pushed in against me. He would help keep us out of trouble.

CHAPTER
THIRTY-
SEVEN

GODZILLA WAS PRESSED AGAINST ME, his head right by my face. He had a serious case of dog breath. I wondered if he thought I had human breath. I turned over and ended up with a rock sticking into my back. I dug into the ground to get it out. This wasn't as comfortable as my bed or the airline seat, the sofa at the colony or even the floor we'd slept on at the farmhouse. I threw the rock toward the river, and there was a splash. Doeun sat bolt upright, startled by the sound.

"It was me. It was a rock. I'm sorry." I cringed apologetically.

"What time is it?" she asked sleepily.

"It's almost ten a.m."

"That's not bad. Four hours' sleep at a stretch is never bad." She yawned.

We'd been doing the same pattern for the last four days. Walk for about six hours, meeting up every two hours, then stop, have a bite to eat in the middle of the night, walk again until an hour or so before the sun came up and then go into hiding—go to ground.

We were upstream from a river and about two hundred yards from the road. We always liked to be close enough to see the road but far enough away that we couldn't be seen. Since we'd first started walking, we'd covered more than seventy-five miles. More than fifty of those had been in the right direction, and the rest were detours to avoid problems. Bridges, barricades, blockades and groups of people were all things to avoid.

We were down to about three hundred miles to go. At this pace it would take us twenty-four more days. We had enough food for five. We'd already cut down on what we were eating every day. Thank goodness for Godzilla. He was like some sort of roadside delivery, a doggie version of Uber Eats. I thought back to what Tom had talked about in the beginning—the rule of three. Three minutes without air, three days without water and three weeks without food. Even if we didn't get any more food, we could still get there.

Most of the people on the road were out during the day. We could see or hear them from where we rested, but we made sure we were hidden. Those we ran into at night were less frequent but scarier. When you couldn't see somebody coming until the last seconds, it was easier to become startled. And startled responses could lead to an exchange of gunfire. That had almost happened a few times. Both Captain Daley and Tom were good at talking people down.

If we heard somebody coming, we'd scramble off the road and they usually would too, in the opposite direction. We'd yell out a hello and try to get them talking. The safest route was for us to go wide around them, through the field or trees or brush. We'd climbed a lot of fences and gotten smacked in the face in the dark by a lot of branches doing that. It was safer but it took up time. That's why we couldn't get more miles in. That and Tom. I just wished we still had a couple of bikes. Even just one for him. I never thought I'd miss that little bike with the pink streamers.

More than once Richard, Julia and Doeun had doubled back when they didn't like the looks of somebody who had passed them. Six people were safer than three. So far, no problems, but it was good to know we had backup if we needed it.

We hadn't seen even a hint of the go-kart people. And while we mostly avoided others, we had talked to a couple of groups of travelers. Despite everything going on, some people still tried their best to be decent to one another. We told them what was in the direction they were going, and they told us what was ahead of us. Things like where to get water and what to avoid. It was as close as anybody could come to a news report.

Doeun got up. "I'm going to check and see how Richard is doing."

Richard was closer to the road, on guard. It was nice of Doeun to check on him. I also thought there was something else going on. If the three of us were in eighth grade, I'd be pretty sure they were almost girlfriend and boyfriend.

I pushed Godzilla over and got up as well. He quickly jumped to his feet.

Tom was asleep under a tree. His rifle was resting across his chest, and if it weren't for the fact that he was snoring quietly, you might have thought he was on guard duty himself. Julia had found a spot on the other side of the tree. She wasn't snoring, but she wasn't moving, so I hoped she was getting some sleep. Captain Daley was nowhere to be seen. That didn't surprise me because he hardly ever seemed to sleep.

I decided to make myself useful. I grabbed the empty water container and took a couple of steps toward the river. Then I had another idea. I doubled back and grabbed my backpack. Godzilla had followed me every step but was now looking at me with an expression like, *Could you make up your mind?* I had. We were headed for the river.

The stream wasn't very wide here, and the water was still. It wasn't the best place to get clean water. I headed along the bank.

It was rocky and overhung with brush, so I had to duck down to move forward. I was heading away from the road, which felt better because I was alone. Then again, with this 120-pound, attack-trained Akita, I wasn't exactly on my own.

I sat down on a rock and opened up my pack. Inside was the small fishing reel. I pulled it out, checked the lure at the end and cast into the river, the little whirring sound ending with a splash. A fish or two would be good in our stomachs. I wanted to contribute, because sometimes I felt like luggage. Everybody else was carrying their own weight. Even Godzilla. If I caught five fish today, I'd still be way behind what he'd brought in. He looked up and wagged his tail.

There was a tug on the line, and I was pulled back into reality. I felt the weight on the line, and a fish jumped out, trying to spit out the lure. It was a big rainbow trout! I reeled it in and Godzilla barked excitedly, offering encouragement. I stepped into the shallows, meeting it halfway. It splashed and flipped, desperately trying to get free. I was just as desperate to not let it. I grabbed it with my free hand and walked back ashore, dropping it to the ground, where it flopped about. It was gigantic and would be a great meal for everybody.

I grabbed my pack with one hand, the reel and the fish with the other. I struggled up the bank and back toward the camp. This was going to make everybody so happy—as happy as I felt.

I came into the clearing to see Captain Daley and Doeun and Julia on their knees—right beside Tom. He was still on the ground, still asleep. Julia turned around. There were tears in her eyes. She got up and ran toward me and threw her arms around me.

"I'm so sorry…he's gone," she said.

Julia kept her arm around my shoulders. I'd stopped crying, but the shaking continued. Richard and Captain Daley put the last rocks on top of the pile. They hadn't been able to dig very deep, and the rocks would help protect Tom from animals. I was happy we'd been able to do something for him. It hadn't felt right leaving Phillip and Fede the way we did, but we'd had no choice. This time we did.

"He went peacefully," Richard said quietly. "I figure it was a heart attack. He just went to sleep and didn't wake up."

I sighed shakily. It was impossible to believe.

"I'd like to say a few words," Captain Daley said.

As he started to speak, my mind drifted away. I'd seen so many bodies, even seen people killed right before my eyes, but this was the first time I'd ever been to a funeral. When my grandfather had died, I was only four years old, and my parents had made me stay home with a babysitter. I remembered everybody coming back to the house afterward, and that they were all dressed in black, but I didn't really understand. I'd just thought I'd see him later. I was too young to remember my grandfather very much. But Tom...he'd been such a huge part of my life. And now I was saying goodbye to him.

"Jamie?" Captain Daley asked. "Would you like to say anything?"

I shook my head. I had so much I wanted to say, but there weren't any words.

"Then I'll end by saying how much we're all going to miss you, Tom, and thank you for all you gave us." He paused. "And I'll keep my promises."

Julia and Doeun sobbed, and Richard had tears in his eyes. Godzilla pressed up against my leg and almost pushed me over.

"It's time to go," Captain Daley said.

We started to gather our things. Richard was going to carry Tom's pack as well as his own. I grabbed my bag and slung it on my shoulder.

"We're going as one group," Captain Daley said.

I felt relieved. I'd been afraid it was just going to be me and the captain. Tears welled up.

"Here, this is for you," Captain Daley said. He was holding out Tom's rifle. I squinted at it. "He asked me to give it to you."

"Me?"

"Tom told me you're supposed to take it hunting someday. You and your dog. That way he can still go hunting with you the way he promised."

I took the rifle, letting a few tears fall. I held it up and then slung it over my shoulder. My left shoulder. The way Tom had carried it.

The sun would be down within fifteen minutes, and it was going to be very dark because there was a thick covering of dark clouds that would block the moon and the stars. In single file we moved along the river and up to the road beside the bridge. We hadn't seen or heard anybody for over an hour, but I had to admit, I was hardly noticing things that were going on right in front of me.

Richard quickly went to the front. Without a word, Doeun and Julia dropped behind, leaving the captain, me and Godzilla in the middle. I put a hand on the strap of the rifle. Tom had taught me to shoot both the pistol and the rifle. He'd talked to me about plants that were edible, how to make a smokeless fire, the best place to gather clean water in a stream, how to use bleach to sanitize it. There were so many things he'd taught me. And I was glad he'd given me his rifle. Wait—how did Captain Daley know that's what he'd wanted?

"Tom died in his sleep, right?" I asked.

"He never woke up."

"Then how did he tell you I should have his rifle?"

Captain Daley looked sad. "He'd told me that a few times. He was struggling. You knew that. He was really feeling guilty that he was slowing us down."

"He wasn't slowing us down!" I protested. "He was keeping us moving forward."

"I told him the same thing. But he was worried. He was trying his best, but it was getting harder and harder. He was in pain with every step, and he knew it was going to get worse."

I sighed. "Like climbing a mountain," I said.

He squinted at me. "Now *I* don't understand."

"That's how Tom explained it to me. He said that each foot higher up a mountain is harder than the foot before it. Not a lot harder but harder because there is not quite as much oxygen and because you're one step more tired."

"That makes sense," he said.

"He told me that above ten thousand feet, you're in the danger zone. Almost everybody gets symptoms of altitude sickness. Each foot higher heightens the symptoms. Then when you get to twenty-six thousand feet, it's the death zone. Stay that high for too long, you'll die."

"And that's like what we're going through now. Each mile, each step, is harder than the ones that came before," Captain Daley said.

"I know. It's going to get worse."

"Not only are we more worn down, but there are fewer resources, people we meet are more desperate, and we can't avoid built-up areas because there's nothing but cities and suburbs and civilization ahead. We've been in the danger zone almost since the start, and now we're in the death zone."

The death zone. That was about right.

"We're going to make it," I said.

"That was another promise I had to make to Tom," Captain Daley said, nodding. "That I'd return you to your family."

"How many promises did you make?" I asked.

"Three, including giving you his rifle. The last one was that someday, when this is over, I would find his family."

"And tell them what happened to him?"

"Well, that." He paused. "But mainly to tell them they were all a bunch of fools and that he was right in thinking the world was coming to an end!"

I couldn't help but laugh, and Richard turned around at the sound.

"I think I'd like to be there when you tell them," I said with a small smile.

Captain Daley smiled back. "Tom would like that."

Richard stopped. "Do you think you two could keep it down?" He raised an eyebrow wryly.

"Of course," Captain Daley replied. "We have to save our breath anyway. We've got a lot of ground to cover before the sun comes up, and there's less oxygen with every step up the mountain."

CHAPTER
THIRTY-
EIGHT

I WOKE FROM MY SLEEP and turned away from the bright sun shining in my eyes. I looked at my watch. It was almost one in the afternoon! I couldn't believe I'd slept for seven hours! I reached down for my rifle—Tom's rifle—and was relieved it was there. But where was Godzilla? He wasn't pressed against me or on top of me. I sat up.

"Good afternoon, sleeping beauty," Julia said.

"Do you know where Godzilla is?" I rubbed my eyes.

"He's not far. There's a briar with some rabbits just up the way. He's been playing hide-and-seek with them for the past couple of hours."

I got up and stretched. Doeun was under a blanket over to the side. She was turned away, and I couldn't tell if she was sleeping or just resting.

"Where are the captain and Richard?"

"Stu went to try to catch a fish, and Richard is up by the road on guard duty."

"Which way is Godzilla?"

She pointed. "It's not much more than a hundred yards. I hope either Stu or Godzilla manages to bring us back something. My money is on the dog."

I pushed myself up, took a few steps, and Julia called out, "Rifle. Take your rifle."

I spun around and grabbed it. I was glad she'd reminded me.

I left our little clearing behind and was swallowed up by the trees and brush. Turning back around, I saw it had vanished. That thought made me uneasy. What if I wandered into the woods to try to locate Godzilla and not only couldn't find him but couldn't find my way back? I almost spun around right there, but I didn't.

I thought about what Tom had shown me. I wasn't just looking for danger but for markers. A forest could be filled with trees and rocks, but they didn't all look the same. I had to mentally mark my way as I walked. I passed to the left of a large rock. I'd pass it on the right on my way back. Directly in front was a large oak tree, and that was the line I was aiming for. The sun was beaming down and warming up my left shoulder. It needed to be on my right shoulder as I returned. I'd walked at least seventy-five yards. It couldn't be much farther.

There was a sound directly in front of me, and I froze. It could have just been the wind in the trees. Then more noise, and closer. I dropped to one knee and pulled the rifle off my back. I clicked off the safety and brought it up to my shoulder and aimed and—Godzilla came through the bushes! I was so happy to see him, though disappointed that he wasn't carrying anything in his mouth.

I lowered my rifle and clicked the safety back on as he ran over and jumped up on me. It wasn't just the humans losing weight. He was getting skinny. I gave him a big scratch at the side and could feel his ribs underneath the fur. Somehow this made his bringing me what he was catching even nicer. He could have easily killed something and eaten it all himself. Instead he brought the kill to share with us. I was so glad, for so many reasons, that he was with us. Especially now that Tom was gone.

We started back toward the camp, and I remembered everything. Sun on my right, looking for rocks and trees. And also listening. We could hear the creek from our clearing, so I'd know I was getting closer when I could hear the water. I stopped to listen. I thought there was something, but it could have been just leaves in the trees rustling in the breeze. And then a loud, angry voice cut through the forest. My spine stiffened, and the hairs on the back of my neck stood up.

I turned all around, trying to figure out where it had come from. Godzilla was doing the same. His ears were up and he stood stiff-legged, the way he did while hunting. And then the voice came again. It was just as angry, maybe even louder and directly in front of me, in the direction of our camp.

I started moving. Slowly. Deliberately. Trying to make no sound. And no sound was being made. Just the leaves blowing. The camp was just past these bushes, over this last little hill. Maybe those voices were from up on the road or even on the other side of the creek, and I was worried for nothing. I moved even slower, watching where my next foot was going to land in case I stepped on a twig and snapped it. Coming to the crest of the hill, I peeked through the trees. There were three men in the clearing! Two of them had rifles, the third held a large machete. Julia and Doeun were sitting on the ground, hands in the air.

It felt like the inside of my head was spinning around. I slumped down even farther. *Okay, I have to think. I have to think.* There were three of them, but also three of us they hadn't seen. If I'd heard them, so had Captain Daley and Richard. When I was closing in from this side, they were probably approaching from the other two directions. I could picture them hiding in the bushes, rifles ready to fire. If I were

Tom, what would I be doing? I used the hill to brace my rifle and took aim on the man who was closest to me.

Captain Daley suddenly appeared. His hands were on his head and there were two men behind him, one aiming a rifle at his back and the second carrying a machete at his side. My heart sank. Automatically my aim shifted from the man closest to me to the man pointing the gun at Captain Daley. He was square in my sights, and I imagined a target in the center of his chest. That was the way Tom had taught me.

I had to rethink this. There were now five of them, three with rifles, and three of us had been captured. That left only me and Richard. Unless they'd already captured or killed him on the way in. No, I would have heard if they'd shot him. But I wouldn't have heard the blow of a machete.

Godzilla gave a quiet whine. "Be quiet, boy," I whispered.

They started yelling again, and one of them pushed Captain Daley, who toppled over, practically landing on Julia and Doeun. Julia screamed, and the man swung his hand—I heard the slap at the same time she flew backward. Captain Daley tried to get to his feet and I saw a machete swing toward him—and I fired.

The gun recoiled back into my shoulder and the sound rushed to my head as the man grabbed his stomach and fell to his knees. A second shot rang out—not from me—and a second man was hit. He spun around, and it looked like the side of his head was missing! It had to be Richard who had fired.

I jumped to my feet, and Godzilla and I charged into the clearing. I fired a second shot and realized I'd fired wildly and hadn't hit anything. A man aimed his rifle toward me, and I saw the flash of the muzzle and heard the bullet whiz by my side. He tried to correct his aim—and then he was hit!

Godzilla flashed by me and leaped toward one of the men. He tried to use his machete but Godzilla knocked him off his feet. The weapon flew from his hands, and he screamed in pain as the snarling dog attacked.

The last man dropped his machete and started running. He was getting away. I dropped to one knee, brought up the rifle and aimed at the invisible target on his back. In a second or two he'd be gone and he couldn't hurt us—unless he was going to get more people. I fired, he staggered, and his whole body seemed to spasm as he crashed, face-first, to the ground.

Then Richard came out of the trees, and Julia and Doeun jumped to their feet. They scrambled for the dropped weapons and snatched them up.

Godzilla was on top of the man. His jaws were wrapped around his throat, and the man wasn't yelling anymore or crying out in pain.

"Let him go, boy," I said.

He shook his head violently, and the body of the man shook along with it. Godzilla released his grip, and the man slumped to the ground. He didn't move. His throat was jagged with blood and raw flesh. His eyes were wide open, but he wasn't behind them anymore. He was dead.

Captain Daley sat up. He was clutching his stomach with both hands. He released his grip, and blood poured through the slash in his shirt.

"How does it feel now?" Richard asked.

"It's not hurting as bad now," Captain Daley said. "I think the painkillers have started kicking in."

Richard had also given him some antibiotics and sprinkled an anti-infective powder into the ugly, open gash in Captain Daley's side. I had no way of knowing how deep it was, and although the bleeding had slowed, I could see red seeping through and staining the gauze.

Doeun and Julia had checked to make sure all five of the men were dead. They'd dragged the bodies one by one to the creek and let the current wash them away. Then they'd gathered the weapons, and now they were just outside the clearing on two sides, watching, guarding, waiting for anybody else to appear. I stood over Richard and the captain with my rifle out, ready to fire again. Godzilla was quietly sitting at my feet, but his ears were up—he was on full alert.

"Now I want you to let me know if the pain is too much," Richard said. "I can stop."

"Best not to stop once you've started," Captain Daley replied, grimacing.

Richard pulled the gauze away from the wound to reveal the gash. He was about to use one more item, but it wasn't from his supply of drugs and equipment. It was the sewing kit from the airplane. He'd removed the largest needle and the thickest of the three types of thread that were in the kit. He would use them to stitch the wound closed. He put the needle into the flesh half an inch below the gaping wound. Captain Daley clenched his teeth as Richard pulled the thread through until its knotted end tightened against the captain's skin.

With his fingers Richard pushed together the two sides of the wound and then plunged the needle in again, pulling the thread through. I could see in Captain Daley's face that he was trying not to scream out in pain. His eyes were closed, like he was pretending he was someplace else. That's how I felt, but I couldn't look away. Stitch by stitch Richard continued, plunging the needle in, pulling the thread through, closing the gap. It was working. The wound was closing, the bleeding seemed to be stopping. Finally Richard tied off the last stitch.

"All done," he said.

"Good," Captain Daley said hoarsely. "We better get moving."

He went to get up, and Richard placed a hand on his shoulder and stopped him. "Look, you can't be moving right now and destroying all my fancy needlework."

"But there could be others, who might come looking when these men don't come back. We have to get some miles between us and here."

"You need to rest awhile. Maybe even a day or two. We're going to go upriver a bit and find a place where we can lie low," Richard said.

"We're going to ground," I added.

"Sounds like something Tom would say," Richard said and laughed.

"Makes sense he sounds like Tom," Captain Daley agreed, "because he acted like Tom would have."

"I just did what he taught us. I only wish I could have done something sooner."

"Your timing was perfect. It's my own fault. I should have just waited and done nothing until you and Richard rescued us. I knew help was coming," Captain Daley said.

"How could you be so sure?"

"There's not much about this world I'm sure about anymore, but I'm sure I can count on the people I'm with."

Ever so slowly he got to his feet. He swayed slightly, probably both the pain and the painkillers affecting him.

"Now let's get going...slowly and carefully."

CHAPTER

THIRTY-
NINE

IT WAS NOW SIX DAYS since the attack, and the captain's wound was getting better. It hadn't bled or oozed for a couple of days. For the first three days after it, we'd holed up in a spot about two miles up the river. It was well away from both the road and our old campsite. We hadn't seen or heard anybody. Captain Daley had slept most of the time. Richard had changed the dressing, and the edges of the wound were starting to heal together. Then we were back on the road and traveling. Not that we'd been traveling fast or far. The most we did on any of those three days was twelve miles.

"You're sure that you're still up to this?" Julia asked, peering at Captain Daley.

"Feeling good today," he said. "Even better than yesterday and the day before that."

"I think the rest did all of us a lot of good," Doeun said.

"It was great to have a few good meals," he agreed.

The river was alive with fish, and staying in one spot had meant we had time to fish. We'd eaten well, and I thought I'd even gained a pound or two.

"To tell you the truth, my foot is bothering me more than my side," Captain Daley said.

He had a noticeable limp, not so much because of the wound but because of his shoes. They were both worn down. The left one had been flapping open at the toe, and was now held together by some of the same thread that held together his side.

"I guess we should have checked to see if any of their shoes fit you before we tossed them in the creek," Richard said.

"Hardly anybody has feet this big, so that's water under the bridge," Captain Daley said, and Richard and he both chuckled.

How bizarre. They were joking about shooting five men and dumping their bodies into the river. Two of those men I'd killed. Godzilla had killed one of them. He looked up at me lovingly and wagged his tail. Who could believe he'd killed somebody? Who could have believed I'd killed two men and hadn't even lost sleep over it? Sure, I'd thought about it, but I didn't feel guilty. I'd done what needed to be done. The lives of my friends were more important to me than the lives of others. Especially others who were there to harm or kill us.

I thought back to something Tom had said in the beginning, after Phillip had killed the first man. I was trying to remember the exact words, but it was something like "hadn't killed anybody *yet*." *Yet* had come and gone for me. Tom always was wise.

We were starting to leave behind the full-on country. Instead of farm fields, forests and little towns, we were sometimes traveling by larger places. We'd always tried our best to move around the bigger towns, cities and suburbs, but now it wasn't completely possible. Doeun and Captain Daley were always studying the maps, looking for the best routes. The ones that were more remote were also much longer. We didn't have it in us to travel many extra miles. We had to risk the shorter paths.

There also seemed to be fewer people on the road now. Instead there were communities that had been walled off, sometimes with barbed wire at the top of those walls, and had guards with weapons. They watched us as we passed by. It was unnerving to travel under their watchful eyes and see their guns, but they also gave me hope. If these communities had come together to protect themselves, why wouldn't my parents have done the same thing? Maybe I'd be going home to a place that was walled, safe and stocked with food and weapons.

The people who were still out on the roads were mainly small groups or families. I wished our group was larger. If only we were the same size as when we'd started. If only some of the group hadn't decided to stay behind at the colony. If only Tom hadn't died and Phillip and Fede hadn't been killed. If only.

Occasionally trucks or cars passed by. I couldn't help thinking that if we could ride in one of those trucks—or capture one of those vehicles—we could be home within a couple of days.

That's what it had come to. I'd actually thought about us shooting at people in a truck. Killing them and taking the vehicle. I'd killed before. I knew I could do it again if that's what I needed to do to survive.

A day earlier we'd paid a "toll" to cross a bridge—some ammunition, some of our medications and one of our handguns. It wasn't exactly voluntary, but there was a business quality to it all, like we were simply paying admission to an amusement park or a toll to drive on an expressway.

We still had weapons—more than we had people. Four of us carried rifles and Captain Daley had Tom's shotgun. Three people had pistols, including me. I wore the holster under my shirt and tucked it away so it was practically in my armpit. It dug into me, and it wasn't comfortable...yet its being there was comforting. I knew it was there. Hidden away where nobody could see it.' Fully loaded. Still never fired.

The pack on my shoulder had gotten lighter. I was wearing my second pair of shoes, so the only clothing I had left was a spare shirt. As well there was the extra clip for my pistol, my blanket, a few potatoes and the frying pan. I'd thought about putting my knife in there, but I'd left it strapped to my left leg. With two guns I still thought I needed the knife.

Inside its sheath I'd also tucked in a few first-aid items and some of the remaining medications. We'd shared them among ourselves, and for some reason I wanted them closer than my pack, hidden away.

My pack also had one other item today. Wrapped in what was once a pair of pants was a dead rabbit. Godzilla had brought it back early in tonight's walk. Along with a couple of potatoes, it was going to be our midday meal once we stopped and set up camp.

The map had shown a river we'd have to cross before our walk tonight was over, and there was no way around it. Sometimes we'd avoided bridges and waded across small rivers to stay farther off the road. This one was too wide. It was the bridge or nothing. We expected it to be blocked and manned. We just hoped the fee for crossing wouldn't be too high.

Richard appeared on the road ahead of us. He'd gone out scouting the route. He was just standing there, waiting. Usually this meant something was wrong or he had a question. Either way I felt anxious. We closed in, and still he just stood there. He was facing us, but his head was down. Now I felt even more concerned. What news was he going to tell us?

"Richard, what's wrong?" Captain Daley asked.

"I'm sorry," he said.

"Sorry for what?"

"I had no choice," he said in a choked voice. "None of us do. I'm sorry."

"All of you, hands up!" a male voice yelled out.

Before I could even think to react, there were lights shining in our faces, and people with weapons rushed out from both sides of the road. There were dozens of them, and they were all yelling orders. Godzilla started snarling and growling.

"Shoot the dog!" somebody yelled.

"No!" I screamed. I wrapped my arms around him to protect and calm him. "It's all right—I can control him."

"Don't resist or you're dead!" somebody yelled.

We all raised our hands as they swarmed around us, taking our rifles and snatching the packs off our backs. I struggled to control Godzilla, holding him as tightly as I could. They started searching everybody—everybody except me. They were too afraid to get close to me, with Godzilla in my arms, and I pressed against him, the holster with the gun staying hidden.

"I'm so sorry," Richard said. "They ambushed me. They told me if I tried to warn you, they'd kill all of us!"

"You had no choice," Captain Daley said.

"He did the right thing," a woman said gruffly. "We didn't want to have to kill you, but we would if we had to. We're not going to hurt you at all if you don't do anything stupid."

The only stupid thing I could do would be to go for my gun.

They laid our rifles out on the road and added the pistols and ammunition as they found them. They opened our packs, removed and commented on items and sorted everything into piles. As my pack was dumped, the frying pan clanged to the asphalt, and the rabbit fell with a thud.

"Fresh meat!" somebody yelled as they held up the rabbit by its back legs. A little cheer went up.

"We're only doing this to provide for our families," a man said.

"What about our families?" Captain Daley said.

"That isn't our worry. You'll be free to leave unharmed if you stay smart." The man tapped his head with a finger.

"We've been smart. We've traveled a long way to get this far," Captain Daley replied. "We started in Chicago."

"Chicago!" The woman looked surprised.

"And is it like this the whole way?" a man standing outside the lights asked.

"Pretty much. Some places are better."

"How much farther do you have to go?" someone asked.

"Less than two hundred miles. We hoped we'd get to the other side of the river before morning."

"Across the bridge?" a man asked.

"Yes," Captain Daley answered.

The man grunted. "Us stopping you might be the best thing that could have happened to you. Those people at the bridge just shoot people and dump their bodies into the river."

"If you take away all our things, all our weapons, we're dead anyway," Doeun said in a pleading tone. "Please leave us something— some food, some weapons. Please."

"We'll leave you with what we don't want."

"Will you leave us some weapons, some way to defend ourselves?" Richard asked.

"That's not going to happen. All guns and ammunition will come with us."

"What about the dog?" somebody asked.

"He's trained. He won't hurt anybody, I promise!" I kept my arms tightly wrapped around Godzilla to make sure he wouldn't lunge. He could maul one person, maybe even kill them, but he'd be shot before he got to the second or third.

"We should take him," another voice added.

"You can't take him!" I protested. My voice came out like a screech.

"Come on," Captain Daley said. "Let the kid have his dog. You don't want him—he's just another mouth for you to feed."

"Or a way to feed a lot of mouths," somebody replied.

What was he talking about? Feeding mouths—he couldn't mean what I thought.

"I'm sorry," a woman said. She stepped out of the semidarkness and into the light. "None of us ever thought it would come to this, but we have to do what we do to feed our families."

"Let the kid keep his dog," another man said.

"It's not your decision!" somebody else argued.

There was discussion back and forth between people I couldn't see, who were hidden in the darkness. A man stepped forward. He was older, and I noticed immediately that he didn't have any weapons. Godzilla growled at him, and he stepped back.

"Son, I'm sorry, but we have to take your dog. I need you to put this around his neck. If you don't, we're going to have to shoot him."

"You can't just—you can't do that to him!" I pleaded.

"Look, we can't stop you," Captain Daley said. "But you don't really want to do that to the dog, do you?"

The man stopped and looked at Captain Daley.

"We're doing a lot of things we don't want to do," the man said, narrowing his eyes.

Captain Daley tried again. "I know you're not bad people. You could have just killed us, but you're not doing that, and you don't have to do that to the dog."

The man looked unmoved. "Hey, we're just trying to survive, that's all."

"We're all trying to do that. Now wouldn't you all rather eat rabbit or turkey or even groundhog than dog?" Captain Daley asked the people around him. "Wouldn't you?"

Nobody answered, but they were listening.

"That fresh rabbit was caught by the dog. He catches them all the time. If you don't believe me, look at the carcass. You won't see any bullet wound, just some teeth marks."

"How often does he catch something?" the older man asked.

"A few times a week. He'll do it more once he's settled in and doesn't have to walk so far each day. Besides, once he gets to know you, he's good security. He's smart and loyal. He'll help protect people. Just give him a chance, okay?"

There was discussion going on that I couldn't hear completely.

"What's your dog's name?" the man asked me.

"Godzilla."

He laughed. "It suits him. Now tie the rope around Godzilla's neck, kid."

I hesitated. I was still thinking about my gun.

"We'll give him a chance to prove himself," the man said. "If he's all that we've been told, he'll have a new home and new people to take care of him."

"How do I know I can believe you?" I asked. I couldn't accept that this was happening. I felt like I couldn't breathe.

"You're going to have to take my word on this."

"We do," Captain Daley said, trying to de-escalate the situation. "We know you could have just killed the dog. Or us. But you didn't."

He walked toward me and bent down. "You have to give him the dog," he said gently.

I didn't respond. How could he ask me to do that?

"There's no choice. He'll go and he'll catch rabbits for them. It's the only way for Godzilla to live." He looked up at the man. "Give me the rope."

He took the rope and tied it to Godzilla's collar.

"Say goodbye, Jamie. Let him know it's okay for him to go with them. You have to trust me."

My whole body shuddered, and I let out a big sigh. "It's okay, boy. They're just going to take you now. You'll be fine," I muttered. I gave him one more big hug, then released him. The man started to lead him away. I almost stood up before I realized that doing so could expose my gun. I put my hands to my face to cover my tears and so my arms covered the bulge of the weapon.

"We'll treat him well," the man said.

Godzilla resisted for a few steps and then allowed himself to be led away.

"How about treating us well?" Captain Daley said. "Can't you leave us with something? Even one rifle and a few bullets?"

"Please. We're dead without a way to defend ourselves," Doeun added.

"A way to cook, even our blankets," Richard added. "Some tools or—"

"We're leaving some of those things anyway." The man turned so he was facing the unseen people surrounding us. "We leave them one rifle—the shotgun comes with us—and six bullets." He turned back to us. "If that gun is aimed in our direction, we'll have no choice but to kill all of you. Don't make us do that."

"We won't," Captain Daley said firmly. "Thank you."

How could he thank the people who were taking almost all of our things, who were taking my dog!

"We're also going to help you in another way," a woman spoke up. "We told you that you can't cross the bridge. There's a spot about a mile upstream from the road where you can wade across the river."

"Thanks for that." Captain Daley bowed his head.

"It's the least we can do. We're not bad people, but sometimes we have to do bad things. Again, our apologies, and son, we'll give your dog every chance to be part of our group. He looks like a good dog."

"He is a good dog. Very loyal," Captain Daley said.

"You need to stay right here after we leave," the man said. "Gather up your things and head straight along the road. In about a mile there's a small dirt road that goes off to the right. Take it until you reach the river. There's a rope that's been strung between two trees, one on each side of the river. Use that as a handhold as you cross."

They started to walk away, Godzilla being dragged along.

"Take care of him!" I called out. "Please!"

"You have my word."

They walked out of the circle of light and then the light disappeared as well, leaving us standing, shaking, alone in the dark in the middle of the road. They were gone. And Godzilla was gone as well. I burst into tears.

CHAPTER
FORTY

RICHARD PICKED UP THE RIFLE and stood guard as we gathered up the few remaining items, stuffed them into our backpacks and hurried away. I wasn't sure what remained, but judging from the lightness of my pack, there wasn't much. I was too stunned to think, and Julia took my hand and led me away.

Godzilla was gone. My dog was gone. At least he was alive. But what if he didn't bring home enough game? What then? I couldn't even allow myself to think about that. In total silence we moved down the road. I felt numb all over as we stumbled along the dark and deserted road.

"There's the path."

We turned onto it. With tall overhanging trees on either side, it was even darker. As we moved along, the sound of the river got stronger. It couldn't be much farther.

"Let's take a break," Captain Daley said. "I want to rest and regroup before we cross."

We followed him to a small space amid some larger trees. It was snug with all of us sitting there, but it did feel safe.

"Let's figure out what we still have," Captain Daley said. "I just wish we had some light."

"Do you mean like this?" Julia said.

A little beam lit the space. Julia was holding a small flashlight. The beam was faint, so there wasn't much battery left.

"How did you get that?" Richard asked.

"I was holding it when they searched me, and they didn't look in my hand. Then I slipped it into my pocket."

"They didn't get this," Doeun added. She held a knife in her hand. "I had it strapped to the inside of my thigh, and they didn't pat me down that well."

"Let's look in all the packs," Captain Daley said.

We opened up and removed all the contents.

"This is a find!" Richard exclaimed. It was the small rod and reel. Either they had enough of their own or they had just missed it.

"They left us three blankets, and there's the frying pan and pot, and four…no, five forks and two knives."

"If only they'd left us some food," Julia said.

"Maybe we should cross and then we can fish. When do we cross another river or go by a lake or—"

We all thought it at the same time, and Richard and Doeun said it out loud. "Maps."

"They took the maps," Captain Daley confirmed.

A sense of panic washed over me. "But how do we get home without the maps?"

"You have two pilots who have been studying the maps for hours every day," Doeun reassured me. "We can get us home even if we're missing a few of the details."

I let out a big sigh. I believed her. My father only had to go to a place once to know how to get there again.

"More important than the maps, they also took the first-aid kit, the sewing kit, the axe and all the medicine," Richard added. He turned to Captain Daley. "I'm worried, because you needed to take antibiotics for another three days, and now they're all gone."

"Not all," I said. I pulled up my pant leg, reached into the sheath and pulled out first the knife and then the three little bottles that were lodged in there.

"Amazing!" Richard exclaimed, his face lighting up. He held them up and looked at the bottles. "Two of these are antibiotics and the third is a painkiller."

"I thought they were important, so I didn't put them into my pack."

"They are *so* important," Richard agreed. "I just wish we'd have stashed away a couple of weapons too."

I hadn't mentioned it. I reached up and undid the top two buttons of my shirt and removed the pistol from the holster. "Like this?"

"The kid saves the day yet again!" Richard clapped his hands together.

Captain Daley gave a smile. "We're a lot better off than we were twenty minutes ago," he said.

"Thanks to Jamie," Julia said. "We've lost a lot, but we're still here. Where there's life, there's hope. We're still moving forward, still all together."

"Not all," I said. I felt like I was going to start crying again.

"I'm so sorry about Godzilla," Captain Daley said. "But I think he's going to be all right. Despite what they did, they're not bad people."

"Yeah, once they get him back to where they live, he's going to settle into their hearts," Doeun added, reaching forward to pat me on the arm.

"And into their stomachs," Richard said, before adding, "No, not that way! I mean he'll bring back so much game. That dog will pull his weight, just like he did for us."

"I just wish he was with us." I stared at my feet.

"We all do," Captain Daley said. "And if there was any other way, we would have stopped them or even gone back to get him. It's just...we can't. You know that, right?"

"I know," I said. "I'm going to miss him."

"We're all going to miss him," Julia said. "But I know he's going to be fine."

"And so are we," Captain Daley said firmly.

Those words sank in. I believed him. I was sad, but I had to believe him.

"If everybody's ready, I want to cross the river while there's still some darkness to cover us," Captain Daley said. "We'll find a place on the other side to hide for the day, get water and maybe catch a fish or two." He paused. "After all, we do have a frying pan."

CHAPTER

FORTY-ONE

THE SUN WAS STARTING TO come up. Usually that was our signal to stop, find a place to hide and grab some sleep during the day before continuing to move during the night. Today was going to be different. We'd been warned by some people we'd met that it was better to travel this section during the day. Our route would take us by fenced and walled colonies—neighborhoods that were like little forts. We were told that at night they might shoot at anybody, but during the day they'd be able to see us and realize we weren't any risk at all.

I hoped we'd at least stop for a bit and grab something to eat. We had crab apples in our packs. It was the only food we had. We'd passed through an orchard four days earlier and found apples that hadn't been touched at the tops of some of the trees, and I'd climbed up and got them. We'd harvested all that we could find, and that's what we'd been eating since then. We probably had enough for another three days.

When this had all started, there'd been a strange sense of excitement. Sleeping in the plane, eating leftover airline food and planning for an adventure ahead. We were like characters in a movie. We were heroes, and like all heroes, we were going to win. It was hard to believe that was only two months ago. It seemed like forever ago. Now we were less like heroes and more like survivors. It wasn't *The Lord of the Rings* and even if it were, my faithful companion, my Samwise, was gone. I had to hope that Godzilla was all right. Maybe he was even doing better than we were. How could he do worse unless he was dead? This was more like *The Walking Dead*. We were zombies walking among zombies.

People we came across as we traveled were thin, limping or at least moving really slowly, almost shuffling, and dressed in tattered clothing. They had dirty faces—water was too rare to waste on washing. There was a look in their eyes. It was hard to establish eye contact, but when I did, I could see that they weren't even scared anymore. It was more like hopeless, or vacant, as if there was nobody there. And worst of all, I knew we didn't look much different. I didn't want to look in a mirror—not that there was one—because I knew what I'd see.

The toe of Captain Daley's left shoe was now almost completely gone and held to the upper with a piece of twine he'd found a few days earlier. Julia's shoes weren't much better. Both the captain and Richard had thick, unkempt beards that made them look wild. Everybody had long hair. The only good thing about this was that we looked so pathetic, nobody really bothered us much anymore. It just didn't look like we had much to take.

We kept moving, but it got much harder with each passing day. Step by step we traveled. Sometimes we'd go hours without even talking. Walking and talking seemed like too much work. We could do one or the other. When we rested, it was hard to get back up. The only thing that kept us moving was hope. We weren't traveling fast or far, but each step brought us closer.

The previous day had been our worst so far. We'd probably walked ten or twelve miles, but only five were in the right direction. We kept having to take detours around blockades on roads. Captain Daley had told us we had at least 125 miles to go. At that pace we still had another twenty-five days of walking. I didn't know if we had that many more days in us.

More and more, it was harder to find what we needed to survive and keep moving. Without our bleach, we'd had to be more careful for the last ten days—no, it had been eleven days since almost everything had been stolen—with what we used as a drinking source. Getting water and surviving on the food we could scrounge from fields or catch in rivers was all we could do. Not that I even felt hungry anymore. That gnawing feeling had chewed a hole right through my stomach.

Somehow, through it all, Captain Daley kept us moving. I didn't know how. He wasn't doing any better than the rest of us, but he just kept believing. He talked about how glad our families would be when we got home, talked about his family, about how we were going to do it. Either he really believed it or he was a great actor.

"Let's stop up ahead and take a break before going any farther," Captain Daley said.

He was pointing at a park. Among the playground equipment and the baseball and tennis courts were tents and crude lean-tos— makeshift homes for people who had taken up residence or were passing through. More and more we were staying in the shadow of other people. There really wasn't much choice now that open country had been replaced by cities and suburbs.

We entered the park. There was an open spot along the side, close to a little creek where people were filling water containers. Did that mean this water was safe to drink? Should we drink and then fill up our container when we left? What choice did we have? We had to drink water even more than we had to eat.

"Everybody, take a long drink," Doeun said as she passed the water container.

"Stu, should we get out a couple of apples?" Richard asked.

"I think it's better we don't eat here. We haven't got much, but it might be more than some of these people have. It's best we appear to have nothing."

"Appear?" Julia said and laughed.

"That's actually something I was hoping to talk to you about," Richard said in a serious voice.

"Both of us were," Doeun said, stepping up beside him.

The two of them had been walking behind the rest of us for a big part of the night. That was unusual, because Richard almost always walked in the front, leading with his rifle. I'd heard them talking a few times, which was also unusual since we almost always moved in silence.

"I—we—want to talk to you about a change in our route," Doeun said.

"Do you think there's a better way?" Captain Daley asked.

"We think there's a better destination," Doeun replied.

"Let me explain," Richard said, putting a hand on Doeun's shoulder. "My brother and his wife have a place. It's sort of a hobby farm. He had some chickens, a cow, grew crops and had a natural spring on his property. It's about forty miles from here." They looked at each other.

"And you think we could stop along the way?" Julia asked.

"I thought we could stop, but it's not exactly along the way," Richard said. "In about fifteen miles there's a way we can get there by heading about twenty-five miles south."

Captain Daley looked as confused as I was. "But that'll add another fifty miles round trip to get home, and I'm not sure it's worth it for a bit of rest and food," he said.

"It's not extra miles if we stay there," Doeun said emphatically.

Captain Daley shook his head. "We have to get home."

"We're not going to make it," Richard said. "I don't even know if we can make it to my brother's."

"Even if we get there, how do you know he's going to be there, that he's going to be able to put us up, provide for us?" Captain Daley asked.

Richard paused, letting out a breath. "I don't know," he admitted. "But how do you know we have homes to go back to either?"

Captain Daley shook his head. "I know my family is waiting for me. It's the only thing that's kept me moving," he said. "That and a promise to get Jamie home."

I nodded in agreement, glad he wasn't backing down. We knew our destination. We weren't giving up now.

"That could still happen. We get to my brother's, and we rest up. Then, when we're better, stronger, anybody who wants to leave can leave."

Captain Daley didn't answer.

"We think it's the best chance we have," Doeun added.

"If we push hard, we can be there in two days," Richard said.

"If we could do twenty miles a day, we'd be home in six," Julia replied, catching my eye.

"There's a difference," Richard said. "We might be able to go flat out for two days, but I don't think we can do it for six."

"It's also the route. Once we make the turn toward their farm, we'll be walking *away* from the city and into the country," Doeun said. "We all know it's going to get harder with each mile in areas that are more built up."

She was right. We all knew that. We were climbing higher up the mountain, and each step was harder. Turning away from the city and onto the route they were talking about would be heading back down the slope.

"Besides, you're talking about the distance to where Jamie and Julia live. My home is fifteen miles beyond that, and Doeun's another few miles. It's still another thirty-five miles for Stu to get home, and he'd have to do that on his own," Richard said.

I had never really thought beyond my getting home.

"And that's right across the city. It's going to be the most dangerous part of the entire journey, and he'll be doing most of it alone," Doeun said, trying to meet Captain Daley's gaze.

"He doesn't have to leave. He could stay with us!" I exclaimed.

"Staying with you isn't any different than staying at my brother's place. He's still not with family," Richard said.

He was right. Captain Daley wanted to be with his family the same way I wanted to be with mine. He wouldn't be able to accept an invitation to stay with us.

"We want everybody to come with us, but we can't force you," Doeun said.

"And we both feel bad for even suggesting that we don't stick together. That's why we think we should all go to my brother's farm."

"But we understand you need to try to get to your families," Doeun said. "That's all Richard wants." She paused. "And I guess I'm part of his family."

She reached out and took Richard's hand, and they both gave an embarrassed little smile.

Captain Daley's expression softened. "I was wondering when that was going to come into the open," he said with a smirk.

"Like you were fooling anybody anyway!" Julia said. She went over and gave both of them a hug, and Captain Daley shook Richard's hand and hugged Doeun. I didn't know what to say. I just knew this didn't change anything about what was going to be decided.

"I understand you two wanting to do this," Captain Daley said. "But in the end, we all have to make our own decisions."

"I still feel bad," Doeun said quietly. "Like it's dereliction of duty for not completing our flight."

"You've gone well beyond duty. We're not on a flight. I'm not your captain or commander. I'm your friend. Friends to both of you. I know you have to do what you have to do." Captain Daley put his hands on their shoulders.

"Thank you for understanding." A tear spilled down Doeun's cheek. "Will you at least think about coming with us?"

"It's probably the only thing I'll be able to think about," Captain Daley said. "At least, for the next fifteen miles."

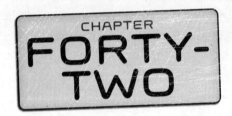

CHAPTER FORTY-TWO

CAPTAIN DALEY AND JULIA WERE behind me, and Richard and Doeun walked in front. They'd been leading the way, setting the pace. We'd been moving faster. We'd seen lots of people, more vehicles and what seemed like a steady stream of walled-off neighborhoods. Privacy fences, sound barriers and backyard fences had all become defenses and boundaries. It felt strange to walk by under the gaze of armed guards on the walls, but it was also reassuring. I tried to pretend they were there to protect us from other people out on the road.

Besides, it was just more reason to believe that when we got home, our neighborhoods would be doing the same. That image was probably the only thing that kept me moving forward. I thought about my family waiting for me. My parents would see me and come running out. I knew they'd be teary-eyed. So would I. We'd go back inside the walls, and there would be food and water and enough people with enough weapons to make sure it stayed that way. I had to hope this was the reality, because hope was about all I had to keep me going. If we decided to change directions, what would make my legs keep moving?

Captain Daley fell in on one side of me, and Julia on the other.

"How are you feeling?" Julia asked.

"Okay. I don't know whether it's good or bad to be away from the walls."

"Really all those people want is to make sure we keep walking and don't bother them," Captain Daley pointed out.

"Hard to believe anybody could see us as a threat," Julia scoffed.

"Or imagine we have anything worth taking. I guess that helps make us safe," Captain Daley said.

I laughed. "If having nothing makes us safe, we're about the safest people in the world." I paused, then added, "And we've come pretty far today."

"We'll be at the intersection in less than an hour," Captain Daley said.

I hesitated before asking, "And what then?"

"That's what we want to talk to you about. What do you think we should do?" Julia asked.

I shrugged. "I really have to do whatever is decided."

"But if you could choose?"

"I want to go home," I blurted.

"We all want to go home—but we also want to stay alive," Captain Daley said in his measured tone.

Did that mean we were going to go with Doeun and Richard instead of heading home? It wasn't like I could set out on my own. Or could I? I realized I didn't know the way. I couldn't go anywhere without them.

"I didn't know you still had so far to go after you get me home," I muttered.

"It isn't that far," said Captain Daley. But I knew he was just being nice.

"It's going to take you at least three days to cover that distance."

"Believe me, when I get that close, I'm going to practically run the whole way. But let's not worry about that now. We have a decision to make first."

🔥

We stood at the intersection. To the right was Richard's brother's farm, and straight ahead was the way home.

"Have you decided?" Richard asked us.

"I think I can answer that," Doeun said. She looked at Captain Daley. "You're not going to come with us, are you?"

Captain Daley shook his head, and my heart leapt. "How did you know?"

"I've been flying with you for enough years to know you weren't going to stop until you reached your destination," she said fondly.

"We really appreciate the offer, but we have to continue," Julia affirmed.

"Jamie, you're free to come with us if you want," Doeun said, turning to me.

"I'm not stopping," I said. "I'm going home." I felt good, knowing I had Captain Daley and Julia on my side. I felt hopeful again.

"We figured that as well," Doeun said, ruffling my hair, "but we had to offer."

Richard held out the rifle to Captain Daley. "You'll be needing this."

"You'll be needing it as well," Captain Daley said.

"There's three of you, and you have a lot farther to go."

"We have the pistol—thanks to Jamie. You'll need a gun to get there and once you arrive. But you make a good point. Let's figure out how we're going to divvy up everything."

"There isn't much to figure. You three are taking all the food that's left, the blankets, the pot and the frying pan," Richard said.

"We'll divide the food into fifths," Captain Daley countered. "We'll take the frying pan and the water container, and you can take the pot as your water container. You get one of the three blankets."

Doeun grinned. "It sounds like you two have been thinking this through," she said.

"Can you even imagine us not doing that?" Julia arched her eyebrow.

"And if we decide to take nothing?" Richard asked.

"Then you'll be leaving your stuff here at the side of the road for somebody else, because we won't be taking it with us," Captain Daley said, putting his hands up.

"And there's no point in arguing with him," Julia said. "He is a pilot, which means he's incredibly stubborn and thinks he's always right." She elbowed Captain Daley.

"I've been learning that's an occupational hazard," Richard said, winking at Doeun.

Doeun leaned over and gave him a playful tap on the arm, and they both smiled and laughed. It made me smile too. "How about if Jamie stands watch while we sort the supplies," Captain Daley suggested. He pulled out the pistol and handed it to me.

They took the packs, including mine, and walked over to a patch of grass by the side of the intersection. I stood there scanning in all three directions. For the moment we were alone.

I stared ahead, to where my home lay. Then I looked right, to see where Doeun and Richard would travel. Behind me was the way we'd come.

If we'd traveled a direct route, we'd have come eleven hundred miles, but with all the twists and turns and detours, it was closer to fifteen or sixteen hundred. I didn't think I'd ever forget even a single one of those miles and the things that had happened along the way. From bursting through the fence on that ridiculous stair car to the first bodies, shots and danger. The places we'd stayed, the people we'd run from. Where Phillip fell, where we'd left others, the murder of Fede, the death of Tom, and Godzilla being taken from me, dragged away on the yellow rope. I remembered every single painful point along the way. Everything we'd been through. And now we were dividing again.

They all walked over to me. It was time.

"You remember all the details, right?" Richard asked.

"I've got it all up here," Captain Daley said, tapping his forehead.

"We hope you won't need to, but if you do, we want you to know how to find us," Doeun added.

"You know you're welcome," Richard said. "You're not just friends—you're family."

"I'll keep it in mind for the fellowship reunion," Julia said, meeting my eyes.

Julia and Doeun hugged, as did Richard and Captain Daley. They changed partners, doing the same. Richard and Doeun came up to me. They both wrapped their arms around me.

"Thank you for being with us," Doeun said.

"I don't think I had much choice," I said with a quiet laugh.

"We're just glad you were," Richard said. "You saved us more than once out there."

Just then I remembered. "I guess I should give this back," I said. I dug the ring out of my pocket.

Doeun gazed at it. "I'd forgotten about that. Frodo should keep the ring, because the road goes ever on," she said, closing my fingers around it.

She was quoting "A Walking Song," which Frodo and Sam always sang. It seemed perfect.

"No, you should take it," I said. "Or maybe I should give it to Richard, and he can give it to you."

Doeun and Richard both smiled. "I think he's trying to pressure us into marriage," Doeun said.

"No pressure needed," Richard replied. He reached out his hand, and I gave him the ring. "Thank you, Jamie."

"I just wish Godzilla was still with you. But who knows? In the story, Samwise came back when there seemed to be no hope," Doeun said.

I appreciated her saying that. But there really was no hope.

"Since I won't be there to watch over people, I want you to promise that you'll take care of these two," Richard said to me.

"I promise." I looked over at Captain Daley and Julia. I was happy with our little trio.

"Well, we better get going," Richard said. He took Doeun's hand.

"When this is all over, I hope you and Doeun can come to our house for a meal, meet my wife and kids," Captain Daley said. "Then you'll understand why I have to keep moving."

"I understand. Family is family. I just didn't think I'd have to go through all of this to find a new part of mine," Richard said, gazing at Doeun.

We started off on our separate ways. I looked over my right shoulder and saw the two of them walking—packs on their backs, rifle on Richard's shoulder, hand in hand. I was sure they were going to make it because they were together.

CHAPTER FORTY-THREE

"HOW MUCH LONGER DO YOU think that shoe is going to last?" Julia asked Captain Daley.

The rip in the sole had become even larger. It was flapping with each step.

"I'm hoping for another forty-three miles." He crossed his fingers. "Until we get you two home."

"That doesn't get you home," Julia said.

"No, but I'm thinking I can get another pair of shoes from Jamie's father," Captain Daley said. "I think trading him a son for a set of shoes isn't too much to ask for."

I shook my head. "His feet aren't as big as yours."

Julia snickered. "Nobody's feet are as big as his. He has to hope we run into a clown!"

Captain Daley winced, pretending to be insulted. "First, that hurts. Second, I'd love that as long as the clown comes with a working clown car. Finally, if worse comes to worst, I'm going to hop on one foot to get there."

"Do you think Richard and Doeun got there?" I asked.

Julia shrugged. "It's been four days. Even moving at the same pace as us, they would have been there yesterday or the day before."

"Do you think they're all right, that they found what they were looking for?" I asked.

"Watching the two of them walking away together, I figure they'd already found what they were looking for," Captain Daley said.

Julia laughed. "I never really saw you as the romantic kind."

"I think that's another side effect of this walk." He smiled. "How about you? Your husband is going to be pretty surprised to see you walk through the door."

"I hope not too surprised," she said. "He's so helpless, I'm positive he hasn't actually taken out the garbage since I left."

"I'm not even sure where you take the garbage to these days or—let's move over this way," Captain Daley said.

I was going to ask why, but looking up, it was obvious. A group of seven or eight men was coming toward us. We moved to the far side of the road, and they instantly changed course to intercept us. That wasn't good.

"I'll be at the back," Captain Daley said.

We shifted into single file, with Julia leading and me in the middle. I knew the reason for this. Captain Daley had the gun. He'd cover us from the back, and we didn't want them to see the weapon at first. We hoped we'd slip by because they'd see we had nothing worth stealing.

I peeked around Julia. As they closed in, they spread out. I knew they weren't going to let us pass. Still closer, I could see machetes being pulled out.

"They're bringing knives to a gun fight," Captain Daley said under his breath.

"They're bringing *lots* of knives," Julia said. "More knives than we have bullets."

"Have you ever heard this math problem? 'There are seven crows on a telephone wire. You shoot one. How many do you have?'"

"Six," I said.

"Wrong. None. The rest fly away."

That was optimistic, I thought. These people looked mean and desperate.

They were getting louder, and I'd heard that tone of voice before. It was like a pack of wolves yipping to give each other courage.

"Get behind me now," Captain Daley said.

He pulled out the pistol, and at the same time Julia removed the knife from the sheath strapped to her leg. I planned to leave my knife hidden. Instead I pulled the frying pan out of my pack and held it up.

"We don't want any problems," Captain Daley yelled out. He held the gun in front of him.

They stopped in their tracks. "Why don't you put that down before we pull out our guns," one of them said.

"If you had guns they'd be out already."

The same guy—he was the biggest, out front and probably the leader—spoke. "You think you can take all seven of us with that little peashooter?"

"No, but I'm positive I can shoot you, and probably one or two more guys as well. Raise your hand if you want to be the second and third guys."

"I can kill at least one of them. I'm going after that one." Julia pointed. "Not only do I think I can take him, but there's something about his stupid face that just irritates me. Don't the rest of you feel like slapping him too?"

They chuckled at the guy. He didn't look happy.

"You think you can scare us off?" the leader said. "The three of you look like a big gust of wind could blow you all over."

"It might," Captain Daley said, "and that's because we haven't eaten for three days."

We'd eaten the few remaining crab apples, and we'd traded the last antibiotics we had for a couple of potatoes, but that wasn't much.

"Come on. It's not like we even have anything worth stealing," Captain Daley continued.

"You have a gun. Give it to us and we'll let you go."

"I have a better idea. Give us that bag you have on your shoulder, and I'll let *you* go."

The guy laughed. "I've got to give you credit. You've got a lot of guts."

"Not that much. Soon we're going to see your guts." Captain Daley raised the gun and pointed it right at him. "I always aim for the stomach. It's a slow death, pretty painful. At least, that's what I heard from the last two guys I shot."

None of them looked so confident anymore.

"We have nothing to give you and nothing to lose. You drop that bag, or I shoot you right now. Heck, I might even do you a favor and put two bullets into you so you die faster. Do you think any of the others are going to risk their lives for you?"

There was some grumbling in the background.

"Drop it now!" Captain Daley yelled.

The man slowly lowered the bag to the ground. Two of the guys behind him looked distracted, like they not only weren't listening but were focused on something happening behind us. I wanted to turn to see what they were seeing, but I couldn't risk taking my eyes off them for a second.

"Josh...Josh...look," one of them said. He was pointing down the road.

I heard a noise. At first it didn't register. After a moment I realized it was a dog barking. Did I recognize that bark?

I couldn't believe my ears, and then, as I turned, I couldn't believe my eyes. It couldn't be, but it was! Godzilla was running toward us, trailing a length of yellow rope behind him.

"Godzilla!" I yelled out, almost too stunned to speak

"That's his dog," Julia said. "He's not going to bargain with you. He's no talk, all action."

They hesitated, hedged, shuffled sideways, and then, as a group, they took off, climbing over a metal fence and running off into the field beyond.

I rubbed my eyes as Godzilla ran toward me. I bent down, and he barreled into me, knocking me backward. The frying pan flew out of my hand as he jumped on top of me, pinning me with his paws.

"Godzilla, you're here! You're back and—" I burst into tears, and his big, rough tongue licked them away. Wait, why was it so rough and dry?

"He needs water! Please get him some water!"

I struggled to move him off me, and he fought back, pushing against me. I wrapped my arms around his leg and pulled myself up.

"How can he be here?" I cried.

Julia held up the end of the rope. "Judging from this, he chewed his way free and dragged it along with him."

"That was almost two hundred miles ago. How is that possible?" I asked.

"He's been tracking you," Captain Daley said. "Following your scent."

"That can't be," I said as I tightened my arms around his neck.

"Their noses are way more sensitive than ours," Julia explained.

I started rubbing him. I could feel his ribs sticking out. "He's just fur and bones."

"He's been running instead of hunting. He wanted to get back to you," Julia said, giving him an ear rub.

"He wanted to be with his family. I guess we all know what that's about," Captain Daley said, pouring some water into a small bowl for Godzilla to lap up.

Julia held up the bag the man had left behind. She reached inside and pulled something out—a carrot. "It's filled with carrots and some potatoes and apples!" She grinned.

"That's fantastic," Captain Daley said. "How about we get moving before they come back to try and claim it. I want to get away from those guys."

I got up and looked anxiously in the direction they'd fled. I didn't see them, but that didn't mean they weren't still around.

I got to my feet. "Come on, boy. It's time to go home."

CHAPTER

FORTY-FOUR

IT LOOKED SO FAMILIAR AND so different all at once. Some of the houses were burned out, and the park had colorful patches of tents. People were living by the playground equipment.

"That's our ice-cream store over there," Julia said. "At least, what's left of it."

The big pink-and-white sign that announced how many flavors the shop used to have seemed to be the only thing left. The other stores looked ransacked, with smashed-out windows, some filled in with plywood and others just wide open. The little mall parking lot was filled with cars that had been stranded, unable to start, since the start of this.

"How close are we now?" Captain Daley asked.

"Less than a mile to go," Julia said. "A little bit farther to Jamie's neighborhood."

"You must be excited," he said.

"Excited and nervous. What if we get there and, well, *there* isn't there?" she said.

"Hope has pushed us forward fifteen hundred miles, so let it bring you the last mile."

Julia bit her lip. "And if he isn't there?" she asked.

"Then you come with us to Jamie's neighborhood. You know they'd take you in. You'll find your husband. Do you think we'd leave you alone after all we've been through?"

We continued to walk, but now it was in silence. I couldn't help thinking the same things Julia was. If Julia's husband was gone, if there was nobody there for her, what would be there for me? I thought I might start to cry. I was so tired, so weak...I couldn't take it if this didn't work out.

"I don't know whether your parents are going to be more surprised to see you or Godzilla," Captain Daley said.

Godzilla's ears perked up at the mention of his name, and he wagged his tail. He was right at my side the way he'd been since the beginning and then since his return. He hadn't even gone out on his own to hunt. It was good to have him so close, but a rabbit would have been great. We'd run out of food completely the day before. We'd deliberately eaten all we had left—not that it was much—to give us the extra push to do the eighteen miles we needed today. We had to thank that guy—Josh—for trying to steal from us but instead leaving his food behind.

We were passing by a cement and stone wall on the left. Peeking over the top were the upper floors and roofs of houses. In the before days, this was a sound barrier. Now it was like the moat of a castle. I could see that some of the homes were blackened by fire. It seemed fire-breathing dragons could fly over walls.

"This is it," Julia said. "This is my neighborhood. The road leading in is just ahead."

I had thought Julia would want to go faster, but instead she slowed down. We came to her road. A couple of cars blocked the way. Both were burned out, and there was nobody manning the barricade. That wasn't good. There should have been people with weapons guarding the entrance.

We slipped around the cars and continued to walk. There were more houses with smashed-out windows, abandoned cars, overgrown lawns and no people. It was like we were walking through a ghost town. Where had all the people gone? None of this was good. How much farther could it be to her place?

Julia had stopped walking. She was staring at a house. It looked to be totally abandoned. And then she walked up the driveway.

Julia sat at the kitchen table. In front of her were a few things she'd salvaged from the house, which had been completely ransacked. There were a couple of pieces of clothing, a Christmas ornament and a framed picture of her and her husband on their wedding day. The glass was smashed.

The kitchen floor was warped from where the rain had come in through the smashed picture window. Captain Daley and I stood off to the side because she'd said she wanted to be left alone. We'd stood there, helpless, as she cried.

We'd searched—all three of us—but there was no sign of her husband. We hoped that even if he wasn't here, somehow he'd left a message for her, telling her where he'd gone. There was nothing.

"Julia?" Captain Daley said quietly.

She looked up. "I can't believe he's not here after all we did to get back."

"Are there other places he might be?"

"His brother lives about five miles from here, and his best friend owns a big place about ten miles away. He might have gone to one of those." Her voice sounded hollow.

"He might have. You can check, but not now. Not on your own."

"I know," she said. "We need to get Jamie home first. Then I'll go."

"I can go with you," Captain Daley said.

"No, you can't! You have too far to go, and you need to get there."

"You can stay with us, and my family can help," I said.

"That's assuming that—" She stopped herself. I didn't need her to finish the sentence. Assuming my family was there.

"Then we stay together. All of us," Captain Daley said. "Understood?"

She nodded her head and wiped her tears from her cheeks. "I understand." She stood up slowly. "We better get going."

This had been the longest two miles. From what remained of Julia's house to what could remain of mine.

"We're almost there," I said.

"I can't wait to see the expressions on your parents' faces when you stroll in," Captain Daley said.

I'd been thinking about that for fifteen hundred miles. It was the hope of seeing them that had kept me moving. Soon that hope might be gone.

"You still have a long way to go to get home," I said.

"What's a few more miles after fifteen hundred?" He gave me a wink.

"It's not just another few."

"I can make that in three days," Captain Daley said. I guessed he was right. We had made it this far. "This must all be looking pretty familiar." He gestured around.

There was the big field, playground and baseball diamond. Tents were pitched along the edge close to the forest. I wondered if my parents could be living in one of those tents.

"I used to play in those woods, and we'd catch frogs in the little creek on the far side." I pointed.

"Probably it's a water source for the whole area now," Captain Daley said. "I've heard that frog legs taste like chicken." He smacked his lips jokingly.

"Maybe I'll find out." I paused, lost in thought. "Captain Daley, do you think this is ever going to end?" I asked.

"Everything ends. Isn't that what Tom used to say? I just don't know if it's going to take two more weeks or two more months or two more years. All I really care about is the next few minutes." He paused. "They're going to be there."

"I know. I hope."

Julia reached out and patted me on the back. She'd been quiet since we'd left her place.

We came to the street that led to mine. It was open, no barricade. That was bad, even worse than a barricade that had been abandoned. Up ahead were a few stalled cars on the road and more vehicles in driveways. The houses looked normal if you didn't look too hard. Some had broken windows and smashed doors—just like in Julia's neighborhood. The lawns were untended, uncut, and flower beds were wild and unplanted. It looked like many of the neighborhoods we'd passed by. Neighborhoods that hadn't been able to survive.

This was so much worse, though. I knew these houses. I'd passed them every day going to school or had ridden my bike by them. I knew the people who lived in some of them. Some were my friends. Where were they now? And, more important, would my parents be waiting or gone?

"It's just around the corner, right?" Captain Daley asked, nudging me out of my daydream.

"Yeah, it is. How did you know?"

"I was at a backyard barbecue at your place when your parents moved in about seven or eight years ago."

"I remember that! There were lots of people from their work," I said.

"I was there too," Julia said with a small smile.

I couldn't believe it. "I didn't know!"

"It was a wonderful party. Even if you don't remember us. We remember you," Julia said. She put an arm around my shoulders.

"Why didn't either of you ever mention that to me?" I asked.

"I guess we had other things on our minds." Captain Daley chuckled. "It's going to be good to see your parents again."

We were coming up to where I lived. It was a short dead-end street with a big *No Through Traffic* sign on the corner. There were only fifteen houses, and it ended in a big open paved section where people could turn around a car and where we'd always played. We used to roll out two basketball hoops or play road hockey or just ride our bikes. Sometimes parents would watch or even join in. On special occasions they'd carry out picnic benches, and families would have a barbecue and eat together. Those were things I'd taken for granted. My parents, people I knew, neighbors, having food, knowing that it was safe. All being together. No matter what was there when I turned the corner, all of that was gone. It was never going to be the same. It was never going to be safe.

I stopped. Godzilla pushed right in against me. He must have sensed what I was feeling.

"I know it's hard, but it's okay, Jamie. One of two things is going to happen when we turn the corner," Captain Daley said, turning to me as I stopped.

"Either they're there or they're gone," I said breathlessly.

"Wrong. Either we're going to find your parents there right now, or we're going to find them in the next few days."

"What do you mean?"

"If they're not there, then we're going to search and find them. They probably haven't gone far, and it shouldn't take long." His voice was clear and reassuring.

"But you have to go home."

"I will go home, but not until I keep my promise to get *you* home. It's going to happen. You have my word."

I knew what he was saying was true. Despite all the things in this world I could no longer count on, I could count on him.

We started walking, and as we made the turn, I saw that the way forward was blocked. There was a high wooden wall where there had been only an open road. My neighborhood—my house— was visible above and beyond the wall. There were two people standing at what looked like a gate, and one of them appeared to be holding a rifle. Both guards had thick, full beards. I tried to see past the beards, looking them in the eyes, hoping beyond hope that I'd recognize them.

"Jamie?" one of the men said.

I knew the voice before I recognized the face. It was my father.

CHAPTER
FORTY-FIVE

"IT'S A MIRACLE," MY MOTHER said as she hugged me even tighter. We sat in the kitchen of my house. It was a place I'd never thought I'd see again. It all looked the same except for my parents. My father was thinner and almost unrecognizable behind the beard. My mother's hair was longer and had gray flecks.

"I'm not surprised," my father said, beaming.

"You're not?" I questioned.

"I knew you were on Stu's flight and that he'd take care of you."

My father wrapped us both in a big hug. It felt so good and so unreal.

"Stu, I don't know how we can ever repay you for what you did," my father said.

"This meal helps make up for it." Captain Daley grinned, his mouth full.

We were each eating a big plate of boiled potatoes and had already eaten an egg each.

"Everything, anything, we have is yours," my mother said. "It's just so hard to even understand what you three have been through."

We'd told them about the trip. At least, parts of the trip. There were so many things we'd left out—mostly the very worst parts. How could I ever tell them I'd almost died so many times and that I'd killed people to allow us to survive? How did you tell something like that to your parents?

"I'm more interested in hearing how you've done all of this," Captain Daley said.

I figured he *was* interested but more than that wanted to change the subject.

"It's been a real group effort," my mother began.

"We've always been a pretty tight community on this street. We all know each other, and when it hit, we banded together," my father added.

"How many of you are there?" Captain Daley asked.

"There are the people from the houses on this cul-de-sac, but some neighbors a few streets over and a couple of family members joined us. We have a total of fifty-eight people," my father explained.

"Actually, those numbers are wrong," my mother said, smiling. "Jamie and Julia make it an even sixty people. Julia, we insist that you stay here."

"And your husband can join us as well," my father added. "Because we're going to find him."

My father saying that was the same as Captain Daley saying it—I knew we would.

"Thank you. That means so much," Julia said, her eyes welling up.

"And Stu, you know the invitation stands for you to stay," my father added.

Captain Daley nodded. "I appreciate that. Tell me, where did you get all the wood for the barrier walls?"

I knew what he was doing—changing the subject again.

"It was already here. We took out the fences that were *between* the properties and used the material to build the wall around us," my mother answered.

"That's what saved us when other parts of the community seemed to fail. We were like a castle, and we built a wall to protect us," my father said proudly.

"Some people had seeds, and we got more and we planted food where there had been grass and flowers."

"The crops are coming up nicely," Captain Daley noted.

"It helps having that little creek right behind us. We've had water to drink and to water the crops," my mother said. It was true, when I thought about it now. Our neighborhood was well situated. We were lucky.

"I wish there was more variety, but we have cucumbers, beans, potatoes and tomatoes. They're coming up just in time, as we run out of whatever food we had stored," my father said.

"Where did you get the chickens?" Captain Daley asked.

"They were already here," I replied. I knew. "Mrs. Fielding has been raising them in her backyard for years."

"That rooster used to drive me crazy!" my father exclaimed. "Especially after a long flight when I needed to sleep. There was even a motion before town council to make it illegal to have farm animals in the neighborhood. Now I hear that crowing, and it makes me smile." I smiled too. I remembered how annoyed he used to get.

"Everybody gets one egg a week," my mother explained.

"It makes me feel bad for eating somebody's egg," Captain Daley said.

"Don't be ridiculous," my mom said, shaking her head. "Anything we have is yours. And Julia's. Anything."

"That's kind of you, but I know that even with everything you're growing and raising, you barely have enough for yourselves," Julia said. "I feel bad for taking some of it."

"Not another word," my mother said. "After what you did, bringing our son back..." She faltered, overcome by emotion. I felt a lump in my throat. I still couldn't believe I was here.

"Your son had as much to do with us being here as anybody else," Julia said solemnly.

"It's true," Captain Daley said, patting my shoulder. "And you know, once Godzilla settles in, he's going to start hunting and bringing back some game. He makes himself useful in so many ways, including security."

"He certainly looks scary, but he's probably as gentle as a puppy," my mother said.

"He is gentle, but he's devoted to your son. He would kill or be killed to protect Jamie," Julia said, gazing fondly at the dog.

"I hope you don't mind my asking," Captain Daley said, "but I saw you had a rifle and a bow and arrow on the wall. How many more weapons do you have?"

"I'm afraid not many more," my father said. "One of the neighbors was into archery, but I'm really not sure how effective a bow and arrow would be in a fight."

"Very effective," I said. "Deadly."

I didn't want to add anything more. Not now. Maybe not ever.

"And other weapons?" Captain Daley asked.

"We have a shotgun, a pistol and a very limited supply of ammunition."

"It only has eight bullets, but you now have a second handgun," Captain Daley said, glancing over at me.

"We can't take your gun," my father said.

"It's really more Jamie's than mine," he explained.

Both of my parents looked concerned. I didn't know what to say.

"It was rough out there," Captain Daley went on. "Everybody had a weapon, and this is the one your son carried for most of the trip. He's a remarkable young man. He saved lives out there."

I bowed my head, thinking about Tom giving me the gun way back at the beginning. It felt like so long ago.

"He's always been remarkable," my father said.

I felt a swell of pride.

"But it doesn't matter whose gun it is," my father went on. "You're going to need it. Your route home from here leads you through the city. It's…it's…not good."

"It's terrible," my mother added. "There are gangs of desperate people preying on anybody they find who's weaker."

"That's what we'd worried about," Julia said grimly.

"It's worse than anything we could tell you…but then again, you'd know," my father said.

"We tried to avoid cities," I explained, turning to Captain Daley. "Can't you just go around it?"

He shook his head. "It's too big, too spread out. I'd have to make the trip at least three times as long for it to make a difference."

"What if you stayed here with us for a week or two or longer?" my mother suggested. "Get some sleep, some meals into you—maybe we can even find you a new pair of shoes."

"And that's not going to be easy!" my father joked. "I never knew how you could use those gigantic paddle-sized feet of yours to work the rudder pedals of a plane!"

They all laughed, and for a few seconds it all seemed better. But I was concerned about the captain. We all were.

"What we can do is get you a pair of shoes and cut out the toes. It'll be better than what you have now," my father suggested.

"And when you do decide you're feeling strong enough to go, you'll leave with a pack full of food, water, some new shoes on your feet and, of course, you'll be taking the pistol," my mother said.

"And one of us can escort you at least partway there," my father said. "It's the least we can do."

Captain Daley didn't answer. I wasn't sure my parents had noticed, but I had. He was listening, but that didn't mean he was agreeing.

"You'll stay for a while, right?" I asked. I really hoped he would. Even just a couple of days, to help prepare him for the next journey ahead.

"I'll think about it," he said. "I want to thank you for the offer but also for giving me hope. Seeing what you've done here gives me reason to think my neighborhood has done the same thing."

"Knowing your wife and how organized she is, I'm sure that's the case," my mother reassured him.

"And her being the police captain means she probably has some resources that can help defend the community she's set up," my father added.

"I'm counting on that," Captain Daley said. "And now, if you don't mind, I'm really tired." He gave a yawn. "I'm looking forward to a good night's sleep on that soft mattress in your guest room."

CHAPTER
FORTY-
SIX

"JAMIE, WAKE UP."

It was my mother. I almost rolled over and told her I wanted to sleep a little longer, before it all came rushing back. I sat up immediately, and a rush of fear and then relief rolled over me. I was in my room, familiar posters on the walls, baseball trophies on the dresser. If Godzilla wasn't pressed up against me in the bed, I could have believed it had all just been a bad dream.

My father was standing beside her. "He's gone," he said sadly.

"Who's gone?"

"Stu. Captain Daley."

"What do you mean he's gone? Why didn't you wake me up?" I demanded.

"We didn't know. We were asleep. He left in the middle of the night," my mother said.

"And Julia?"

"She's here. She didn't know either."

"But why would he do that?" I asked. "Why would he leave without saying goodbye?"

"He left this with the guard at the gate." My father handed me an envelope. My name was on it.

I rubbed my eyes, trying to push away the last remnants of sleep. "What does it say?"

My father shook his head. "It's for you. We didn't open it."

I took the envelope.

"Do you want to be alone to read it?" my father asked.

I shook my head. "I'll read it out loud." I opened it up and removed the letter. I took a deep breath and started reading.

"Jamie, I'm sorry to say goodbye this way, especially after everything we've been through, but I didn't have a choice. I knew if I told everybody that I was leaving, your parents would give me too much of your food and try to force me to take the gun."

"He left the gun on the kitchen table," my mother said.

Of course, I thought. "Did he take *anything?*" I asked.

"From what I can tell, he took some potatoes, a couple of cucumbers and some tomatoes. Maybe enough for a few days."

I swallowed. Not much at all. I wished he'd taken more.

I turned back to the letter. *"I could have stayed two or three more days or even a couple of weeks, but I just wanted to get home to my family. I know you understand."*

I took a deep breath, released it slowly. He was right. I did understand.

"If nothing else, I should have stuck around long enough to get a new pair of shoes. These ones are going to have to do me for the last part of the journey. If need be, I'll hop the last few miles, like I said I would."

I could picture him doing that. Or walking with one shoe. Or crawling. He wasn't going to stop.

"Jamie, I hope you forgive me for leaving like this, but we didn't come this far and go through so much for me to take one of your parents away

from you. I couldn't have your mother or father endanger their lives and accompany me."

"I would have gone," my father said quietly. "Maybe I still should. He couldn't have gotten that far. Maybe I can catch him."

"No, you can't," I said. I'd skimmed ahead, and now I kept reading to my parents. *"That's why I didn't leave the note in your house but with the guard. It gave me a big head start. I was pretty sure by the time you got it, I'd be hours ahead. There's no way anybody could find me even if you left now—so please don't try."*

I couldn't help smiling. Typical pilot. Just like my parents. Stubborn but logical. Covering all the bases. There was no way to follow or find him.

"I want you to make sure you take care of Julia and help her find her husband," I continued reading. *"You have to help her believe she'll find him. Hope got us this far, right?"*

My mother sat down beside me. "You have our word we'll help her in every way we can," she said, putting her hand on my arm.

"I know," I said. I sighed. *"Jamie, you're a fine young man. You remind me so much of my son, Adam. I think the two of you would really get along well. Someday I hope we'll find out."*

I felt myself tearing up. I took a deep breath in order to read through to the end.

"I want to thank you for being a big part of what kept me moving forward. You did more than that, though. You were as big a part of us surviving as anybody else. I know you'll keep on being the same person and helping your parents and your community survive. You and that big dog are going to help everybody."

I reached down and rubbed Godzilla's neck, and he looked up and then gave me a big lick across my face.

"I made you a promise that I'd get you home. I'm going to make you another promise. I'm going to get home. Guaranteed."

I looked up at my parents. They were both in tears. Even though I'd miss him, I wasn't going to cry. Because I knew that, although it wasn't going to be easy, he was going to make it. He always kept his promises.

The Original Group

CREW
Captain Daley
Doeun
Julia
Fede

SECURITY
Phillip
Tom
Sara
Noah

MEDICAL
Dr. Singh
Richard

OTHERS
Amber
Nelson
Me
Calvin

EXPLORE the UNKNOWN

with

the TEEN ASTRONAUTS series

by award-winning author
ERIC WALTERS

ORCA

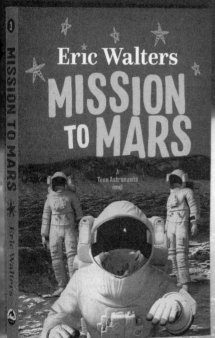
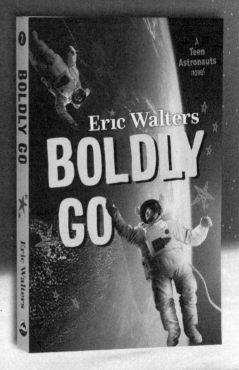

ERIC WALTERS is a Member of the Order of Canada and the author of over 125 books that have collectively won more than one hundred awards, including the Governor General's Literary Award for *The King of Jam Sandwiches*. A former teacher, Eric began writing as a way to get his fifth-grade students interested in reading and writing. Eric is a tireless presenter, speaking to over one hundred thousand students a year in schools across the country. He lives in Guelph, Ontario.